PRAISE FOR
# These People Are Us

"George Singleton has the singular voice of a down-home schizophrenic. His stories are crazy mad fun."

—*Playboy*

"George Singleton writes about the rural South without sentimentality or stereotype but with plenty of sharp-witted humor.... A raconteur of trends, counter-trends, obsessions and odd characters."

—"Morning Edition," National Public Radio

"I laughed out loud. A lot.... Practically every page has a sentence worth reading over again just to savor the image.... Singleton's characters have a solid presence."

—*Winston-Salem Journal*

"These are fine stories—odd, amusing and insightful."

—*Publishers Weekly*

"It's as if George Singleton grasped America by the heels, held us upside down for a sound shaking, then collected the daffy oddments that fell out of the pockets. *These People Are Us* is funny and funky, trendy and counter-trendy, wild and accurate."

—Fred Chappell

"George Singleton is the only writer I know who can make me, in a single moment, laugh out loud and weep."

—Cathy Smith Bowers

"These characters try to get through the day as best they can. They muse and complain and fight with each other in a manner that brings Flannery O'Connor to mind. Singleton's superb ear for dialogue makes this book a joy to read."

—Scott Ely

"Here is a stunningly singular blend of humor and humanity. Tipped hats and hoisted fluted glasses to *These People Are Us*."

—Dale Ray Phillips

# These People Are Us

# These People Are Us

### STORIES BY
## George Singleton

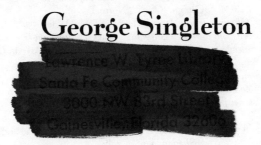

A HARVEST BOOK
HARCOURT, INC.
*San Diego   New York   London*

Requests for permission to make copies of any part of the work should be mailed to the following address: Permissions Department, Harcourt Inc., 6277 Sea Harbor Drive, Orlando, Florida 32887-6777.

www.HarcourtBooks.com

Grateful acknowledgment is made to the editors of the following publications in which these stories first appeared.
*American Literary Review:* "Directions for Seeing, Directions for Singing"
*Apalachee Quarterly:* "These People Are Us"
*Chariton Review:* "Rentals"
*Cimarron Review:* "Cleft for Me"
*Denver Quarterly:* "Dialectic, Abrasions, The Backs of Heads Again"
*Georgia Review:* "Normal"
*Glimmer Train:* "How I Met My Second Wife"
*Greensboro Review:* "Santayana Speaks Through Me"
*New Southern Harmonies:* "I Could've Told You If You Hadn't Asked," Outlaw Head and Tail"
*New Stories from the South — The Year's Best — 1994:* Outlaw Head and Tail"
*New Stories from the South — The Year's Best — 1998:* "These People Are Us"
*New Stories from the South — The Year's Best — 1999:* "Caulk"
*Ontario Review:* "Crawl Space"
*Playboy:* I Could've Told You If You Hadn't Asked," "Outlaw Head and Tail"
*Shenandoah:* "Caulk"
*Southern Review:* "The Ruptures and Limits of Absence"
*Writers Harvest 2:* "Remember Why We're Here"

First published by River City Press in 2001

Library of Congress Cataloging-in-Publication Data
Singleton, George, 1958–
These people are us: short stories/by George Singleton — 1st Harvest ed.
p.    cm.
"A Harvest Book"
ISBN 0-15-601274-X
1. South Carolina — Social life and customs — Fiction.    I. Title.
PS3569.I5747 T48 2002
813'.6—dc21     2002024030

Designed by Linda Lockowitz
Text set in Electra
Printed in the United States of America
First Harvest edition 2002

A  C  E  G  I  K  J  H  F  D  B

*For Glenda, with love*

# Contents

# Acknowledgments

I would like to thank my writer-friends Dale Ray Phillips, Ron Rash, and Marlin Barton for knowing and talking about things other than writing. I am indebted to the valuable minds of Fred Chappell, Richard Bausch, Jim Clark, Robert Watson, and Gil Allen, though maybe I didn't listen to them enough. I wish to thank the magazine and journal editors, especially Christopher Napolitano, Alice K. Turner, Stephen Corey, and Michael Griffith.

Thanks to Jim Davis at River City Press, and of course to Wayne Greenhaw—bon vivant, fine writer, humanitarian—for making this book possible.

Beverly Singleton deserves a sweeping bow for being a patient, understanding, flexible, know-when-to-look-the-other-way mother.

And finally, I remember my father—merchant seaman and wild storyteller—for forcing me to listen closely and watch peripherally at all times.

# These People Are Us

# Remember Why We're Here

M<small>Y WIFE KEPT TALKING</small> about convection ovens. I thought
she said *conviction* at first—which brought up weird capital punishment visions—and then I thought she said *confec-
tion*, even though we don't eat that much candy outside of the
holidays. Already we owned a microwave, and a regular electric
thing that didn't broil full in the house that she bought outright.
On the porch was a hibachi I'd had since before meeting her,
and a larger gas grill I didn't trust, seeing as flames seemed to
pour out of the bottom more often than not. I'd read an article
one time about some poor insurance salesman or banker outside with a spatula in his hand when a stray bullet hit his tank.
His family saw everything, too.

My wife said, "There's a new self-cleaning convection wall
oven out that can cook a thirty-five-pound turkey. It can cook a
dozen loaves of bread. It has a convection roast mode, and a
convection bake, and a thermal bake."

I said, "*Thermal* bake? What does that mean, Jerilyn? What
do you want to cook that needs a setting called thermal? Why
don't you wait a couple years and I bet they come up with something catering to people who need different circles of hell." It
just came to me, like that.

She said, "For piping-hot casseroles," and from the way she

said it I knew she'd been memorizing some advertisement. Jerilyn said, "Convection ovens use circulating heated air around foods, which roasts meats faster while leaving them beautifully browned outside and juicy inside."

I kept a can of Sterno in my backpack, too. There were dry sticks out in the yard, and probably pieces of flint scattered around somewhere. I'd never been in the Boy Scouts, but a couple of my buddies growing up were, and they taught me how to build a fire, tie a knot, and skin a snake. I said, "I don't know how to say this. I know I said when I came into some money it was yours for what you wanted, Jerilyn. But I thought you'd have something more in mind like a swimming pool or a good minivan. We don't have a swimming pool or a mini-van. But we do have ovens. We have stoves. We got us some appliances, is what I'm saying."

Jerilyn did not stick her bottom lip out and pout. She stared me in the face and made it clear how circulating heated air was the best thing for us. She said, "I want the convection oven to go in the kitchen of our new mountain cabin up past Tryon," and unrolled one of those free real estate guides she always picked up off racks outside of places we went that served all-you-can-eat buffets. She said, "Some guy just bought most of the whole top of White Oak Mountain where there used to be a Baptist church camp. I called the real-estate agent, and she said they tore down all the old stone structures and strategically placed the rocks in the lake so bass and bream would bed better." She said, "The developer started in on a dozen little cabins around the lake, but ran out of money and wants to sell them off fast."

Jerilyn nodded and kept eye contact. For some reason, I said, "Why'd the Baptist church camp go under?" I thought Baptists still thrived hard here. I said, "I bet there are a bunch of rattlesnakes and copperheads up on that mountain, and I bet those Baptists were a little on the charismatic side." I didn't go into more detail about probable snake-handling and lack of antivenin.

"You said you're finally the man of the house, Spoon," Jerilyn said. She wouldn't take my last name when we got married, but she sure used it more than my first.

"Circulating heated air that roasts meats faster. Thirty-five-pound turkey," I said, walking towards the answering machine. "I better think of more and better things for the babies of America."

"Uh-huh," she said.

WE'D JUST GOTTEN BACK from visiting Jerilyn's cousins down in Charleston. They wanted to throw a little party for me, seeing as I'd finally made it, in their eyes. In the past, I'd always tried to find a way out of these visits, seeing as I felt somewhat the oddball. I didn't have family money, I went to college and tried to do well, and I didn't have two houses on the same island. I said, "Well, I guess that hot-air theme kind of runs in your family, doesn't it, Jerilyn?"

The week before, I'd gotten my first check from the lawyer who took care of whatever needed getting done. I'd come up with a line of baby diapers that had LOADING ZONE emblazoned on the back side. The people up in New York said that it was perfect timing—that kids now had a new fascination with heavy equipment, and that a tiny picture of a dump truck releasing its load on the back of a kid's butt was just what America needed to remember its blue-collar roots. I even got an offer for a regular 9-to-5 job with an ad agency up there, but said I'd rather stick to teaching at the technical college where I had enough time to come up with new ideas. Jerilyn said something about how I must not have that much time or I'd've come up with more than one idea in a decade.

Anyway, we went down to Charleston and ended up with cousin Dargan—who went by "Dar," which always sounded kind of stupid and Cro-Magnon at best—and his sister, Ashley. Ashley's good-hearted doctor-husband, Sam, and their two kids were there, plus Dar's latest girlfriend named—get this—Anise, who got some weird theology degree from a place I'm sure sent diplomas through the mail, but it gave her the right to preach at a church way left of the Unitarians. I'm no psychiatrist, but I'd take bets that Anise got called Anus a bunch of her life, and joined the odd church in order to cast hexes on old high school classmates.

We sat there at a table for however many people we needed, one block off of the Market. The waiter came up and took our drink orders. This was not a typical tourist restaurant, either. There were no fishnets filled with starfish hanging from the ceiling. There were no fake sailfish on the walls.

There were no prices on the menu, is what I'm saying.

Dar was last and said, "I'll have one of your house micro-beers, but don't bring it with so much attitude, man." Dar'd sold real estate in the past, but now talked about going to New Mexico in order to learn about pressure points, channeling, acupuncture, aroma therapy—you name it. Dar still had a broken-off needle in his arm, if that matters, from the old days when he went to college and didn't care about doing well 'cause he knew he had family money and would end up owning two houses on one island.

Sam leaned over the table and said, "Don't start up, Dar. Remember why we're here." We were there, of course, to celebrate my newfound success. "While I'm at it, could you please watch your language around the kids?"

Well, this didn't go over well at all. Even though Dar cherished the wayward-family-member archetype, he always bowed up when confronted with his behavior in public. Dar said, "Why we're here? I thought we came here to have a good time, man. The waiter acted like he had to go stomp hops and barley by himself. I don't need that."

Sam and Ashley's girl said, "Your name's Anise," pronouncing it the wrong way.

Dar said, "Goddamnit. You tell your own girl to watch her mouth. I did not come to wish Spoon well, and then have to listen to people talking about buttholes all night long."

I said, "Hey," all diminuendo.

Dar sat back and stared at his knee.

Ashley said, "Loading Zone! That's so cute. It almost makes me want to have another baby. How much money are you going to make off this deal, Spoon?"

The waiter brought our drinks and served Dar first. He didn't say anything. I squeezed Jerilyn's knee under the table twice to let her know I wasn't comfortable. I may not come from some kind of aristocratic family, but my parents knew enough about minding their own business. I said, "I get a lump sum up front, and then a penny for each diaper sold. They're going to be marketed in twelve and twenty-four packs. I got a good lawyer." I squeezed the leg again, once and long, which I consider the international sign for "keep quiet." My parents taught me to mind my own business—and lie big.

"That's great," Sam said. He came from a working-class Chicago family, and out of everyone in Jerilyn's family I connected with him best. When he talked about my liver, he didn't preach.

I said, "Thanks." Anise looked at me and moved her lips. I said, "What?" but then realized that she chanted or something.

5

Dar said, "When I was in college, I beat off into a sock so much I grew a toenail on my pecker." He held his right hand in a loose fist, poured beer into the cup he'd made with his fingers, and said, "Look at me—I'm getting my date for tonight drunk!"

Sam got his children up first, then Ashley ran after them. Anise said, "Your family doesn't understand that you offer them unconditional love, Dar. They don't yet know agape."

Dar held his eyebrows high, shook his head in disbelief, and said, "Did you see those entities coming out of my sister's chest? Man, no wonder her husband's projecting so much. I wish they could see what I can see. I can tell two things—when meat's gone bad, and when a bad marriage is going on."

I caught myself nodding up and down until we finally left for that hotel room my wife said we'd checked into, but hadn't really. We'd always stayed with Dar before. Jerilyn talked about how our suitcases were already inside the Holiday Inn, et cetera. I caught myself thinking about a more peaceful time, like when I got hit by a car at age twelve, or like a couple years later when I cut off my thumb up at my dad's shop and had to get it sewn back on.

This, of course, happened before my knowledge of convection ovens. Had it happened after, I'd've caught myself thinking of perfect heat, too.

THE MAN WHO YEARNED to transform most of White Oak mountain from a defunct Baptist camp into a circle of modern tin-roofed A-frames with lofts had got caught poking a female contractor who'd come down from this experimental design school in Vermont to work on the project. That was the real estate agent's story. That was why the cabins had unfinished interiors and low prices. She said that ours wasn't made by that developer, though, that ours was bought and unfinished by another man totally, like it'd matter. The big developer didn't get his hands on everything, was her story.

About two minutes after I gave in to the oven, Jerilyn and I drove the sixty miles north to our cabin. The real estate agent's name was Penny. Although I normally don't trust people named after currency, or people in the same line of work that Dar'd been in before getting all spiritual, she and I hit it off well. Penny offered my wife and me cigars.

"Is your real name Spoon, Spoon?" Penny said when we got out of her car. She drove a regular car, a Ford something.

I said, "My last name's Spoon. Everybody's always called me Spoon. My first name is normal. Call me Spoon."

Jerilyn walked alone to the edge of the lake and turned around. She said, "With all the trees, you can hardly even see this cabin here."

I said, "Trees have limbs that get heavy in winter. They crack and fall on the roof."

Penny said, "You could cut them down. Or you could learn how to lay tin. Your insurance will pay for it, Spoon."

Jerilyn yelled, "I've always wanted to grow a shade garden. We're not cutting down any of these trees. Our other house doesn't have trees, and I'm tired of planting only corn, tomatoes, and peppers."

There was no one on the lake. That made me think that maybe some dead Baptists were submerged and it spooked people away. Penny said, "This lot here is three-quarters of an acre, and you have the creek on your property." She held out a map. The land wedged right into the lake, almost halfway in.

I said, "I can roof. I can also nail down one-by-twelve planks on the particle board for the floor, and insulate the walls, and

7

put up drywall. I know how to do those kinds of jobs. A lot of people think pine's too soft for flooring, but you get a good kiln-dried southern yellow pine and it's good. I don't want no tongue-and-groove."

Penny folded up the map. Jerilyn skipped toward us. "You'll have to get a licensed electrician and plumber. There's a permit for the septic tank. I think it'll go over there," Penny said, pointing to the side of the property farthest from the creek. She said, "You can get something called builder's risk insurance until the cabin's finished. It'll cover if the place burns or if someone gets hurt."

I said, "I only believe in car insurance. You see, if you start feeling puny and think you've come down with a major illness, all you got to do is get in a car wreck and yell out, 'Ow, I got whiplash! I got cirrhosis of the liver, too!' I'm pretty sure it's a scam you can get away with."

We walked inside and within a minute Jerilyn figured out where the sink would go and the refrigerator. She told Penny how she'd seen a glass-doored china cabinet on sale at one of the junk stores in town already. My wife held her hands out three feet, pointed to the wall as if she were bringing in a 747 at the runway, and said, "This is where the convection oven will go."

I looked up at the hole in the ceiling. I would have to make a staircase, or buy one of those pre-fab wrought iron spiral things. I'd have to invest some of my "Loading Zone" diaper money into that series of do-it-yourself books sold on late-night television. "This might be too much for us, Jerilyn," I said. "We can afford something that costs a little more and takes less work."

Penny said, "People never plan to die, but they die to plan." I didn't know what that meant. It sounded like something taught at a pep rally for insurance agents. "You can do a lot with this place. If you want to cover the area underneath you'd have basically a three-story house," Penny said. "I think that's a good idea about what you mentioned about making a patio under the front porch," she added. Then she held her hand to her mouth.

I said, "I've been here the whole time and haven't heard about any patio. Who said something about a patio? I didn't say anything about it. Jerilyn was down at the lake doing her thumb like some kind of old master portrait artist. She didn't say anything about a patio."

Penny tried to cover herself. She turned her back to me, looked at the wall, and said, "What do you teach at the tech college, Spoon?"

I said, "Logic, speech, and rhetoric," which wasn't really true.

Penny turned around and looked at my wife. Jerilyn said, "I've been up here a couple times already, Spoon. As a matter of fact, I've already written a check for the earnest money for the place and agreed to what the man selling wants to get."

In the old days I'd've gotten mad. Well, in the old days Jerilyn could've pulled out a hundred grand from one of her trust funds, which were growing at the same rate my student loans were, because of the default, and she could've bought anything. I'd've pouted then, feeling that I wasn't man enough to be a man. But now just catching her and Penny trying to act suave gave me enough satisfaction. I said, "Earnest money?"

Jerilyn said to Penny, "Spoon doesn't know what that means." To me she said, "I had to put down a check that said we wanted to hold it until we checked everything out. Earnest money isn't cashed, and it goes against the bid."

I looked at that big hole in the ceiling where the stairwell would go. I said I knew what "earnest" meant. I said, "Did you check to see if there're termites, Jerilyn?"

Penny said, "Termites don't eat into cedar siding, Spoon."

I said, "I know. I'm just checking on you two, again," and caught myself nodding just like in the priceless restaurant. I said, "I can probably afford to quit teaching for a year and finish this place off." I made a point of saying I wanted to close the deal as soon as possible.

My wife and my real estate agent did some kind of double holding-of-hands thing I'd only heard about. It looked a little like this contra-dancing special I'd seen on the local news. On the way home I said to Jerilyn, "How long have you known Penny?"

She said, "About a month. Actually I met her outside of all this. Right before you got the good news is when we met. Right after, I happened to pick up the real estate guide and see the cabin. It was some kind of synchronicity thing, Spoon."

We took all the switchbacks slowly, and stopped completely for vistas and waterfalls. I said, "Some kind of karma thing, huh? Some kind of predestination, that's what you're saying."

Jerilyn sat there. She looked out the window. In the distance, a redtail hovered, almost still. My wife said, "Don't compare me to Dar. I see what's coming."

"So how did y'all meet before? I want to know this story about y'all meeting before I sold the diapers." A work truck pulled over so we could get by. I waved, as neighbors-to-be should.

Jerilyn said, "The first day I came up to the cabin there was this old man on the other side of the lake pulling fish out every time he threw in his hook. Is a pound a good-sized bluegill? He said he'd caught eight one-pound bluegill. I didn't know if that was good or not. I told him my husband once caught a four-pound brown trout fly-fishing. Remember that time you caught that big thing, Spoon?"

It was a gravel road, and every vista point had a house owned by the same people Zarathustra passed on the way down, I'm sure. It came to me, just like that. I said, "Hey, hey, don't change what I asked you. Where'd you meet that real estate woman before you met her again?"

When my wife told me she'd not really joined a bowling league, that she really joined a church of women that only met on Thursday nights, and that the congregation sat in a circle and talked about their bad childhoods, I wasn't surprised. Per usual, I didn't mention that my father spent some time unemployed, or his physical disability, or how he whipped my butt when I needed it.

I drove and paid attention.

Jerilyn said, "We've been married ten years this Halloween, Spoon. You can't hold it against me for wondering if things could be better. I just wanted to hear other women tell their stories. I'm not in love with anyone else, if that's what you want to know."

Of course I didn't exactly hear her, and asked where she got the address for women meeting to complain. I asked her if she'd been watching all those talk shows in the afternoon. I said, "What, have you seen some entities flying out of my chest or something?"

My wife put her hand on my leg. She laughed and patted and shook her head like a wet dog. She said, "Spoon, we're not on this land for very long, considering. It's okay to strive for more. What I learned when it comes to marriage: it's better to ditch a plan, than plan a ditch."

I damn near missed a curve right then.


BY ACCIDENT I CALLED the lawyer's dog the lawyer's first name. The lawyer kept her cocker spaniel in the office for some reason.

11

I don't know if she did a bunch of work for the SPCA. The lawyer's name was Baiba Brousseau. Jerilyn couldn't come close to saying it, really. I'd taken enough French in my lifetime to say the last name, but I still wasn't sure about the first.

I practiced, "Ba-ee-ba, Ba-ee-ba, Ba-ee-ba," forever. It seemed like a trick to me.

We went in to sign the papers, and the dog came up, and Baiba said, "That's Daisy Mae. Say 'Hey,' Daisy Mae," et cetera, et cetera.

I petted the dog and said, "Ba-ee-ba!" like that, stupid. I said, "What a nice dog you have. Hey, Daisy Mae," trying to cover myself in a way that only wives and real estate agents can, evidently. I probably looked at the wall or ceiling, I don't know.

I doubt it mattered.

That's not the big thing. At the time it seemed like the hook to a good country song, but my self-revelation wasn't close.

Baiba couldn't afford air-conditioning, and it must've been two thousand degrees there. I didn't like lawyers in the first place—none of them, not even public defenders who supposedly cared about people like me—and one with a dog on the sofa seemed overly obvious. She said, "On my sixty-five-acre farm we have horses, goats, cows, cats, and dogs. Daisy Mae just got kicked, so I'm keeping her here. I've got her on herbs."

Jerilyn squeezed my leg once, knowing what I'd say, which was, "You ain't got no manatees or emus? We want to raise a litter of emus under the house and manatees in the lake." I didn't smile or anything.

Baiba said, "My husband and I have an order in for llamas. I'd like to raise some llamas, and some angora rabbits. You can make a bunch of money off them. Unfortunately, y'all have a zoning law up on that mountain that keeps you from raising anything. You'd need three acres before you could think about a farm. Now, there's the chance you could jigsaw a farm — there's a lot ten lots away from your cabin that you could buy, and in time you might be able to buy all the lots in between, one by one. But for now the homeowners' association will take care of making sure no one oversteps the rules."

We sat around a big table, waiting for Penny and the guy who sold the land. Baiba had on an electric fan down on the floor that didn't help whatsoever. I felt in my coat pocket for the certified check. I said, "Uh-oh. There's a homeowners' association?"

"You don't want any trailers next to you, do you? That vacant lot right next to yours might come up for sale. You don't want someone plopping down a single-wide within your view, believe me."

Now, I know all about depreciating land values and whatnot, but I still didn't like people telling me what I couldn't put on land I own. I'm no member of one of those militias or anything. Occasionally I catch myself thinking how I'd like to own and drive a tank, but that's about it. I said, "I was born in a trailer, Ms. Brousseau. I'm probably not the person to tell what I would or wouldn't want to see outside my window. As a matter of fact, I'd probably like to have a good neighbor in a mobile home next to me, as opposed to the smell of horses, goats, and cows."

My wife Jerilyn said, "You weren't born in a trailer, Spoon." She looked at the lawyer and said, "He's just kidding." She said, "I wouldn't be surprised if we got up there on the mountain and he decided to become a stand-up comedian."

Baiba Brousseau stared at me as if she'd just noticed horns sticking out of my scalp. Penny walked in with the owner of the cabin and said, "Sorry we're late. Hey, Spoon. Hey, Jerilyn. Spoon and Jerilyn, this is Reverend Jimmy Splawn." We shook hands all the way around. I thought about shaking my own wife's hand, but Marx Brothers routines probably don't go over well inside a lawyer's office during the signing period.

I said to the reverend, "Hey, I know you. I get a letter from you once a month asking me for money. You run that Faith Ministries place, right?"

Understand, if I'd've known that a preacher once owned my unfinished cabin, doubt I'd've gone ahead with Jerilyn's bid, et cetera. Call me a bigot.

Reverend Jimmy pulled out some fake tears and said, "We loved that cabin. It gave us so many memories. But my wife's mother got real sick, and my daddy died, and I just don't know if we can go up there anymore." He said, "We felt so lucky just getting a part of the old camp before the developer could yank it up."

I said, "I send y'all ten bucks a month to help run your food bank. I'll be damned. It's a tiny solar system, ain't it?" I said, "Did you use to run the Baptist camp up on the lake? Man, I bet they really had an assembly line up there doing baptisms."

Penny sat next to Reverend Jimmy. She was on the seller's side, of course. It was some kind of North Carolina law. We even had to sign a document, that day when my wife and realtor did their odd dance, saying we understood how the lines were drawn.

Baiba went on and on about things I didn't understand concerning deeds, septic tank placement, moving the driveway, permits, et cetera. I looked over at the reverend and knew he didn't sell the cabin because of sick relatives and too many memories. I knew, too, that I'd met destitute men outside of bars down in Greenville, and offered them a ride to the shelter that Faith Ministries operated, but no one took me up because they didn't like having to feign guilt, humility, and obedience for a plate of mashed potatoes and green beans. More than once I'd given a man two dollars and said, "Don't lie to me about what you'll spend it on. I don't really care. Booze or BLT—it doesn't make a difference."

Now, I'm not saying this to prove some kind of martyr thing. I just don't care. If things don't go all that well for you here on the planet, it's probably best to forget. That's all I'm saying, now.

Reverend Jimmy said, "Miracles happen up on the mountain, Mr. Spoon. Miracles. It's not just the clouds flying by, or the sunset. You will see things that will change you forever."

Baiba said, "Sign here," and handed me whatever she'd been talking about earlier. She said, "As they say, it's better to stake a claim than it is to claim a steak." She said, "First you got to plan your work and then you got to work your plan," like that.

I withered in my humid chair. I cannot explain the lawyer's voice, but in that moment I realized that the preacher'd gotten caught doing illegal things with a boys' youth group, or a member of the choir, or he'd had an uncomfortable revelation about the Truth, and that's why we got the deal. At that point I knew I'd spend time scared and paranoid in the cabin, waiting for Reverend Jimmy's regretful and holy and rationalized return. I'd look down at the lake and wonder why our bodies seemed more water than dirt, more dirt than air or fire. I knew right there at the lawyer's miserable conference table that if Jerilyn and I lived to be two hundred years old, we'd never figure out those old metaphysical questions, and that I'd stoop to ask Dar or Anise if they'd picked up on anything at some kind of weird gathering in Asheville or Santa Fe.

I signed. My wife performed Morse code on my thigh: I didn't understand anything whatsoever. The only thing I would've bet on that day was that I'd bend my thumbs odd with a hammer soon and have to come up with another patent or copyright

15

to help all of us against people afraid of mobile homes and strangers.

When Jerilyn and I left the lawyer's office, we drove straight up the mountain like we planned and unrolled our two sleeping bags over the particle board in what later would be our den. I went downstairs and built a fire from fallen trees, caught and cleaned four bluegill from the lake within an hour, and placed the fish on ice after I pulled a champagne bottle out. My wife and I sat there quiet until pure darkness set in, until we couldn't make out bats flitting overhead. We didn't mention money or morality, cause and effect, or luck. We didn't niggle each other to remember a time when our marriage wasn't so secure. I talked myself out of thinking about the times when I insisted on eating nothing but sardines and Slim Jims just to prove how poor I'd grown up.

I said, "I don't want to sound holier-than-thou or pessimistic, but I didn't come out feeling so good about sitting in Baiba's office to buy a place without floors or walls from a preacher. Did you see that guy's hair? I don't believe a word he said."

Jerilyn put her arm through mine there at the fire and said, "I smell fish. You need to wash your hands."

I nodded. I thought about how there wasn't a place to wash my hands outside of a lake that smelled of fish already. We didn't have a sink yet, of course, much less a hot-air hand dryer. It wasn't the time to bring up disagreements we might have about major appliances, and what we could or couldn't hook up in the cabin, conventional or not.

Instead, I pointed upward and didn't pretend to distinguish stars, planets, and satellites shining above, or to explain why some are brighter than others.

# Outlaw Head and Tail

NORMALLY I COULDN'T have made the tape that Saturday. Right away, right there during the job interview a few weeks before, my soon-to-be-boss had said, "Ricky, is there anything about this job that you have a problem with?"

I didn't say, "I can't work for a man who ends sentences with prepositions." I couldn't. It was a job bouncing, or at least talking. I was going to be something called a "pre-bouncer." If some guy came into the Treehouse and looked like he meant trouble, I was to go up to him and start a little conversation, and let him know this wasn't the kind of place to throw a punch without inelegant and indubitable consequences.

I have a way with words. I'm synonymous with rapport.

I said to Frank, "Well, I'd rather not work Saturday days, 'cause my wife has to go to temple and I have to drive her over there. I don't go to temple. Hell, I don't even go to church," I said. "I don't mind working Sundays, but I'd really like it if you could get someone to work afternoons on Saturday for me. Night?—Saturday night—I'll be here. The only thing I ask of you is that I don't work Saturday afternoons, say, until six o'clock."

Frank said, "You know, you talked me into it. Man, what a way with words! It's a deal. You're a godsend, Ricky. I lucked out getting you as a pre-bouncer."

Frank had opened the Treehouse a year earlier, but didn't hire a bouncer or pre-bouncer right away. About the same time his insurance agent told him his payments would soon double, though, he hired me and a guy named Sparky Voyles to keep things down. During his first year, Frank put in claims for a whole new set of glasses, from shot and snifter to the special two-foot beer glasses he ordered, plus twelve tables, sixteen chairs, another tree stump to replace the one that caught on fire and caused smoke damage to the ceiling, and forty-two stitches to his own head one night after a fearful brawl erupted over whether Chevys or Fords would dominate the circuit in the upcoming season.

Frank bought the Treehouse because of insurance, ironically. He'd worked in the pulpwood trade and one day a load of logs slipped off a truck he stood behind, came rolling right off like a giant wave, clipped him behind the knees so hard they said he could run as fast backwards as forwards there for a few days.

Of course, he couldn't run at all, and had to get fake knees installed. His lawyer also got him another quarter-million dollars or so due to a lifetime worth of pain and subsequent nightmares. Frank took most of that money and made the Treehouse, a regular small warehouse he furnished with tree trunks from floor to ceiling, so if you blindfolded someone and took him inside the bar, then took off the mask and showed him around, he'd have the feeling that the whole building was up above the ground, built into the forest.

So during the first year there were fights and insurance claims, but the second year started right off with me and Sparky there to quiet things down. Frank didn't want us to be too heavy-handed, though. He didn't want the bar to end up so quiet it looked like a flock of mute birds built their nests in the Treehouse. He only asked for stability.

Sparky went the same route as Frank—he worked at the railroad before becoming a bouncer, getting paid under the table because he took in disability checks from when both of his thumbs got cut off between two boxcars that clanged together and weren't supposed to, and he erroneously thought he could prevent it from happening. He couldn't. Sparky had been a brakeman originally, out of Lexington.

Anyway, I worked hard pre-bouncing, and kept up with what I had to know, which was mainly words. This is how I get back to the tape and that Saturday. What I'm saying is, because I'm so conscientious about my job, it could've killed my marriage.

On the previous Thursday, Jessie went in to her doctor's office to have him finally go ahead and do that sonogram thing. She couldn't wait to know what our first baby was going to be, building her argument around the fact that we didn't make all that much money, and if it was a boy we needed to pinch even harder and save up for his circumcision.

Jessie works as a freelance interior decorator. She got her degree in art history and felt like it gave her the right.

I took Jessie down to the doctor's office, but she couldn't get an appointment before four o'clock in the afternoon. I got clearance from Frank to get off work on Thursday, but that meant I had to come in Saturday morning at eleven 'cause the guy who normally worked Saturdays needed to go to a wedding anyway. It ended up a simple and clean swap. There didn't seem to be that much of a problem.

So I took my wife to the doctor and she did what she had to do, but the doctor still couldn't even take a stab at it, for the baby kept turned around the whole time. I was hoping it'd be a girl. I never have seen myself as being the father of a shy son.

Two days later I drove Jessie to synagogue. I drove back

home in time to throw in a tape and set the VCR so I wouldn't miss *Bonanza*, which showed in syndication every Saturday on one of the cable channels. I set the station and time to record, then left for the bar.

I WATCH BONANZA every week. That's where I get my ways. That's where I get my ability to talk people out of starting fights. One time this burly truck driver–type came in and seemed upset that a white guy came into the Treehouse with an African-American woman. There'd been a similar episode on *Bonanza* one time when Hoss piped up to a stranger, "Well, would you rather be blind and not have to see the ways of the world?" He said it to a redneck, of course. Words of wisdom, I thought right there and then. I'd thought "words of wisdom" on more than one occasion while watching Ben Cartwright bring up his boys the best he could. I remembered watching *Bonanza* when I was a boy, too, and how I admired the way Little Joe and Hoss and even Adam handled themselves in town. My father, though, used to throw beer cans at the television set and say, "What them boys need to use a little more often is their trigger fingers, not their tongues."

It's that kind of thinking that makes it almost amazing that I grew into being a pre-bouncer. If I'd taken my father seriously back in the sixties, I'd've ended up being something more se-cluded and self-centered, something like a bookkeeper, or a jockey.

I said to the burly guy, "Hey, there's two things that can hap-pen here: either you can learn to understand that love is blind, or I can get Sparky to come over here with his eight remaining fingers and blind you himself, so you don't have to live with see-ing interracial dating in your midst. *Comprende*, amigo?"

I pointed at Sparky. Without his thumbs it looks like he

could use his fists as skewers. The truck driver looked over at Sparky, back to me, then to the white guy and black girl. He said, "Well, okay then," just like that. I stood my ground and tried not to shake. The little voice in my head kept thanking the Cartwrights over and over.

So I put the tape in the VCR, and I set the station and time, and drove off to the Treehouse. The bar doesn't open until noon, but I got there at eleven in order to help Frank clean up from the night before and to set out our specials in the plastic stand-up signs for each table. Frank said, "How goes it, Ricky?"

I said, "Okay, I guess. You?"

Frank said, "Uh-huh. Fine." He said, "You know, we didn't really get to talk last night. I mean, I heard you say that you still didn't know if you'd have a little boy or a girl, but what else did the doctor say?"

I wiped off a table. Friday night had been pretty slow at the Treehouse. Down the road there'd been a yearly festival with a battle of the bands and a tractor pull. I said, "He didn't say much. He asked if she'd been taking care of herself, whether she'd quit drinking and smoking. She said she had, which is true—and, goddamn, it ain't fun around the house, by the way. And then he said he thought her delivery date might need to be changed about a week early. Not much else went on. He dabbed some goo on her big stomach and we saw this little crooked Vienna sausage–looking thing on the television screen. Then he gave us the tape."

Well, no, I said, "The *tape!*"

I didn't say goodbye to Frank. I didn't tell him I'd be right back. I just left the Treehouse, got in my car, and drove fifteen minutes back to my house.

It was too late. Right over the image of my as-yet-sexless

child, the floating little thumb-sucking thing inside Jessie's body, Hoss now talked to Little Joe about how skittish the horses seemed to be all of a sudden.

SPARKY SAID, "WELL, it could be worse, Ricky. At least she still has the baby. One time when I was working Amtrak, this woman came screaming out of the bathroom saying she'd miscarried in the toilet. We were flying down the track about sixty miles an hour, you know. I had my break and was eating an egg salad sandwich in the dining car. I remember all this 'cause I had a mouthful of egg in my mouth when this woman made the announcement."

I nodded my head and shoulders quickly, trying to get Sparky to finish the story. I needed to make some phone calls, or talk to some of the customers.

Sparky said, "She came running out of that bathroom saying the thing came out of her, she thought, but she wasn't sure. On a train, you know, it goes straight down to the track, and at sixty miles an hour you don't have time to exactly check what came out in the bowl underneath you. One time I had a kidney stone and I was supposed to be pissing into a strainer, but I kept forgetting. So I have a stone in between the tracks somewhere from Lexington to Danville."

I nodded hard, waving my right hand like a paddlewheel for Sparky to finish up. A group of four women came into the Treehouse, all of them in their mid-thirties. I needed to find a way to talk to them.

"This woman on the train—her name ended up being Brenda—had a nervous breakdown right there and then. She fainted. Two men who were afraid of airplanes and traveled on business trips up to New York all the time got up and grabbed her, checked her heartbeat and breathing, and put a pillow behind her head. I said, 'Damn, you don't see this everyday on an Amtrak train, do you?' Well, as it ended up, we took her off the train at the next stop and sent her to the local hospital. That would be Gaffney—we were doing the run down to New Orleans—and then on our way back up she waited there at the station for me. She got on board and said, 'I want you to tell me exactly where we were when I miscarried. I want you to take me to the spot so I can give my baby a proper burial.' I told her that by this time—a couple days had gone by—surely her miscarriage was gone. But she got on board the train and took it up to Charlotte, and then we got out and started walking back south on the tracks. My boss said I had to do it, and that I'd probably get a raise for the whole thing."

Two more women walked into the bar. I waved my arm faster for Sparky to get to the moral of the story.

"We found about twenty turtle shells," said Sparky. "You would not believe how many turtles get stuck in between the tracks, especially snapping turtles when you're near a lake or in the swamps. We found turtle shells, and that was it. I wasn't even sure what I was supposed to be looking for. And if I did run across anything that looked like a baby, I didn't want to see it, or point it out to Brenda. So as it ended up, after I finally convinced her that we'd gone past the spot where she miscarried, she walked over into the woods and got some sticks. She borrowed my shoelaces and fashioned a small wooden cross, stuck it a few feet from the track, and said she felt better. And an hour late this gandy dancer came from the station to pick us up to get us back to the station. I wonder whatever happened to old Brenda?" Sparky asked, like I'd know.

He walked off with his hands in his pockets, straight down like trowels were attached to the ends of his arms. I lost all pride and any bashfulness whatsoever and started asking women if they had any of their sonogram videotapes around their houses. I offered a hundred dollars to buy one of them.

Teresa Smiley said she'd be right back. Teresa Smiley said she kept hers on her bookshelf, stuck between a 12 Step program book and a Stephen King novel. Since her husband had gotten custody of their little boy, she got depressed thinking about it, but said, "A hundred dollars! Hell, I won't sell for less than *three* hundred."

It was one of those occasions when I didn't have time to check out the going rate for sonograms on the black market. So I said, "One-fifty." I said, "Lookit, unless you had your sonogram on Thursday, there's going to be a different date down there on the screen. I mean, I'm going to have to go to great lengths of finding out a way to forge the video."

Teresa Smiley stared hard at me, then sat back down at her table, a table filled with women who worked third shift at the mill. Teresa said, "The memory of a child is worth more than a hundred and fifty dollars, Ricky. And your wife won't even notice the wrong date down there. We women are interested in the baby, not the time of day. I'm insulted, and I think you should be really ashamed."

"A minute ago," I said, "you were saying how you got depressed even knowing the tape was around. Come on, Teresa, you don't know how much I need this tape." I told her my story, but didn't explain about *Bonanza* over the image of my baby. I told her it was professional wrestling, so she could understand why I might be a little distraught about having to work on Saturday in the first place.

Teresa said, "Two-fifty," I said, "Two," and she left to get the tape. I didn't even ask her if her child, too, was turned away from the camera, and if it wasn't turned away, was it real obvious as to the sex of the child. When I saw ours, I wasn't even sure where was the head and where was the tail. To me, Jessie's sonogram looked like a picture of an ulcer or something on her stomach wall. I couldn't make out a meaning whatsoever. I didn't have that art background that Jessie could boast about.

Sparky came over to me a few minutes after Teresa left and said, "You might have some trouble coming at you, but I'll be there for you."

I said, "What do you mean?" The worst thing that could happen, I thought, was for Jessie's meeting to be canceled and her coming to the Treehouse to spend the day.

Sparky said, "What I'm trying to tell you is, don't turn around immediately, but there's a guy down at the end of the bar staring a hole through you. It's Teresa's ex."

I didn't turn at all. I could feel the guy staring straight into my brain. The Treehouse had its regulars who came in every day—house painters, self-employed body shop men, the disabled, people who only really worked on Wednesday mornings over at the flea market—but there were people who came in haphazardly, maybe once a month, to sit by themselves and get over whatever it was that stuck in their craw. I never had to prebounce any of those people. First, it wouldn't matter—if they wanted to fight they'd fight no matter what I had to say. Second, most of them were so consumed with whatever bothered them, they didn't have the energy to actually get off the barstool and start a fight, though they'd probably like to see one.

I said to Sparky, "The one who got custody? Are you talking about Teresa's husband who ended up with the kid?"

He said, "That's the one. Name's Ted, but everyone calls him Slam. He won the state wrist wrestling championship four years in a row, and the southeast tournament twice."

I said, "Goddamn it." I thought, if only I'd taken the time to look at the videotape before I threw it in to tape *Bonanza*. I thought, if only the baby had turned around so we'd know the sex of it. I thought, if only Jessie hadn't gotten the appointment on Thursday, and almost caught myself thinking, if only I'd put on a rubber that night.

Sparky said, "I arm wrestled him one time, but it's hard for me to get a grip, what without a thumb. Hell, it was hard for him, too. I kept sliding right through his hand."

"Shut up, Sparky," I said, and walked straight over to Slam. I said, "Your ex-wife's about to save my life, man. I screwed up and taped over my child-to-be's videotape inside the womb, and Teresa's going to get y'all's so I can make a tape of it." I said, "My name's Ricky."

Slam said, "Wife."

I said, "Excuse me?" He didn't look my way. He seemed to keep staring at where I stood talking to Sparky.

"Not ex-wife. Wife. Just like a piece of paper can't make a marriage, a piece of paper can't end one, neither," said Slam.

I said, "Are you Catholic?"

This is no lie. Slam said, "I'm an American and it's the American way of being."

I said, "Oh. Well, then your *wife* is about to save my skin."

*Tape* the *tape*, I thought. I thought, you should've asked her to tape the tape. I mean, there wasn't a reason for me to pay so much to more or less swipe hers. I tried to think of a way of getting to her before she even got inside the Treehouse so we could at least renegotiate.

Slam said, "What?" He held his beer in a way I'd not seen before, a half-inch from his face and a quarter-inch to the right. At first I thought he used the can as a mirror to check out someone who walked up behind him. Being a pre-bouncer, I notice things like that.

I said, "Your wife's saving my ass."

There's this look that only certain people can give. There's this look some people can give that's somewhere between smoke in their eyes and hand grenades in their pockets. Slam had that look. I turned my head towards Sparky but he'd already started punching a guy named Hull who came in drunk and wanted a piece of another guy named Dayton for not painting his house evenly earlier in the summer.

Slam said, "Well, I guess that's better than *humping* your ass, Bo." He said, "Glad to hear it," grabbed his beer and left the bar, either unaware of the law, or unconcerned about the police that regularly parked across the street.

Sparky came over and said, "You got a way with words, Ricky. Whatever it is you said, you did it, man."

I sat down on the bar stool next to Slam's and concentrated so as not to actually pee in my pants like in the cartoons.

AS SOON AS JESSIE had taken that one-minute-and-you-know-if-you've-really-missed-your-period test in the bathroom, she pulled a Walkman out of the bedroom closet, put in new batteries, and slipped a tape of Mahler's Fourth Symphony in the cassette holder. She pulled the earpieces of the headset as far apart as possible, strapped them around her sides, and put the volume on full blast. Jessie said, "We're going to have a baby, Ricky."

I'd just been watching her from the other side of the room. I didn't even know about the bathroom test. I sat there on the side of the room reading my thesaurus. "A baby?" I said. "Are you sure?"

She said, "I have this theory. I believe that if you play music inside the womb, the fetus absorbs it and when the baby comes out, instead of crying and screaming, it'll make noises similar to an orchestra."

I said, "What?"

She said, "The reason why a baby always wails is because it absorbs the noises of the outside world for nine months. In the city it hears horns honking, people screaming, the conglomeration of people's conversations all going into one big drone, dogs barking, cats crying out in the night, the hiss of a teapot. . . ." She had a list of every possible noise, it seemed. She finally finished her dictum with, "So if I keep playing classical music, when the baby's in pain or wants a bottle, we'll be serenaded with French horns and oboes, and violins. Bassoons!" She said, "Bassoons! And piccolos and flutes and cellos."

Hell, to me it didn't sound like all that bad a theory. I mean, it's logically possible. I said, "Why don't you order some of those books on tape, and then at night the baby can tell *us* stories."

Jessie put another Walkman on her own ears and left the room. She kind of left the room a lot during her pregnancy, for that matter. I'm not sure why. I've always tried to be sensitive to her needs.

Ted, or Slam, whatever, kept standing outside the Treehouse. He was waiting for his ex-wife Teresa, I knew. Just about the time I started to go outside to tell him I wouldn't make a tape of his pre-born child, she tapped me on the shoulder. Like every intelligent woman with a lunatic ex-husband in her life, she sensed danger. She parked the Buick a few blocks away and took the back entrance. I said, "Ted's here."

She looked around. She said, "Ted was in here earlier but I don't see him now."

I said, "Out front."

"Oh. Well. Good," she said. "That'll be two hundred dollars up front, no check."

I only had a check. I said, "Hey look, I got this better idea.

Why don't we find another VCR, and do a tape-to-tape so you don't have to lose yours totally. I mean, some day you might want it back." I kind of saw a big confrontation ahead, like when birth mothers arrange for adoptive parents, then change their minds in the delivery room.

Teresa said, "I won't change my mind, believe you me. I've had it. I want a new life, Bubba. As a matter of fact, I've already contacted the paper to advertise a yard sale for next weekend. I'm getting rid of my old high school yearbooks, too."

I said, "Well, okay." It was nearly three o'clock and I couldn't take the chance of Jessie getting a ride home from the synagogue with one of her friends, slipping in her tape, and fainting when she came to believe that her baby had suddenly gained a clear and distinct shape and form which looked like Hoss. I said, "Hold on a second."

I bought Teresa a drink on my monthly tab and walked over to where Sparky stood in the corner of the bar, scanning the slim crowd. "Sparky," I said, "look, do you have one of those teller cards by any chance? I lost mine in the machine—not 'cause I didn't have any money—because the back strip got dirty or something and it's Saturday and the bank's closed and I need two hundred bucks right now to buy the tape. I can give you a check today, or if you wait until Monday morning I can go over to the bank and get cash for you."

Sparky said, "I hope you remember this when you go and name your child."

I said, "I can't name my kid *Sparky*."

Sparky said, "I wouldn't expect you to." He reached into the wallet he kept chained to his belt loop and pulled out two hundred 1-dollar bills. He said, "My given name's Earl. Earl for a boy, Earline for a girl."

I don't know why I said okay, but I did. I figured if I could get Sparky drunk later on in the evening, maybe he'd forget the promise.

"Here you go," I said to Teresa. She handed me the tape. She handed me her own personal sonogram videotape of the only child she'd ever had and said, "I hope I picked up the right one. Slam and me did some amateur strip stuff one night, but we never sent it off to any of those programs on cable."

I asked Sparky to cover for me, told him to use the word "discretionary" or "castigatory" should a fight seem eminent, and I took the back door out, too.

THERE IS A SUPREME BEING. Someone powerful exists, or at least existed for me that afternoon. I pulled out my tape filled with *Bonanza*, plus a half-hour special on the NASCAR season at the halfway point, and pushed Teresa's baby's video in my machine. It didn't need rewinding. I wondered if she'd ever really watched it.

It wasn't her strip show. Right there on the screen, in brilliant shades of gray, was a form. I couldn't make out eyes or genitals. There was no way possible Jessie could see the difference between her womb and that of a woman who grew up and lived in a mobile home.

I felt good about living in America.

The Supreme Being stayed on my side, 'cause while the tape still played, in walked Jessie, home from what ended up being a committee meeting of a group called Sisters of Bashemath, Ishmael's Daughter. She said, "I thought you had to work."

I moved closer to the television screen, down on the carpet, and held my forearm parallel to the date and time logo down at the bottom. I said, "I went and got things going, but I started feeling a little nauseated."

Jessie came up to me, all smiles, and put her hand on the back of my neck. She said, "That's so sweet. You have sympathy pains."

I knelt on the floor in front of the TV screen. I could hear Mahler's First Symphony playing out of the cassette attached to Jessie's stretched sash. I said, "Well, yeah, I had some pains alright, but I'm feeling much better now."

Jessie asked me to rewind the sonogram. I clenched my teeth, rewound it, prayed to all the superior beings ever invented for her not to notice the difference.

And she didn't. While I watched Teresa's child float around in her belly, Jessie lowered the volume on her Walkman and pushed her chin in towards her stomach. She said, "We're watching you right now, honey."

I didn't say anything about any kind of name recognition, like, "We're looking at you, Earl or Earline."

I sat and watched. And I thought to myself, certainly I want my own child to grow up and be happy and famous and healthy and intelligent. I thought, I want to be able to spend time with my kid, go to games, teach him or her how to communicate, take long trips across the country to see how different people live.

And deep down, oddly, I kind of wanted the kid I watched on the television screen to end up a bandit and a folk hero. I wanted that obscure head and tail I saw on the screen to grow up and be an outlaw of sorts, a fugitive. At that very moment I knew that I'd always keep up with Ted and Teresa's boy, and help him out whenever it seemed possible. I'd tell him to keep moving, always, in order to stay content, and to talk to strangers no matter how scary it may seem.

# How I Met My Second Wife

Because I had not grown up to be a sensitive, long-term-thinking, folk song–singing American, I didn't remove my caps. I didn't rinse the containers, and had gone ahead and stuck all my goddamn newspapers in paper grocery bags. I'd dropped all of my bottles into one fifty-five-gallon drum, and they had broken into brown, green, and clear shards. Only a month earlier I drove five miles down the road to a series of graffiti-ridden dumpsters, but then some environmentalist made up a story about bears showing up, and the next thing I knew the closest green boxes were across the state line, forty miles away. That meant I had to save my cardboard, aluminum, plastic, and glass—plus any tires, batteries, motor oil, and antifreeze—and drive them off to be separated at the recycling center fifteen minutes away from my pathetic house.

This is the country, in South Carolina. There is no garbage collector in my area. There's also no newspaper delivery, and I'm convinced the mail lady doesn't show up on Wednesdays because she readies herself for church. There's no cable TV this far out. Sometimes I see pterodactyls flying overhead. I think my closest neighbor owns some slaves. Down the road is a house full of Arena Football League players, that's how far from civilization I live.

I drove my pick-up truck around back of the house and

loaded up all the plastic Pepsi, orange juice, and milk jugs I'd thrown out the kitchen window. I got the big metal drum filled with beer and liquor bottles, and took what few newspapers and junk mail I kept in a log holder next to the fireplace. My regular garbage can was only half-filled, mostly with coffee grounds and some leftover catfish I threw away the night before.

I got my dog and said, "I doubt we'll be finding any good furniture or appliances like at the dumpsters, Hubcap."

My dog jumped in anyway. A couple of minutes later I eased into the recycling center parking lot. There were bins everywhere: Tires, Miscellaneous, #1 Plastic, Magazines, Cardboard, Newspapers, Scrap Metal, #2 Plastic, Aluminum, Batteries, Clear/Brown/Green Glass, Household Garbage, Plastic #3 through #5, 4 Tires Maximum, and Yard Waste. Off in the corner was a sign that read, "Small animals must be in plastic bags." I looked at my dog.

"That there's high-density polyethylene. Man, don't throw that in the polyethylene terephthalate," this woman yelled out me. I was the only person there, and I stood at the #1 Plastic bin.

Listen, I might not have been the Ralph Nader of saving our planet, but I knew enough about beauty and chance to understand that this woman shouldn't have been working the recycling center. Because I keep up with women daily, I knew that this woman could've walked down any runway in Paris, New York, or Miami wearing the latest see-through evening gown. My job required that I work six feet away from half-naked women forty hours per week. I knew women.

I could barely talk. I said, "I don't know. I didn't know. This bottle had the number 1 on it, so I thought that's what it meant." I wished I'd gotten dressed up before taking out my garbage.

The woman walked across the pavement as if her shoes were made by Hovercraft. There was not a more striking woman in all of the Southeast, I knew. Her yellow hair was back in a careless bun so that inch-wide streams framed her face haphazardly. She stood six feet tall, and although she didn't possess a physique paid for at the local aerobics center, I bet that she weighed in at about 130 pounds of solid muscle. Pinch a test tube in the middle; that's what she looked like, instead of an hourglass shape.

I held an empty orange bottle of Fab. I shook and tried to think up some good lies. My dog even wagged his tail, and he trusts nobody.

"Look at the bottom of the bottle. There are numbers on the bottom, One through Five. If there's not a symbol, just put it in the household garbage. It doesn't matter about any numbers on the paper label. A lot of products say they're number one, on the label."

She wore a light blue thin cotton jumpsuit. Also, a chain stretched to both ankles like some kind of geometry law. "I'm Mel Dantzler," I said. I didn't stick out my hand. I didn't put the detergent bottle back in my truck. "I haven't been much of a recycler, to be honest. I don't use that much stuff, though, I have to admit."

The woman turned around and looked at the ten-by-ten-foot shelter. PCDC—Pickens County Detention Center—was printed on the back of her jumpsuit. "My name's Violet." She pulled up her sleeve to show a tattoo of a flower on her forearm, which I supposed was a violet. She laughed. "I'm Violet, or 45207, I think." She took the bottle from me, unscrewed the cap, and threw it into the #2 Plastic bin.

"I'm Mel," I said again.

"Now is that short for Melvin, or is it short for Hormel?" Violet asked. She smiled and shaded her eyes. "I've had a lot of Hormel in jail. I can't say I've had much Melvin."

Later on that night I thought about how I should've said my name was short for Melodious, or Mellow. I should've said it was short for Meltdown. "Yes, ma'am. Melvin. My daddy was a Melvin, and I am, too. I'm Melvin, Jr. I don't have any kids, though. If I ever have any kids I'm not going to name him Melvin. I'll name him something normal like Gene, or Doug. Or her. If I have a little girl I'll name her something normal, too. My wife and I split up two years ago."

"That's nice, Mel," Violet said. "Don't ever call me 'ma'am' again, though." She picked up a 2-liter bottle of RC Cola, took off the top, blew into the top like a poor man's ocarina, and tossed it into the #1 Plastic container. "I ain't thirty years old yet." Violet stepped away from me and pulled her head for me to follow. "Pull on up and I'll help you dump your problems. I'll let you take a look at what other people needed to lose."

I DON'T WANT TO GO into a lot of detail, but a year earlier I lost my good job about a week before my wife left me, and soon thereafter answered an ad in the paper for a responsible driver. It didn't say anything about how I needed to know something about the medical field or welfare. I responded, proved that I could drive a truck the size of a twenty-foot U-Haul, and ended up getting the job as driver of the Mammo-Van. Pretty much I went around from poor area to poor area, backed into driveways, and let a doctor and nurse take X-rays of women who couldn't afford to pay a regular doctor. I wrapped myself in a lead blanket at each stop, and listened to the radio. Everyone said early on that I had nothing to fear, but after I proved to be a safe and prompt employee, one of the nurses brought me what I wanted.

I'm not allowed to get out of the cab, open the back doors, and watch what's going on, of course. From what I saw out of the side mirrors, I wouldn't want to. I don't want to make any generalizations about poor white women who can't afford regular doctor mammograms, but most of them probably needed a wide-angle X-ray to fully scan their torsos and whatnot.

The week before my wife left me I traveled around the hinterlands of South Carolina and taught poetry for some kind of Outreach Program. Pick up a rock. Throw it in any direction. Watch where it stops. That's a hinterland in South Carolina. Poetry Outreach was supposed to heighten the language skills of 5th through 8th graders. Maybe it did. I only know that it made me find roadhouses and hotel bars more often than not. It made me understand the health profession indirectly, and then I got the job driving the Mammo-Van. I can't explain some mysteries of the universe.

I got home from the recycling center that Saturday morning and immediately washed my clothes. I'm talking that I washed my dirty clothes, and then took shirts off hangers and washed them again. I emptied my chest of drawers and re-washed everything until my detergent bottle, made of high density polyethylene—#2 plastic—was empty. I went out and bought a six-pack of little Cokes, a tub of margarine, a coffee can with a plastic lid, liquid dish soap, peanut butter, and straws. I bought a newspaper, and reached inside the grocery store's cardboard box where conscientious people threw back their plastic grocery bags. On the way home I pulled over and picked up beer cans thrown sideways the night before.

That night, right before I fell asleep, I wondered if maybe I misheard Violet, that perhaps she swallowed last syllables like bad poets do, that she only said to me, "I'm *Violent*."

I checked my locks again. I sat down at the kitchen table, took out a notebook, and wrote down everything I owned that I could possibly recycle, from the dingy gray screens on half my windows, to the black plastic underneath my mulch. At dawn I went outside, cut half my yard, and put the clippings in plastic bags.

THE RECYCLING CENTER was only open from 1:00 until 4:00 on Sundays. There was a sign on both sides of the gate. I showed up first, my pick-up filled only with the empty detergent bottle and a sandwich bag filled with cut grass. I'd left my house loaded up, but then thought about how I needed to conserve the things I wanted to dole out once a day.

I also brought along an unopened bottle of wine and a handful of daffodils I managed not to cut in the corner of my four-acre briar-and-blackberry yard. I had cigarettes, nicotine patches, and a couple mini-bottles of vodka.

"Drive on up here, Mel," Violet said. She stood by the shelter thirty yards away from the #1 Plastics bin, and her supervisor—or at least the recycling center foreman—stood next to her. He eyed me like I was a nocturnal animal out in daylight.

I pulled up short and set the handbrake. I got out of my truck, got down on the asphalt, and pretended to look up at the chassis, as if I'd drug a deer beneath me for the last hour or something. Violet walked up. Peripherally I noticed her supervisor jam a metal rod in the mouth of the Household Garbage compactor. "I brought along a few gifts for you. Something about seeing you yesterday made me bring along some gifts. I don't want to get you in trouble or anything, but I made a decision about four o'clock this morning." I kept looking at my chassis. My tailpipe needed some welding work.

"Are you talking to me?" Violet said. "You've seen too many jailhouse movies. Move your lips. Make eye contact, man." I got up and whisked my pants. Violet looked in the cab and saw the wine, et cetera. "I ain't got that much time left locked up. Don't tempt me, Mel. The last thing I need is another six months lopped on."

Violet appeared to wear the same jumpsuit from the day before. "I don't know what's come over me," I said. "I apologize."

She walked over, picked up the baggy of grass clippings, and took them over to Yard Waste. I opened the door to the truck and popped the hood, then pretended to look for a rotten hose. Violet came back holding the empty bag and said, "Stay here another half-hour or so. The man's going to call his girlfriend. Drive up to the Aluminum box like you want to throw something in. I'm going to fill up what cans we got in the back of your truck. I want you to take it down to the scrap metal place in Pickens. They pay about forty cents a pound. I'll split the money with you. Come here everyday before six o'clock. The Alcoa truck shows up a little after seven. The jail van comes and gets me right after."

Maybe my eyes had gone bad, but I'd gotten some kind of 3-D vision and her pelvis seemed to almost poke out and touch me. Violet pulled out the dipstick, looked at it for a second, then wiped it off on her leg. "I'll do it," I said.

"Fucking idiots come in here and throw away a dollar's worth of Coke and beer cans about every fifteen minutes. I don't know if they don't know, or if they just don't care."

"I've always saved my beer cans. If you remember from yesterday, I didn't have any cans. Or at least I didn't have any aluminum cans. I take them off to a scrap metal joint about once a month. I put the money in a piggy bank, and at the end of a year take that money out and buy a case of beer." This wasn't exactly true. I turned in my aluminum, took the money, and threw it in an old Charles Chips canister. When it filled to the brim I planned to take the money to the Cherokee reservation and play poker. I made a point to eat vegetables and vitamins regularly so I could live that long.

"Some pinhead wife brought in twenty pounds of copper wire one day. I didn't know anybody like you back then, Melvin. If I'd've known you then, we could've split ten dollars."

I touched my radiator cap. It burned my finger. Violet turned around to look for her supervisor. I said, "What're you in for?"

Violet turned back towards me as if I asked her what size feminine hygiene napkin she preferred. "Things most people do and get away with. It's a long story. I know that business partners probably need to know each other, but I won't ask about your life if you don't ask about mine. I'll tell you this—I got another two months to serve. I'm no math wizard, but I imagine you and me can make about four to six hundred dollars each. I know you won't cheat me. I got your license plate memorized, and the computer I got in jail lets me know where you live, Melanoma."

I put my hands on the hood to pull it down. "Someone's going to notice how there's no aluminum in the bin every day."

"We'll leave ten or twelve cans a day. Trust me. I won't tell on you if we get caught. I know all about injustice, and I don't want to shove it on somebody who's brought me a bottle of wine and flowers." Violet stepped back. The recycling center supervisor was inside his little office. "Put the wine in the green glass bin. I don't want to hurt your feelings or anything, but go ahead and throw the flowers in Yard Waste."

When Violet filled the bed of my truck two feet deep in aluminum cans I didn't say anything about how maybe I deserved better than a fifty percent share, seeing as it was my gasoline, my time, my Hefty outdoor garbage bags I would be using. Like an idiot I only thought about how everyone has a past, and I'd forget about hers as soon as she got released from whatever she did—whatever we all did, but kept from getting caught.

HUMAN-CAUSED CONTAMINANTS are called "nonpoint-source pollution" according to something I read. Evidently this includes everything from throwing an empty hamburger wrapper out the window at seventy miles an hour, to letting crankcase oil drip out on the driveway with the transmission in park. It includes beer cans in the ditch, and refrigerators toppled down a ravine. Antifreeze on the store shelf almost qualifies as nonpoint-source pollution. Used disposable diapers floating in the Atlantic fit the definition.

I learned all of this from a pamphlet given to me by a woman who wore a two-pocketed uniform shirt with "Carla" stitched above one and "Pickens Scrap" above the other. She kept a flat toothpick at the edge of her flat lips. Carla said, "They's a lot of things we all need to know about. They's a lot of things we bring in for scrap that people pay good money for at the flea market." She pointed to a shelf of green telephone insulators. "I'm saving up for the day I can break the all-time record for one table over there. I think some woman sold a Beanie Baby for thousand dollars a few months ago. That's what I heard. That's what come down."

I wanted out of there. In the past I had only brought maybe ten pounds of beer cans in to a scrap metal operation, placed them on the scale, and gotten my receipt and three to five dollars, depending on market price. "I'm going to bring in a bunch of cans every Saturday. If y'all stayed open past five o'clock I'd bring them in every day."

Carla looked out the window. "Is that a real Mammo-Van? My cousin's boyfriend's sister had to go inside one them. She said it gave her creeps. She said reminded her of a drive-in date, being in close quarters with a man's hands on her titty."

"It's a real one. I'm just borrowing it. I can't get a week's worth cans back my truck without five trips over, and that'd defeat the purpose, what with miles per gallon and whatnot."

Here's the map: the closest dumpsters were now forty miles away, over the border in North Carolina. The recycling center where Violet worked was fifteen miles away. Somewhere in between was the Pickens Scrap place where Carla wore her shirt proudly. If you stood thirty Carlas upright, and put thirty Carlas horizontal with the ground on top of them, you'd have Stonehenge in the early days. "Well," Carla said. "We can't all live in a hub."

I drove straight to the recycling center after I got cash money. I drove in like I owned the place and passed more than a few Broncos, Suburbans, Jeep Cherokees, and even a couple Range Rovers, so the drivers could get out and discard what they no longer saw as necessary. I skidded two feet from Violet, who helped a man shove his La-Z-Boy into the Miscellaneous bin. "I got us the first dividends," I said.

Violet gripped the recliner's wooden adjustment lever and leaned over in a way that wasn't good for the back. She wore an orange suit on this day, with thicker fabric. Her shackles showed moreso. She said to me, "Sir, paper products are divided into magazines, office paper, pasteboard, cardboard, newspapers, and junk mail. Figure it out immediately."

The man that Violet helped wore a tweed jacket and handed her paper money for helping him. He tipped her, is what I'm saying. She nodded, smiled—and although I couldn't tell from where I stood—probably pumped his crotch a couple times. That's what it looked like from my vantage point, there with two handfuls of quarters. I said, "Hey, listen."

The man with the chair opened the back-seat door and both he and Violet leaned inside as if they puzzled over marijuana seeds. I stuck my full hands in my pants pockets, walked backwards five or six steps, and got back in the truck. I'm not sure why I thought how some women deserved the scare of meaningless benign fatty lumps and others didn't deserve lumps whatsoever.

I was crushed momentarily. I felt the same as a caveman who brought back an entire elk or something, only to have his cavewoman wife say she'd decided to go vegetarian. If I still wrote poetry, I might've written a poem about it that started off something like, "I felt the same as a caveman who/brought back an entire elk, only/to have his cavewoman wife say/she'd decided to go vegetarian."

I'll be the first to admit that I may have lost my Poetry Outreach job for reasons other than drinking nightly at places with warped pool sticks.


THE DOCTOR AND NURSE working the Mammo-Van both come out of a rural clinic network that one of the Democratic governors started back in the 1970s. There's about twenty Mammo-Vans in the state, each covering a two- to three-county area. I don't want to make any judgments about the doctor, but I bet he graduated towards the bottom of his class and could never get a job above some one-story hospital on a Gullah-speaking island. The doctor's name was Dr. Mulkey, and he took himself way too seriously for a man who spent most of his day holding on to a subway-like handgrip in the back of the Mammo-Van because I took sharp turns at thirty miles an hour.

The nurse, though, saw her job as meaningful and respectable—which it was—and could communicate with people as if they were human beings, which they were. The nurse understood the fear on women's faces, and oftentimes held their hands between the front doors of their small houses, trailers, or apartments, and the back door of the van. Her name was Ms. Frankie to our clients, Francine being her first name. She even wore a gold metal name-tag pin with that etched onto it. I never knew her last name. Frankie sat with me in the cab between mammogram stops; she said she got nauseated in the back, but I knew she couldn't take the doctor.

"You're not your jovial self, Mel," Frankie said to me the day after I found Violet making deals with every recycler in Pickens County. "I hope you're not unhappy with this job."

I kept my eyes on the road. Each morning I tried to memorize our route, seeing as sometimes we ventured down dirt roads without street signs. "I got a weird story to tell you, if you promise not to tell Mulkey or anyone else. I got a story I just can't puzzle out. I think I made a big mistake."

Frankie said, "You're not going back to writing poetry, are you?"

I passed a series of rusted drums on the side of the road, probably once filled with some type of chemical that shouldn't seep into the ground. We weren't far from my house. "Good Lord, no. It's almost that bad, but not quite." Then I went ahead and told the entire story, starting from my first wife leaving, and ending with Violet's hands inside the La-Z-Boy man's recreational vehicle.

We took a turn down a gravel road. Frankie held directions for a place where supposedly six grown women lived together, all old-maid sisters. In the back of the Mammo-Van I heard Mulkey's weight bang against the lead-lined walls. Frankie said, "This will sound a little New Age, maybe. But I believe in fate, Mel. I can't help it. It's the way I got brought up, and it's the way I've noticed things throughout my life."

I hit the brakes to let a blacksnake cross. I didn't want Frankie bringing up karma, or what-goes-around-comes-around. I'd learned juju while teaching those outreach things. I said, "Go on, snake," and blew the horn.

"You must know bad to understand good. You must know good to understand evil. You must know fear to understand peace. That's how I see my job, Mel. You have to understand pain and disease to understand satisfaction and good health. I don't know if it's possible, but when our patients undergo their X-rays, I try to think all of this over and over, and send my thoughts into the minds of our women."

We came upon a large wooden house, porch sagging, two or three pecan trees in the front yard. A handful of mixed-breed dogs came out of nowhere, barking and wagging their tails. A half-naked middle-aged woman waved at us, then turned to yell towards the open door. Presently five other women emerged, older, all limping in one form or the other. I said, "You got your job cut out for you," because I couldn't think of anything unfamiliar.

Frankie patted my leg. "No. You got *your* job cut out for *you*, Mel. You have to find a way to understand that meeting Violet is going to be a way for you to find the woman you were meant to meet. It worked the same way with your first wife, I bet. I know. Think about it."

Frankie got out of the Mammo-Van and waved to everyone standing on the front porch. She reached down and pet a number of curs. I thought about meeting my first wife, in the college cafeteria, where I drank coffee and she flicked fried okra at a table full of sorority members.

I CONTINUED TO VISIT the recycling center with an empty truck bed. Violet filled it, and I went home. Somewhere in between, always, she'd shuffle off in her shackles and talk close to some rich guy's ear, often laugh and touch the guy's shoulder, chest, or lower back. Understand, for me Violet continued to be the most alluring human being I'd ever seen — she even got smarter and prettier each time I came in pretending to discard a pizza box or swizzle stick. She said things like, "Hey, Mel, I'm glad to see you again." I said everything from, "Last week's take was $106.68," to "I love you."

I saw Carla on Saturdays, and even brought her a box of toothpicks the last visit. Carla gave me money and never asked questions. She flexed her biceps, that's all.

This was five weeks into the scam: "Violet, I've been keeping the money in an old globe I bought somewhere with a slit in the top. I'm keeping our can money in the world. It's old. It's still got the USSR on it intact. It's still got Burma there."

"That's good to know," she said. "In case you die or something, I'll know where to look after I get out. In case I need to go over and break into your house."

I threw a plastic bag into the small-animal bin. A rabbit had gotten creamed in front of my house the previous night. I said, "I know I don't have a right to be jealous or anything, but I can't help feel that way when I see you whispering to these other men coming in here. I know you have the right to cut deals with anyone you want, but goddamn it's eating me up for some reason." At the time I didn't realize that I'd said the exact same thing to my first wife right before she left me. My first wife worked as a librarian.

Violet placed about a dozen steel Sapporo cans in the back corner of my truck bed. "You can hide these in the middle of a garbage bag and they won't know the difference at the scrap metal yard. Listen, Mel. I'm in jail. I got sentenced to six months for something that, at worst, should've gotten me a job with the Department of Treasury. Those men I talk to are either lawyers or investment bankers. I know all of them. I knew them in the past, and I'll know them in the future, believe me. I can't ask somebody of their status to take aluminum in to get recycled for me. It wouldn't look good. I don't want to hurt your feelings any, but that's the way it is. That's the world. That's economics, the caste system, and a chapter in sociology, all wrapped up in one." She pulled up her sleeve. Below the tiny tattoo of the violet was a new one, homemade-jailhouse obviously, that gray-green color of crooked knuckles.

It was a plain dollar-bill sign. Violet had put a $ on her forearm, which pretty much told me all about her.

I DROVE THE MAMMO-VAN daily, got off work, and went to the recycling center. I didn't let Violet get to me. I took Hubcap the dog wherever I went, and talked to him about the mysteries and intricacies of human behavior.

In the middle of Violet's last week of incarceration I got off work early. Because I didn't really want to see her after she got out, I loaded up what beer cans I had bagged in my shed out back and went to Carla's scrap place. I planned to take Violet half the money and say that was my last delivery.

Carla stood there with one of those scales of justice things, placing pennies on one side. "Look at this, Mel," Carla said. "Left side right here all wheat pennies. The gub'me't quit making wheat pennies in 1958. Right side, pennies minted after 1981. Shit. It ain't close. It's getting to the point it'll take twicet many new pennies to equal a pound of wheat pennies before long. Mark my words. Hey, it ain't Saturday."

I said, "Maybe shine doesn't weigh as much, Carla." I pointed at the new pennies. The door opened and a woman wearing a normal, old-fashioned gray jogging suit came in. What I'm saying is, she had on sweatpants and a sweatshirt. She had her hair up in a haphazard bun, too, with inch-wide streaks framing her face, and it didn't take a logician to figure out that I thought how she looked similar to Violet, when I first met

Violet. I thought of bacon strips, too, for some reason. I said to Carla, "I got off early. No one needed a mammogram this afternoon."

Carla jerked her head upward towards the stranger. "Ma'am?"

The woman said, "I don't know if you can help me or anything, but I'm cleaning up what my husband left me with. I got an air conditioner and a dehumidifier I don't want to take time to sell in the newspaper. Also, I got this old Valiant he left behind. I'd just as soon sell it for scrap than admit I have it in my driveway."

I turned around and looked at her. She looked familiar. She looked like a woman you'd notice poring over a foreign newspaper in the library—trim, serious, with just enough veins in her hands to show she knew the difference between pain and boredom. "I'll pay you a hundred dollars more for the car than whatever they'll pay for it here," I said. I didn't even ask her if it ran.

Carla said, "If we got to tow it in we don't give but fifty dollars. Takes money breaking down a broken-down car."

The woman looked at me and smiled. "I know you. You came and taught my kids one Saturday about two years ago. I used to teach down in Beaufort. You came down and taught my kids poetry."

I said, "That's where I know you from. I'm Mel." I stuck out my hand. "I'll give you $150 for the Valiant, if you want."

She said, "Mel. That's right. I'm Lorraine. Are you still writing poems?"

Carla said, "Poems?" and laughed. "He's a truck driver, going around, looking at women's boobs."

I said, "I will."

I got my money from Carla. I helped Lorraine unload her dehumidifier and air conditioner. Later I followed her home,

48

looked at the Valiant, and paid her cash money on the spot. Hubcap got in it, and I drove the thing home. Lorraine followed close behind in my truck. When we got to my house she kept bringing up things I'd told her kids, things I didn't remember whatsoever. Evidently I brought up both the notions of Chance and risking sentimentality—two things I imagine every poetry teacher brings up one week into any class.

I made a pitcher of margaritas. Lorraine told me how she moved upstate from Beaufort, how her first husband was a man whose breath whistled lies more often than not. I told her how I drove around most days with not much on my mind, until I needed to stop at a place of pure fear and anxiety.

I thought about mentioning my new theories on incarceration, but didn't want to scare her off. Neither of us made a toast. Lorraine looked around my half-bare house and didn't let her head bob one way or the other. We reached over simultaneously to wipe salt from the other's lip, just as the poor tired sun slumped towards more people needing light.

# Directions for Seeing,
# Directions For Singing

I KNEW THAT SHE WASN'T all that keen on leaving me. Why else would she want the tape? I've never heard of a woman who left her husband, said there was no other choice, and yet she wanted what might be their most sacred possession—unless they had kids or something.

The one thing she wanted was the videotape. She told me that I could keep the other car, the appliances, the flatware. I could take sole possession, without interference from a lawyer, of every pot and pan, the "his" and "hers" towels, the television, the furniture. She only needed her own clothes and the Subaru wagon her father gave her for a college graduation present. And she wanted the videotape of our wedding ceremony.

Lilly said, "I'm sorry, Eston. But you shouldn't have told me anything like that. I have to leave you now. There's no other choice. I feel confident that my counselor would agree with my decision."

I said, "Look, Lilly, this was all your idea. I mean, I didn't cheat on you or anything. And it was for your own good—not mine."

"Give me the tape, Eston. I want the tape."

"You don't need the tape, Lilly. I'll keep it. And I'll watch it every morning before I go out on the road."

"I don't really want it, Eston. I just want to put it in the drive-way and back over the thing on my way out of our life."

She had never talked this way before the counseling sessions. The whole reason she left me had to do with something Margie, her therapist, suggested. We were to sit down once or twice a week and tell each other something about ourselves that the other person didn't know. This was supposed to strengthen our marriage.

Lilly said, "Eston, I had this dream last night. I didn't even tell Margie about it."

What kind of name is Margie for a therapist, anyway? I wondered. Shouldn't they be called Doctor something?

"In this dream," she went on, "you were standing in the corner of the bedroom. You were trying to hide from me or something, but both of us knew you were there. I mean, you knew I saw you there, and I knew you knew I saw you, but we both pretended not to know."

I said, "Lilly, is this supposed to mean something? Did Freud say something about people hiding from each other in their dreams?"

Lilly said, "Hold on, that's not it. So you were in the corner, just standing there, and I took off my clothes and got on the bed. All of a sudden, the door opened and this woman with scarlet hair comes in. She's naked, too, and she gets into bed with me. I look over at you in the corner and you start to cry. But I go ahead and make love to this woman anyway."

Lilly sat there at our kitchen table, nodding. She kind of smiled, too. I said, "That's what you have to tell me?"

She said, "Uh-huh. Now it's your turn."

Well, I had something to tell her all right. Two months earlier Lilly had come home to tell me that our marriage—or at least her life—needed some help. Some women's center in town was conducting seminars twice a week, taught by honest-to-goodness counselors who had M.A.'s in psychology and certificates for conducting these kinds of seminars. It cost two grand for the course, and the participants would learn how to visualize, how to use crystals more effectively—that kind of stuff.

Lilly went through the first two-month seminar. But she said she needed a follow-up course—on the advice of Margie—that was a sort of an advanced class in reading Tarot cards to plan the future. There was also an intensive session for anger therapy, where the women hit each other with Nerf bats. They pretended that whoever they bashed was whatever pissed them off. It could've been housework. It could've been their husbands. It could've been this year's spring fashions, I don't know.

It seems to me that a crazy woman shouldn't hang around other crazy women if she really wants to be cured. I've heard that people who work around autistic children for a long period of time start picking up autistic mannerisms. Put a pig in the henhouse from the start and you'll end up with a clucking pig, et cetera. So having a group of loony, lost women meeting twice a week didn't seem like a good idea to me in the first place.

Not for $2,000 a seminar. I didn't have that kind of money for the advanced course. But I wanted a happy wife. What an idiot I was.

I said, "That's good about your dream, Lilly. I think that it's a healthy thing to dream about women—in your case. It's all that anima-animus stuff, probably. Does Margie ever mention that?"

"No, I don't think so. She said it probably had to do with what I ate for supper."

"I thought you said you didn't tell her about the dream? I thought we were supposed to tell each other things that no one else knows."

"Oh. Well, I lied, then. So that's two things I've told you tonight that you didn't know about me."

Great, I thought. Suddenly my wife had transformed into a lying bisexual.

"Now it's your turn, Eston. Tell me something about yourself."

I met Lilly five years ago. I managed a bookstore in town and she went to the local community college. She would come into the store and tell me everything she learned about split infinitives, comma splices, and transitional phrases, as I showed her our selection of novels her English department was too conservative to teach. We started dating a few months later. In the summer we got married with her parents' blessings, provided I promised to quit the bookstore where I made just above minimum wage. Lilly's father retired early, pulled some strings, and got me his old sales route from Savannah to Fayetteville.

My ex-father-in-law sold ethnic panty hose. That's what I do now. Each year I give a thousand bucks to the United Negro College Fund. I want black women to do well in college, graduate, be successful. I want them to go out and buy a pair of panty hose every day. I even support two kids in Africa through one of those missionary funds. It costs me a buck-fifty a day, but, as I figure, these kids will grow up healthy and intelligent—maybe get a grant to come study in the United States, buy panty hose, and so forth. Or, one day, my territory might expand past Fayetteville and across the Atlantic.

THE DAY BEFORE Lilly and I started doing that truth-therapy crap, I had driven home from Savannah. It'd been a bad trip. In the back of my van were 864 pairs of panty hose. Either the company had to start making the things less defective or no one in the area could afford them any more. I'll be the first to admit that Republican administrations are the downfall for the ethnic panty hose salesman.

Anyway, I was driving up I-95 visualizing a better, more peaceful existence. Lilly learned how to do it at the Women's Center and taught me how important it was. Whenever stress builds up to the point that a stroke seems the only way out, it's good to pretend that you're in another atmosphere. With another payment coming up for Lilly's new course—and with no black, Hispanic, or Chinese women buying my products—I couldn't think of anything else except our financial situation.

So there I was driving up the interstate, pretending that I was aboard the Titanic, standing right on the bow. Then I was on a fourth cross next to Jesus, giving directions to my accusers on how to hammer better. Then I was Custer, Hemingway's gunsmith, Amelia Earhart, Gauguin's Tahitian women. I was arrested for spitting on the glass of a drive-in teller window at the bank, sentenced to life in prison, and placed in a cell with Charles Manson.

I don't know if it was some kind of cause and effect, but right there I came back to reality and saw the exit ramp to a little town called Coward. The town had one general store. A few years ago the owner, a man named Harley, refused to sell my product because he didn't want more black people in the town—or pretty black women who might entice his son—and he said that I should be lynched for being in this line of work.

I took the exit. I guess I should've been more patient and selective. When I parked I didn't even check to see what I grabbed in the back of the van.

"OKAY, LILLY, I'LL TELL YOU something about myself that you don't know. Here it is," I said to her. She sat forward on the chair. I stared at the coffee maker for a moment, wondering why

I no longer taught in college, why I had let her father talk me into changing professions.

"Don't feel afraid. I feel much better after telling you about my dream, Eston."

I said, "I love you very much, Lilly. I don't want you to be miserable, or depressed, or whatever. I want us—when the time is right for you—to raise a family, get a house at the beach, the whole fireworks stand."

"I already know that, Eston," Lilly said. She kind of frowned, like if I didn't come up with something along the lines of infidelity, I was worthless at this little project.

"Hold on," I said. "Because I love you so much—because you've made my entire life worth living—I want you to continue with your classes over at the women's thing. I don't agree with a single aspect of anything that goes on there, but I don't feel threatened by it, and I want you to be healthy."

She rolled her eyes again. She asked me if I'd ever dreamed about being with a man.

I ignored the question. "So tonight on the way home I tried to rob a store, so we could come up with the money for that next semester of therapy."

What I needed to use for a mask, as it ended up, was our garter line, maybe in ivory or taupe. Instead, I threw a five-x, queen-sized pair of black panty hose over my face. Those things fit women from 180 to 300 pounds, hips to sixty inches.

Sixty inches is five feet of hips, and that's a lot.

So I went into old man Harley's store, waving around an empty bottle of Crown Royal stuffed into a paper bag. I yelled out, "Okay, buddy, hand over all your cash."

He was in the back of the store, putting drinks in the cooler. He yelled out to the front, "I'll be with you in a minute, partner."

I pulled up the hose and peeked around to see if anyone else was in the store. I was alone, and the door to the stock room opened. I put the hose back over my face.

"Hand over all your money," I said to Harley. I couldn't see a thing, but I moved my head to the sound of his footsteps, like I knew what makes sense.

"You don't know the woman who wore those things, do you? Good God, man, you could hang a whole hog in those things."

I started to tell him to shut up and just hand over the money, but a customer walked in and startled me, and I dropped the bag, breaking my Crown Royal bottle. Harley said, "Well, that makes sense. You'd have to be drunk to put a fat woman's lingerie on your head—in public, at least."

I picked up the bag and broken bottle and left. I drove in reverse out of the parking lot and down the road until I got to the ramp to get back on the interstate. I could have had a wreck, or gotten a ticket. I did it all for Lilly.

So when I finished telling her all about my one attempt at armed robbery, she told me that she couldn't trust me as the father of her children, even though we didn't have any. Then she said that I'd probably be a good father after all, but I'd be the kind of husband she couldn't trust. And almost every man is one or the other, according to Margie.

I said, "Lilly, this was your little game. And I did it all for you." She was out of the kitchen, haphazardly collecting her crystals and clothes, chanting something I couldn't understand.

It sounded like the wedding march.

MY NEIGHBOR EUGENE likes me so much he cleans my windshield every night. Eugene teaches entomology at the community college. Every night when I come off the road, he shows up to identify and collect any insects I've amassed during the day.

57

He says that my van is like some kind of magnet for moths and dragonflies. One night I came home with a luna moth stuck in my grill. Eugene was so happy he cooked dinner for Lilly and me that night.

"She just up and left, huh?" he said when he learned that Lilly was gone. He came over to complain that I hadn't been to work in a week and that he needed more bugs—except he called them specimens instead of bugs.

I said, "Yeah, Eugene, she just left. A week ago tonight, as a matter of fact. Said she was miserable and that she couldn't trust me as a husband or a father. You want a drink?"

Since Lilly left, I'd been putting away about a bottle a day of Jim Beam. I poured mine over a tumbler of ice and added a jigger of water. I didn't want to be hard core about it.

"Do mine the opposite way," said Eugene. "I got a couple of nice praying mantises next door I need to work on tonight."

I didn't take his advice and gave him a half-and-half of bourbon and water. It felt good to be drinking with the boys again—or even just one boy. I hadn't done it since getting married.

I said, "I can't figure it out, man. She didn't want to work when we got married, so I told her she didn't have to. She sat here at home and read books for the first year of our marriage. Then she wanted to get a job working as an editor, and I set up an interview for her with Hosiery Today in Greensboro. I even offered to move up there, but she didn't want to move so far away from her family. Then she finally took that job writing for the weekly shopper. She seemed fine. She liked doing human-interest stories."

"I was really happy with the piece she did on me," Eugene said.

"And then two months ago she decides that her life is miserable and that she needs a sabbatical from the paper so she can go find herself. Hell, Eugene, the girl is twenty-six years old. That's not old enough to get lost, if you ask me."

Eugene stared into his glass. He probably pondered the molecular structure of the ice cubes or something. One thing about scientists—they're on a different biological clock than humanities professors and salesmen. Scientists only use the bathroom right after they get out of bed in the morning, I think. A person could read all of Dostoyevsky in a science building's men's room without any distractions. In the humanities building, and out on the road selling, a person doesn't have time to read the graffiti. Or the religious tracts.

"How old are you now?" Eugene finally said.

"I'm thirty-six."

"Me too. At least you've been married. There aren't a whole lot of women in this area I can go up to and start talking to about worker bees and cicadas. Man, you can talk about literature. You can walk right up to a woman in a bar and identify her panty hose. You've got it made, Eston."

I feel kind of sleazy admitting it—and Lilly never knew, I don't think—but I kept a collection of clear fingernail polish in my van. Sometimes I'd be stocking a store with my product and notice a customer with a run. I'd ask her to stay put and I'd go out and get a bottle. Twice I'd applied the polish myself—once to a blind woman who trusted me, and once to a hooker in Charleston who propped her foot on my shoulder while I knelt down by my rack. It took me damn near all afternoon.

I said, "Maybe you're right, Eugene. Maybe I'm a lot luckier than I realized." I went to the sink and made another bourbon. My neighbor took his first sip and made a face. "Maybe God will tell me when I die, 'Eston, you taught a bunch of kids who came into your bookstore how to like poetry that they didn't have to know for their classes. You taught a lot of women with sixty-inch hips how to feel good about themselves. You allowed one woman to leave her parents, find herself, and move back in with her parents. Good job, take a front row seat, buddy.'"

"At least you stuck to your vows. And you didn't turn into a bank robber or anything," said Eugene.

I said, "Change the subject."

Lilly's parents made us get married in their Methodist church, by their minister. I had a friend from college who went on to Yale Divinity School and became some kind of Unitarian or something, and I wanted him to perform the ceremony. My in-laws-to-be said that Unitarians weren't really Christians, that God wouldn't acknowledge a marriage done by the leader of an intellectual discussion group.

I said okay.

Lilly's Methodist minister wasn't all that Methodist. He kind of swayed toward the charismatic. He didn't mind people yelling things out in church or speaking in tongues. He made Lilly and me answer a series of questions before we even went through with the actual wedding, talked to us about goals in life, wanted to know if we planned to bring up our kids in the church. When I told him it seemed more practical to bring the kids up in the same house where the parents lived, his eyes rolled back a little and he started coughing. I told him it was just a joke, and he told me that I shouldn't joke around. Otherwise, he would see to it that Lilly and I never got married. I said okay.

Two years ago this same minister took a group of teenage boys up to a retreat in the mountains of North Carolina, stripped them down, and tail-gunned them all. During the trial one of the boys said that they were forced to sing "Rock of Ages" while the preacher raped them. Somehow the court said the minister only needed psychiatric counseling and parole, not a jail term. The church took away his license to preach, and about a week after the trial he had the nerve to come to me looking for a job selling ethnic panty hose. I told him I didn't have a line of hose for pederasts. He told me I'd fry in hell. I walked away, not wanting to beat the guy up and have to face Lilly and her parents.

Eugene got up and poured another drink for himself. He said, "You know, I've only been to one wedding in my life, and I don't even remember being there. This cousin of mine got married when I was about five. I was the pall bearer."

"Ring bearer, Eugene."

"Yeah. Yeah, sorry, Freudian slip."

"Don't bring psychology into it, buddy."

"I was the ring bearer, but I don't remember anything, except I see the pictures from time to time at my parents' house. There's this great one of the flower girl shoving cake into my face. I wonder whatever happened to her."

"She's probably doing research on boll weevils, Eugene. You missed your chance."

He looked like he was going to cry for some reason. I don't know why, but I felt like he'd feel better if he watched the videotape of Lilly's and my wedding. I said, "You haven't missed much. Come into the den with me."

I got a couple of coasters out for our drinks. In case Lilly came back to her senses, I didn't want her complaining about how I let the furniture die. I got the tape off the bookshelf, noticed how it had been placed between a copy of Kant's Prolegomena and a critical study of Marcel Duchamp's anti-art work. I think I put it there on purpose sometime during the week, drunk and dusting.

"Here's a wedding, Eugene. Notice all the lies."

We didn't even get to the point where Lilly and I said all that

61

stuff about having and holding, rich and poor, sickness and health. Eugene sat up close to the television and said, "Your in-laws are reading the front of the United Methodist Hymnal throughout the whole ceremony."

I said, "Huh?"

"Back up the tape. Whoever did the camera work got a close-up of Lilly's parents reading the front of the hymnal. I'm a Methodist, and the front of the hymnal has a page with directions for singing a song. There's like ten or twelve steps, I think."

I backed it up and saw my in-laws sitting in the front pew, heads down, reading. I said to Eugene, "What's it say that's so important?"

"Not to drown anyone out. Not to mumble. Hold your head high and keep your eyes focused towards God. Don't sing like you used to sing when you sang to Satan. You know."

"Great," I said. "Lilly's gone back to some people who won't even be able to remind her of the vows she made. They'll tell her how to sing a song."

When Lilly and I made love—which was only when she wanted to—she used to let out these aria-sounding notes. She'd fling her head back, sometimes getting it stuck between the mattress and the headboard. I'd watch her focus out into nowhere. Afterward she'd say that I possessed a musical root that made her sing. During our marriage it made me feel like a man. Now it makes sense, I suppose. Maybe she felt like she shouldn't sing for me, like she should sing for God and God only.

Eugene said, "You know, church might be the place for me to go meet a woman. I can sing pretty well."

He got up, left my house, and hasn't been back since. He hasn't cleaned my windshield either. Every Sunday morning I see him, though, dressed in a suit, on his way to the same church where Lilly and I were wed. Sometimes I stick my head out the door and belt out a rich tenor voice, my head aimed toward the morning sun.

Last Sunday I was outside getting my newspaper as Eugene left. My head banged from the bourbon the night before, so I didn't wail out anything. When I got inside, I discovered Lilly's picture on the front page of the "Living" section. She'd graduated from the Women's Center, along with six others, and had received a certificate stating that she was now licensed to conduct seminars. As I was reading the article, she called me for the first time since she had left.

"Can you hear me, Eston? I think I have a bad connection," Lilly yelled into the receiver.

I said, "I can hear you, Lilly. I can see you, too."

She thanked me for understanding her need for a change. We spoke for fifteen minutes; then I went outside, rearranged my panty hose, and made out a plan for Monday's deliveries. I didn't catch myself singing "Amazing Grace" until the final verse.

# These People Are Us

THE TROUBLE STARTED when my wife admitted that she dreamt of shallow graves regularly. Maybe it wasn't as much trouble as it was truth. We started getting to the root of our problems when she got to Question 11 of the At-Home Marriage Repair test we'd bought off of one of the channels. There was a guarantee stating that if the results didn't come out that we should either split or remain together, then we'd get our money back. Besides the 100-question test and dual answer sheets, there was a teacher's manual explaining what all the various answers meant, and a graph to chart out our progress or lack thereof. There was even a 1-800 number to call in case we got sidetracked or confused.

Alexis did all right up to Question 11. She'd not had any traumatic childhood problems, she'd not felt teased as a child, she didn't think her spouse—that would be me—gave her an inferiority problem, ever. She didn't trouble with the way I dressed, or the way I ate my food either.

My problem cropped up right at Question 1, so we pretty much had me figured out. Question 1 was "At any time in your life did a family member do anything that drew attention to you in such a way that the entire community in which you lived would later think of you as a leper, loser, heathen, or un-American?" At least that was the gist of it, I swear.

I had to answer yes, but I never thought of the event as so detrimental to my overall psyche that it'd ruin my marriage. I was eight years old, and only two or three months into living in South Carolina. My father'd lugged my mother and me here from California. It was 1966, and he'd already survived a bout with cancer, overexposure to radiation, a forty-five-foot fall into the empty hold of a merchant ship, fifty-seven broken bones including both hips, back, knees, ankles, and so on. We moved to South Carolina because my father was disabled, but his father—my grandfather—agreed to take him on as an under-the-table employee at the textile supply company that he owned.

So there we were suddenly, trying to fit in. We went to the Baptist church my grandparents attended Sunday mornings and Wednesday nights. I shuffled off with the other kids for Sunday school classes and did my best to stay in between the lines when we used crayons to color pictures of Jesus. I'd never even heard of the guy up until this point in my life. I'm not saying that my parents were un-Christian or immoral or anything. I think they just didn't like fighting the traffic on Sundays back before.

When I think back to this point in my life in a cause-and-effect kind of way, I owe the church everything. Because we went to church, I had to get a suit. Because I got a suit, I started noting how I looked like this tap dancer on the Lawrence Welk show, except I was white. Because I started secretly tap dancing down in our cement basement, I assume I took an interest in the arts, which later followed me throughout school, which kept me from being scared of writing, which ultimately came in handy when I went into that field. What I'm saying is, without the Baptist church, I wouldn't be the scholarly researcher that I am today.

My first book will be an annotated, non-scholarly, human interest bibliography on Job. I know every work ever written that mentions Job somehow.

Anyway, on one of those Wednesday nights the preacher decided to have a Q-and-A session with the congregation. Some old lady asked when the choir could get new robes—there was an Andy Griffith episode just like this—and some other old woman asked everyone to pray for some other old woman who had gout. No one mentioned Vietnam or other global issues.

The civil rights movement did pop up, though, and that's what got me treated like a leper, heathen, loser, and un-American for the rest of my stint in the town. Some man stood up and said, "What do we do if a black man comes into our church?" except he didn't quite use the term "black." He didn't use the term "Negro," and this was long before the notion of "African-Americans" came into being, of course. He didn't even soften up and say "a colored fellow." He used that racist term my father told me to never use, right before first grade at a multi-cultural elementary school in Anaheim, along with words I'd picked up from a guy named Frenchie when I got to visit my father on the ship when it came to unload its cargo at the dock down in Long Beach.

This guy at the church asked the question, and someone else stood up to said, "Ignore him and hope he doesn't come back!" Everyone laughed and applauded.

Except my father and mother. I can't say that I didn't laugh, because I did. To tell the truth I wasn't really paying all that much attention, but I'd learned to kind of do as everyone else around me did. I learned to say "Amen" with the rest of the congregation at the right time. So when everyone laughed and clapped, I laughed, thinking it was appropriate.

I'd stopped by the time my father jerked me off the pew, right there beside his father and stepmother. He still used crutches at this point, three years after falling into the hold, and two or three years before going through a succession of replacement hip operations. I remember my mother slipping her arm through his elbow as we walked down the aisle and out of the place, and I remember being on the other side, with my father's index finger holding my wrist right up against the rubber knobs where his hands fit on those wrap-around-the-forearm-style of crutches.

People turned around and stared, I'm sure. I just kept looking down at the wooden floor. People took notes, said things like, "Those are them Sheltons from up North," I feel certain, what with the way I got treated between second and twelfth grade by every kid except those who'd also moved with their parents from other exotic heathen places like New Jersey and Georgia.

I do know that my father made an awkward multi-shuffled pirouette when we got to the front door of the church, turned to the congregation, and said, "Ignore this," and gave everybody the finger. Even my mother, of all people, let out this little squeak not unlike a gerbil or chipmunk being squeezed too hard—her way of saying, "Up yours."

I know that for a while my father and I dressed up in black and re-visited the same church on Saturday nights for a couple of years so he could paint Coca-Cola around the door frame and front steps, so that on Sunday mornings the congregation would have to enter through a swarm of yellow jackets, if they had the faith.

SOMEHOW I'D FORGOTTEN to tell Alexis about the church incident, so after I explained Question 1 to her she said, "I think this explains some things about our marriage." She said, "Don't think I've not noticed how you always swipe the Gideon Bible out of hotel rooms when we're on vacation."

I said, "I just do it to be funny." I said, "If someone thinks he or she has the right to force religion on me, I feel I have a right to take it away. Simple."

She said, "I'm no psychologist, but it's pretty apparent that you have this enigmatic sense of duality," or something like that. Then she said, "I find it amazing that you grew up in a Christian-paranoid household and ended up trying to write a book on Job." No, Alexis wasn't a psychologist. She worked directly with the garment industry as a buyer. That's why she didn't have any particular problems with the way I dressed. She pretty much knew the ins and outs of fashion.

I said, "Uh-huh. If you want to add on to that, I'm kind of glad that my father's dead. He'd kill me if he knew."

It's not that Alexis and I had that big a problem with our marriage. It's not like I was out whoring around, or she couldn't "find herself" suddenly. It's not like she had to go to Al-Anon. We both liked kids even though we didn't have any. Basically we wanted to find out why she went to sleep crying oftentimes, and why she woke up in the middle of the night in tears, and why I kept making scenes in public unknowingly.

I didn't quite get past Question 2, either, which was "Have you ever had a relative frighten you so much that you didn't know how to react?" Alexis said, "My aunts and uncles and grandparents are normal. I have a cousin who acted odd as a child, but she ended up being a violist. She just didn't talk much."

I said, "Oh, fuck," when it was my turn.

I knew I didn't have the time to tell Alexis about how my grandfather later showed up with a gun to shoot my father after we walked out of church, and how my father ended up getting fired from the under-the-table job. I knew I didn't have the time to tell about how I got summoned to the office over the intercom in the seventh grade so the secretary could tell me that my grandfather would be picking me up from school—which ended up being a kidnapping ploy that failed when I asked to use the phone, called my mother, and she came and got me out of school right then. I only said, "My father's biological mother was kind of odd."

My grandfather and my father's real mother divorced in 1941. My father was 16, and he ran away from Dallas to join the merchant marines. He told stories about his escape, usually with different reasons, endings, road stories, and so on. When I was about 16 and complaining in my snot-nosed way about Hungarian goulash for supper again, my father told about how his parents were so poor they ate grass soup. When I brought up the grass soup incident again a few years later, he said I was nuts, that I must've dreamt it, that he never ate grass soup in his life.

He told me he bought a duffel bag of marijuana for ten dollars one time back before anyone knew what it was, but that he quit smoking the stuff because he got too hungry and thought he'd fall off the deck of the ship.

Anyway, we drove from California to South Carolina in this cool red and white Oldsmobile, with mostly my mother driving, seeing as how my dad's hips hurt and he'd vowed to quit morphine. We stopped in Dallas to see his mother, a woman who played a honky-tonk piano in a bar once owned—I found out later—by Jack Ruby. She played honky-tonk, and she wore purple dresses and a stole. Her name was Nelta, and she caked white make-up on her face and wore lipstick as deep red as thin blood.

This was the beginning of August, understand. I got out of first grade some time in mid-June, and my parents flipped coins whether to move or not. Social Security and the Sailors Union of the Pacific provided my father something like $300 a month all together, which wasn't quite enough to keep a household together, even if my mother went back to work for Western Union. Without morphine, my father needed bourbon. Without bourbon he needed cigarettes, and the doctor'd already made him quit smoking, what with the cancer a few years earlier. A fifth of bourbon a day cut into $300 a month living expenses, even in 1965 dollars.

We packed up what we owned and moved, stopping outside of Phoenix to see friends of my parents who gave up and moved into a trailer so they could look for copper. We maybe stopped another night, I don't remember. I recall El Paso at 110 degrees in the shade, and I remember stopping at an apartment building to meet my father's mother. She wore purple, and had hair dyed the same color as her lipstick. She said, "Little Enloe, the Easter bunny knew you were coming and he left something for you."

She didn't have a piano in the apartment. She had a couch with stuffing coming out of the upholstery at both arms. She didn't own a cat. My biological grandmother wore high-heels and went into the kitchen. She opened the refrigerator and pulled out this hollow chocolate bunny in a box with the cellophane window. It'd turned white, and the head had been eaten off.

My father said, of course, "What do you say, Enloe?"

I know what I wanted to say. I knew I wanted to say, "This is stale," or "My parents told me not to take candy from strangers," or "The Easter bunny must get really tired by the time he makes it to Texas."

My grandmother Nelta said, "You don't have to thank me, honey. Come here, and sit down on Grandma's lap, and let me sing you a song."

I knew I didn't get the "thank you" out as fast as I should've and had no choice but to do what she wanted. I swear to God she took me over to the couch and sang me a song about a woman named "Soft-hearted Sally Tucker," a song she said she wrote herself for the club where she worked.

I knew what the words meant, too. I'd heard the words from Frenchie, remember.

I AM NOT LYING when I say Alexis moved her chair back from me inch by inch subconsciously as I explained the answer to Question 2. I noticed it the way a person watching a movie notices how the victim keeps stepping backwards as the attacker wearing a mask nods a knife up and down.

We went through questions 3 through 7 together on a par. I'm not sure what they meant, but they were easy, and graphing the answers—we cheated by looking at the Teacher's Manual—we ended up side by side: "I tend to wear blue more than brown," "I like dogs more than cats," "I'd rather read a book than cut the grass," "At night voices call out my name and it bothers me," and "I like to travel to distant cities," all with yes or no answers.

Alexis and I felt pretty good about our chances of mending the marriage for about two minutes. She even scooted her hard-back chair back towards me halfway. We sat in the den face-to-face, like the opening instructions said we should do. We drank water.

"Do you want some supper?" Alexis asked me. She said, "I'm hungry. I can go outside and mow the grass so we could have some grass soup."

I said, "You're funny." I said, "Let's get this over with. I want to get to the bottom of whatever it is we're going through." Alexis and I'd been married half a decade and I still liked her looks. She wore a thin skirt and kept her legs open when I told the stories of my childhood. I could see right up there, is what I'm saying. I said, "I'll fast a day if it'll keep you from crying, and me from standing in the middle of the canned-meat section of Winn-Dixie, singing out the lyrics to Johnny Mathis and Tony Bennett songs."

Alexis said, "It's the George Jones that has everybody thinking you're just drunk out of your mind."

I said, "What's the next question?"

She held the booklet. We kept separate answer sheets and short pencils that came with the package, pencils that looked like they came straight from a miniature golf course. She said, "For the next question, I answer 'No.'" She said, "Question 8: 'Did one of your parents ever force sex on you?'"

I said, "Yes!" right away. I didn't take the time to think about how ambiguous the question was. I didn't think about how it could've sounded like your parent tried to rape you, or how he or she just tried to set you up with a member of the opposite sex, which is how I interpreted it.

Alexis stood up and said, "You shouldn't've told me about the tap dancing! You shouldn't've told me about the tap dancing!"

I understood what she thought I meant. I said, "No, no, no!" I said, "What I mean is, my father wanted me to go to bed with this Waffle House waitress!" like that.

My father stayed at his father's business long enough to figure out how to make replacement aprons, which were leather belts that went on spinning frames. He figured out better ways to make them, and started up a business in my mother's name, seeing as he was so-called disabled. My dad made me work weekends and summers, but mostly we just drove around. I mean, we'd go to work and tinker for an hour or so, then go out back and shoot a pistol or two at whatever we decided looked like a good target—a roll of butcher paper, a gross of unfolded die-cut boxes, a spare tire he thought wasn't needed, a poor dying sweet gum tree out off the highway.

When we didn't shoot, we drove. When we didn't drive, we stopped and drank coffee. My father always said he'd pay me five bucks an hour, and at seven o'clock that night in the kitchen I'd say things like, "You owe me sixty dollars," to which he'd relate to me how we only worked in the shop an hour and drove around, drank coffee, and shot a pistol for the rest of the time.

When we stopped off for coffee, we stopped at this Waffle House on Business 25 in town, and always—always—some pimple-faced twenty-year-old woman with three kids and no wedding band would serve us, and my dad would say, "You ain't married?"

She'd say, "Was."

And he'd say, "This is my son Enloe, Jr. He ain't got no girlfriend." He'd turn to me and say, "Whyn't you ask her out?" The waitress would always smile, and shake her head from side to side, more than likely thinking about how she needed a high school sophomore in her life about as much as she needed only one finger on each hand, thus keeping her from being able to pour from the pot.

I'd turn as red as the plastic tablecloth and look away, outside, way past the city limits. I'd look out the window and see a land where only my cast of buddies from outside South Carolina came from, and how we could all live in peace, not worrying about what other kids our age had to say about us being un-American heathens.

Well, maybe I just looked out the window. Maybe I just turned red and kicked my father under the table and muttered, "Dad, please shut up," under my breath.

After the woman left, my father would say something like, "She liked you, son. I could tell by the way she was looking. She wants you. She wants to take you home when her kids are gone and play a game of ring-toss, you know what I mean."

Of course I knew what he meant, seeing as Frenchie called sex "ring-toss." I knew what my limping father meant because more than once he'd say things like, "Those Baptists pretend to be so goddamn superior to everyone else, but I bet you there's more ring-toss going on between the congregation than there is at a kindergarten field day."

I usually kept pretty much quiet around my father. I knew what he could do with yellow jackets. By this time, too, he'd had a couple hip replacements and could walk only using a cane. A quick cane to the back of the thighs is something a son remembers.

Alexis said, "I don't know if we can get through all these questions." She said, "Do you mind if I skip around to what kinds of food you'd rather eat, or cars you'd rather own? Do you mind if I go on towards question 100? I'm not sure I can take all this. Why didn't you tell me before?"

We'd gotten married by a notary public. Instead of a honeymoon we just held a party for friends. We didn't have a china pattern. People brought us paper plates. My mother made a toast. She didn't really mention anything that happened when I was being brought up.

ALEXIS AND I MARRIED LATE. We married, probably, out of nothing else to do. I'd already worked in an ad agency for a year, gone to graduate school, taught college, and tried writing fiction before settling on applying for year-long grants so I could work on annotated bibliographies. She'd gone to college, and worked as a social worker, and modeled when someone discovered her, and gotten the job as a buyer through a guy named Bernie Sachs up in New York. We'd already gone to bars and art gallery lectures thinking we'd meet people who'd be compatible. I met Alexis when I was thirty-one and she was thirty. We'd both needed tune-ups, oddly. Some religion professor or massage therapist could go on and on about the symbolic and ironic implications of the event, but the simple truth is we sat in opposite chairs at a Lube-World, waiting for mechanics to get the job done.

She owned a Toyota wagon, and I had a big Chevy pick-up for no real reason.

We sat there reading old magazines. I asked her if she minded if I smoked. She asked me if I could smell her perfume—she thought she'd put on too much. I said I liked the smell of perfume better than oil. She told me her name and held out her hand. We shook. I am not lying when I say I didn't really make eye contact at the time. There was a glass partition between us in the waiting room, and the shop. I could see my truck and Alexis's Toyota, going up and down the hydraulic lifts, randomly, like pistons, like sex between two pessimists.

It didn't take that long a courtship, and it didn't seem like all that long a marriage before we sat there across from each other answering the questions. Alexis said, "Do you trust people who don't drink?"

I said, "Not always. I'm sorry to say I don't always trust them. I hate to say those kind of people who always brag about how they're on a natural high or whatever also seem to be the kind of people who're either really boring, or who want me to be exactly like them for some reason. Like there's an exclusive club. People who brag about not drinking are just like people who brag about living in gated communities near Asheville." But I added, "People who don't drink and just live without mentioning anything, I respect."

Deep down I figured I shouldn't tell the truth, but Alexis

and I'd made an oath to each other. She said, "I feel the same way!" all excited. She said, "Question 10's easy—'Does your spouse ever seem to be more interested in inanimate objects than you? Does your spouse ever seem to care more about the garden, or the eaves, or the car?' I want to answer first, Enloe. I want to say 'No!'"

I said, "I've always thought you cared more about me than you did about lawn ornaments or farm implements."

I penciled in "No" on my answer sheet and assumed Alexis did the same. She didn't respond to me, though. Alexis put down the booklet and her pencil. She walked back towards the kitchen and I swear I heard her let out this little noise that I'd only heard her make right before she cried in the middle of the night.

I said, "Is the pollen bothering you?" That's how much I had the situation figured out.

She said, "I want to know what you have to say about Question 11. Pick up that booklet and tell me what you think."

The question was, "In your dreams, have you ever noticed any kind of symbolism you could interpret as wanting to hurt your spouse?"

I said, "While you're in there, could you get me a beer?" I said, "Oh, wait—that was some kind of reflex. I forgot we agreed to drink water while doing this thing."

Alexis came back with a good cup of vodka, straight, one ice cube floating in the top of the glass. She brought the same for me, plus the can of beer. Alexis said, "I have some theories. I'm not sure it has to do with you. I've been thinking," she said.

I said, "You're dreaming of killing me?" like that. I couldn't believe it. When we first met she kept a sawed-off shotgun under her bed, but took it away once I told her how it made me feel uncomfortable.

Alexis said, "I don't think I've killed anyone in my dreams." She didn't make eye contact. Right away I knew something was up, and at first I kind of felt good about it, I hate to admit. After having to spill out all the things about my chocolate bunny without a head and whatnot, I felt like Alexis was about to start catching up with me.

I said, "What did you dream, honey—you got real mad at me and stepped on my foot or something? You spank a dog that you think is symbolic of me? What?"

Then she told me about the shallow graves. Alexis said, "I keep having this nightmare. In the dream I'm walking down a path in the woods, and then I'll come to a clearing where there's a cemetery. I walk through the cemetery looking at all the head-stones—really nice headstones, too. But then I keep walking back into another part of the woods further ahead, and finally I get to this shallow grave with a hand sticking out, or a piece of a flannel shirt. A couple times it was hair sticking out from the dirt."

I said, "When did you start drinking straight vodka? This is terrible," and put my glass down.

"All that crying in the middle of the night is from this dream, Enloe. Every time I have the dream I say to myself in it, 'I need to go get some fill dirt and cover the body.' I promise I don't ever say, 'I better cover up Enloe,' or 'I better cover up my husband.' I just know that I've done something very wrong, and I don't want to get caught."

She still looked away from me. She didn't reach out her hand for me to hold, like in the movies right before the psycho-analyst makes his unethical move on a patient. I said, "So I guess you'll be entering a 'Yes' on your answer sheet."

Alexis got up and said, "I can't finish this tonight."

I told her it was okay. I told her we could get back to it

whenever she wanted, that we had time. I tried not to think about synchronicity, about how if I'd never taken such an interest in Job I'd've never been able to show such patience.

OF COURSE I DIDN'T SLEEP that night, and neither did my wife. I couldn't sleep on purpose, and Alexis couldn't sleep because I kept pumping her full of coffee. I lied. I told her about watching a fascinating and timely documentary on how large amounts of coffee have been known to purge human beings of visions. We sat together in the den, apart.

Alexis said, "It's all me. There'd be nothing wrong with our marriage if I wasn't involved," pathetic-like.

I said, "Well, true, if you weren't a part of this marriage I doubt we'd be talking about what's wrong." I tried not to laugh. I tried not to think about getting a third-shift job so I'd be gone from the bedroom when Alexis dreamt.

Alexis said, "Maybe I need to go to a real psychologist before we can go on with the test. Maybe I have some problems stemming from deep in my own psyche I need to resolve before we can even think about getting our lives together back on track."

I said, "I don't want to sound like an ingrate or anything— I'm proud of you for wanting to get everything in order—but I have about the least amount of confidence in psychology as a science. I'd just as soon we went up in the mountains and have some woman place gemstones on our nerve endings. Honey, if you think that psychology's going to solve your dreams, then I can tell you right now what your problem is."

Alexis said, "I know."

I said, "There is no hope. Listen, when I get through with the book on Job—and it should be really soon—I'll go back and get a real job. When the grant money's gone, I'll get out of the house more often. That'll cure things, I bet." I said, "I love you," and got up to kiss her.

Alexis said, "I love you, too," and grabbed the channel changer away from me. It was four-thirty in the morning, and she wanted to see the news. She said, "What do you mean there's no hope?"

On one of the 24-hour news channels a guy stood in a small workroom somewhere in the midwest. He told about how he had these solar-powered engines that could provide electricity for the entire country if only the government would give him a large chunk of the Mojave desert.

I said, "This is a perfect example of what I'm saying. Let's pretend the government gives this guy all that land. And let's say that his solar-powered engines are such a hit that somehow every nation is able to use them, so we don't have to suck oil and coal out of the earth any more. Pretty soon the whole entire center of the world will be filled with oil, and it'll creep closer and closer to the surface, and then one day some jackass will throw a cigarette butt out his window, which will catch some of the oil on fire that's seeped through the surface, and the entire planet will explode from the inside out." I said, "I think there's something about that towards the end of the Bible, but not so detailed."

Alexis just looked at me. She handed me back the changer and went for more coffee. From the kitchen she said, "Don't get weird on me, Enloe."

I flipped over to watch bowling on the sports channel. I flipped over to watch an old movie where the shadow of the microphone was visible at the top of the screen. I turned to that infomercial channel that advertised the booklet we bought on how to repair a marriage.

Alexis came back in with her cup and I said, "Look."

There was a blue-suited motivational speaker-host talking to various people in the audience about their addictions to home-shopping networks. One couple from Mesa, Arizona, told how they went into bankruptcy after the wife bought every doll ever advertised. A man from Columbus, Ohio, stood up and said, "I had this dream that when I retired I'd open up a small wood-working and baseball-card store. I bought every drill bit and every table saw advertised, plus autographed baseballs and bats and eight-by-ten photographs, not to mention complete sets of baseball cards from the fifties up until now. Well, I retired, and then I rented a little place in one of our strip malls. To make a long story short, I couldn't sell any of the memorabilia for half of what it cost me, and I cut off my thumb trying to make an ar-moire."

He showed his left hand. Alexis said, "Who are these people?"

The host came running back down to the stage and said, "I've heard these stories all across the country where I give my seminars. Peer pressure, last straws, and that old notion about the Great American Dream is running all of us into the red." He walked over to a table and picked up a book and said, "And that's why I want to tell you about my new book, How to Stop Buying Useless Quick Fix-Its off Late-Night Television." He said, "I know what I'm talking about, and I have documentation to prove it."

At the bottom of the screen it read, "Dr. Barnes is a direct descendant of Franz Mesmer, the father of Hypnotism."

I didn't want to sound melodramatic or anything, but I said, "These people are us."

I turned off the TV. Alexis and I sat in the dim light of the room. I wondered about questions 12 through 100, and knew that somehow both of us would have to bring up our college years, and things we'd done, and things it'd be better not knowing. I thought of Job's seven sons and three daughters, and wondered if there was any way possible to research our family trees so one day Alexis and I could go on that channel with my book and plug the concept of Patience. I wanted a subtitle under my face saying, "Enloe and Alexis are direct descendants of Job, the father of Patience."

Alexis moved to the couch. I scooted way over. She kind of laughed and said if I rubbed her feet, she'd promise not to kill me and dump my body in a two-foot grave. I thought of that poor woodworker man without the thumb. My wife and I mentioned nothing. Eventually it got light outside again, like it had for my parents, and theirs.

# Normal

I MET MY WIFE ONE DAY and married her the next. Of course she wasn't my wife when I first met her: back on that day she was just a friend's friend, coming to visit with my buddy Jack. Jack's friend happened to be a friend of Jack's ex-wife Lalla— Jack should've known right away that marriage would vanish, because of her weird name. Anyway, Jack's friend and ex-wife's ex-friend is named Penny. Jack and Penny and Penny's friend Jane—my wife, now—came to visit because I lived close to the Atlantic ocean. As people who have a friend who lives next to a large body of water tend to do, they called and said they'd be in for the Labor Day weekend.

Actually only Jack called. I didn't know Penny all that well and hadn't even met my wife yet. He said, "We're bringing Jane with us. Y'all will get along real well. As a matter of fact, she's just like you, Bose—cynical and sarcastic."

I said, "I don't believe you." No one was as cynical or sarcastic as I was back in those days. As a child a lot of kids had called me Bozo instead of Bose, and I pretty much took it all out on the rest of humanity, now that I look back on it.

Jack said, "Jane works with Penny at a law office. You'll like her."

"I hate lawyers," I said. "You and Penny and Penny's friend

are welcome, but don't make me try to like her. People who work in law offices tend to think they're lawyers, too."

I knew all of this for a fact 'cause I'd just gotten through dealing with some lawyer's gofer, trying to get money out of a factory for throwing ice on my car every night. The factory didn't even have a name on the outside of the building, and they built something secret and special for the government. Every night the factory smokestack let out a chemical steam that, I'm positive, interacted with the humidity and caused hail to dump on my house and car. The lawyer's gofer said it wasn't an airtight case. My insurance agent said he couldn't cut me a check every twenty-four hours to deal with the pings in my hood.

My landlord knew all about the factory—the risks, etc.—and he'd tried to sue for ten years or so before just giving up. He moved into a condominium with a waitress from Colonel Frank's Fireworks Stand & Truck Stop a month after his wife died. He only charges me a hundred dollars a month rent, which isn't so shabby a deal as long as I don't go outside after midnight without protective headgear.

So I'd been living down here for six months when Jack and Penny and Jane arrived. I'd moved down because construction crews were sought, now that some insurance agencies had begun paying off on hurricane damage claims. Six days a week I worked with a man named Lassiter, doing everything from loading a scrap-heap truck, to mitering molding, to cedar-shake shingle roofing. One paranoid couple, who bought and moved into their beach house a week before the hurricane hit down in Garden City, asked Lassiter if one of his boys could go to the library and read up on some voodoo rituals to protect the house. I got that particular job, of course. Lassiter remembered on my job application that I'd earned a degree in philosophy, and he reasoned it was the closest thing to voodoo. I went down to the Piggly-Wiggly and bought some chicken feet, buried them in the sand all along the house's perimeter, then went up to each foot and said to it "Carpe diem" or "Veni, vidi, vici" until the owners were convinced that if another hurricane hit, their house would be spared miraculously. They tipped me a couple hundred bucks, and I took some pings out of my car roof.

Jack and I first met back in college where he studied English and then went off to Texas to work oil until the bottom fell out in the early eighties. Jack returned to graduate school and completed his dissertation, then got married to Lalla and competed with the malls and her rich daddy until she finally left. Jack knew he'd get nothing out of the marriage—none of the silver or furniture or even the love seat I'd built for them that had indentions in the arms to hold drink glasses and ashtrays. So he decided he'd just go to bed with Lalla's best friends, all of whom more or less sided with him in the break-up. Jack was a sympathetic fool, all of Lalla's old friends concluded. Jack didn't really care what they thought as long as they slept with him and drove his ex-wife crazy.

Jack and Penny and Jane drove in around six o'clock on Friday evening. I'd just gotten home and taken my shirt off. My tool belt pulled my blue jeans down a little, and exposed the developing beer belly a little more than it should. I said, "Hey, Jack."

Jack said, "All right, Bose," and started laughing.

The first thing my wife-to-be said was, "Bose is the sexiest man I've ever seen in my life." She stood next to my old Triumph motorcycle, one hand and one hip on the seat.

Now, the first thing I remembered was that Jane was supposed to possess a sarcasm right up there with mine. She kept looking me straight in the face, and I noticed she couldn't have been much more than five feet two inches. I said, "You look like you might've played some basketball in your time, Jane. Or maybe done some runway modeling over in Paris."

Jack forced a laugh, and Penny remained in the front seat of the car, as if she didn't want to use up any energy getting out only to repack and get back in and leave. Jane stood and smiled exactly my own smile, more of a grin than anything else. She said, "I think that's where I met you, Bose. Weren't you doing some hair modeling over there?"

I showed Jack and Penny to the spare bedroom and gave Jane my bed—saying that I planned to sleep on the couch or, what with the way she had been making fun of my receding hairline, maybe outside naked during a hailstorm. Then I excused myself to the shower. Jack said he'd fire up the barbecue, while Jane and Penny started in on a salad and baked beans.

In the bathroom I unknotted every strand of my hair, washed and conditioned it, checked the mirror for any signs of graying or balding in back. For some reason, I thought of Friedrich Nietzsche.

ONE TIME A WAYS BACK, when I was painting a house down here, the wife of the guy who hired me decided that I needed company. Either that, or she wanted to inspect my work every minute I stood on the ladder. Her husband was an architect and full of new ideas, now that the hurricane had demolished everything he'd ever made before. I liked the husband.

On the first day on the job the architect's wife said to me, "You're a Taurus, aren't you?"

I yelled back, "What's it to you, anyway?"

She laughed and said, "I knew it."

"This paint looks more green than blue to me," I said. It did, it really did, I wasn't trying to change the subject.

She said, "You're changing the subject. Or you have the classic male blue-green color blindness. Do you hate women?"

I noticed that I'd missed the whole side of a shutter. If another painter talks to me while I paint, I do okay. But anyone else distracts me. I think it's because I have to think with anyone else, but I'm not sure.

I said, "I love women. I've always loved women. Women don't always care for me all that much, but I love them nonetheless. I can't even think of the concept 'ugly woman.' Now, I'm not all that keen on women who try to make me go back to school, or get a regular job, or make me quit drinking and smoking, or buy a new car that has a sunroof, or don't even know me but tell me what kind of man I am."

I thought that last jab might've been a little mean, but she made me say it. She made me paint randomly, and in this game a random painter is about as good as a gourmet chef with no taste buds and a case of the palsy.

"Well, Bose, it seems to me that all women try to change their men into what's best for them. Best for the man, I mean. That cliché about what's behind every man is a woman isn't all that far-fetched, really. Look what Eleanor Roosevelt did for her husband. Think about Yeats's wife, or James Joyce's."

I said, "Do you think Nancy told Ron to say he forgot everything? Is that what you mean?" I would've said her name, but I always make a point not to know too many family members' names when I paint. Then they come and talk.

"If you think he was a great man, then I guess she did."

Like my wife-to-be, who I hadn't even heard about yet, this woman was way ahead of me. I said, "Do you believe in reincarnation?"

"I most certainly do. I'm a Gemini."

I didn't make the connection. So I said—and I thought of it

all by myself, right off the top of my head, at that very moment— "Better hope you don't come back as a paintbrush or I might slap you all over the house."

I remembered all of this story right after I got out of the shower on the night before I married my wife because there was a connection that I made. I came out of the bathroom wearing normal old khaki pants and a blue shirt. Jane said right away, "That shirt looks really good on you. It matches your eyes."

My eyes are green.

Penny came in and told us to come eat. She smiled like a good person, no sneer, like a woman who'd take fig preserves to a senior center and be willing to listen to all the stories that fig preserves conjure up in people.

"Are you hungry, Bose?" Jane asked me. Penny left us alone. I didn't know if it was a sign. I heard Jack outside cursing about something.

I said, "I'm hungry." I said, "I eat."

"You sound defensive," Jane said back. She positioned her body straight towards me. If I shifted left or right, she moved in that direction also, fluidly, unconsciously.

"I just thought maybe Jack might've told you I normally drank. And don't really sleep."

"I'm twenty-two years old. Did they tell you I was only twenty-two, Bose?"

I said, "You seem mature for twenty-two, Jane." We stood in a hallway. I wasn't comfortable.

"Really I'm twenty-six. Are you saying I'm immature?" Jane walked up to me and touched the bottom parts of her breasts on the middle of my stomach, which was not beer-bellying underneath my blue shirt.

I didn't notice she held two drinks until she handed me one. I kissed her for the first time, then.

"YOU HAVE A WASP NEST under your grill," Jack said. He wasn't wearing his shirt and a welt stood out above his nipple. I took a cigarette out of my shirt and unrolled some tobacco. Before I could lick my palm, though, Jane came up and spit on my hand.

When I thanked her, she said, "It's the least I could do for both of you."

What the hell. I couldn't figure her out and decided to quit trying.

Jack put the wet tobacco on his sting and said he felt better, so I took the platter of hamburgers away from him. Jane walked in with me and said, "Have you ever been in a pharmacy and bought some condoms and found one of your old girlfriends standing right behind you in line?"

"No, I can't say that I have. Do we have any onions in the refrigerator, or relish or mayonnaise? I forgot to go shopping."

"That happened to me one time."

"That's too bad," I said. I didn't want to know if she was buying the condoms or if she was in line behind her ex-boyfriend.

"Kind of," said Jane. "I was in line, but my ex-boyfriend stood ahead of me buying chewing gum for people with dentures. That kind of gum that won't stick to your teeth, you know."

I couldn't take it. I knew not to ask, but I said, "Jane, for some reason I'm attracted to you. And I think Jack's right in that you and I might have the same sarcasm and all that. But I don't know what the hell you're talking about."

"My mother wears false teeth. Do you know how difficult it is to be paranoid about things like that? How a person's mind might work overtime?"

I said, "Do y'all want to eat inside or outside? I think if we don't put on the light, it'll be okay outside." The hail storms wouldn't hit for hours.

Jane put her arm around my waist ... and an index finger one inch down the front of my pants. She kissed my cheek and said, "Against the floodlight, you'll even be sexier than you were when we first drove up." And then she started laughing.

I said, "In the floodlight, your shadow will be even shorter than before."

Penny said, "Let's eat inside and play Spades. I want to play Spades. Girls against boys, let's play Spades. Do you know how to play Spades, Bose?"

Again, I thought of Nietzsche. He once said, "A man's maturity consists in having found again the seriousness one had as a child, at play." I said, "Penny, I failed kindergarten 'cause when the teacher said 'Let's go outside for recess,' I said, 'Hey, lady, I don't play.'"

Jane said, "My, how things change over the years."

WE ATE AND DRANK and Jack talked about his new crop of students, and how he was going to some language conference to present a paper on the excesses of twentieth-century writers vis-à-vis the minimalist movement. At the same time, Jane and I said, "That sounds fascinating!"

"Did you happen to pack the paper in your bags, Jack?" I asked. He scratched his welt with his middle finger, towards me.

"No, I left it in my office, Bose. Sorry."

"I really would like to hear it. I would! What I'd like more than anything else is for you to practice your paper, and we— Penny, Jane, and I—could be your panel."

"It starts off like this," Jack began.

Penny got up and grabbed a deck of cards off of the kitchen counter. "There sure was a lot of traffic coming down here. I guess a bunch of people go to Myrtle Beach on Labor Day." She began shuffling, loudly, while Jack said something about a French philosopher.

"They're going to Darlington," I said. "The old Southern 500."

Jane said, "Bose, you won't believe this, but I went to the race last year. We had these seats down in what they call the Chicken Row 'cause all the people above start throwing their used fried chicken legs down near the wall. But I don't remember that much of the race. I had to leave for about a hundred laps. During the national anthem this little retarded girl behind me started . . ."

"Throwing up," I said. "I was standing behind her. I threw chicken bones on you, more than likely, Jane."

Jane stared at my face and did one of those overused drop-jaw looks. I remember the moment of the girl throwing up, because at the very same time there was all that to-do about burning the American flag, and when I heard the retarded girl start in, it sounded like someone urinating. I had thought to myself at the moment, "Now, that's unpatriotic."

Jane said, "No way. Come on, Bose. Did Jack tell you about that story? I mean, I threw up, too, but in the ladies' room."

Jack said, "Synchronicity also plays a major part in twentieth-century writing."

I said, "That little girl had on blue jeans and a Richard Petty T-shirt."

"The girl I saw," said Jane, twisted grin back on her face, "had on . . . green jeans." Then she said, "I'm just kidding. This is amazing. This was meant to be. Hey, to hell with the boys and girls. Bose and I want to be partners."

We played cards until two in the morning. Jane and I bid

low—both of us, during the same hand—more times than in the history of the game. Jack and Penny won by an average margin of 600 points in games that only went to 500.

Jane started whining one time, and when she lipped to me, "I have the queen of spades," I thought she said, "We have it made." So I threw out the six, Penny a nine, and Jane her queen and Jack the king. Then Jack threw out a heart, I tossed my ace of spades, Penny her ten, and Jane an eight. Jane said, "Damn you, Bose, didn't you hear me say I had the queen?"

I didn't answer. It was the last game of the night and I went to bed, thinking Jane would come in later. In other words, on the night before my wedding, I slept alone, my wife-to-be on the couch. I thought that with all the weird karma or whatever, she'd know we belonged on the same mattress.

WELL, MAYBE I DIDN'T sleep. I kept the light on. I turned on the radio to a local AM station that rotated between blues music and auto-repair information. I noticed the difference between crickets and tree frogs outside.

At four o'clock in the morning I got up and walked around my bedroom. My tool belt looked as though it might fall off the hardback chair, so I straightened it out twice. I counted nails, and sorted them into different pockets.

I sat on the bed and wondered if I really needed to be involved with a woman who cheated in cards, and why my friend Jack would think that Jane was perfect for me. We'd never played cards before that I could remember, so cheating wouldn't have been something to build a hypothesis on concerning a possible attraction and commitment between Jane and me.

I went into the den and asked her: "Jane, why are you asleep on the couch?"

She rolled over and shaded her eyes against the floor lamp I'd turned on, plus the light out of my room. "As far as I'm concerned," she said, "you rejected me."

One of her breasts hung out of the V-neck T-shirt she wore to bed. I didn't look directly, but I could see. And I could see way into the future—not that breasts mean all that much to me, (not everything, at least)—and I saw us waking the child and getting him or her off to school. I saw myself draping large terry-cloth towels on a rack next to the heater in the bathroom so Jane could be extra warm after her shower. I saw myself enrolling in classes so I wouldn't have to depend on hurricanes to give me construction jobs. Maybe I would go back in philosophy, or maybe I'd become something like a technical writer, or a consultant, or a public-relations star. If Jane wanted to work, she could. If not, we'd find a way to make ends meet. I could do most of the home repair. There'd be a good chance the banks would be willing to give us large loans for fix-me-up houses in the inner cities of the United States. And at the end of every day I'd hold Jane in my arms, on the couch, with her breast hanging out and our child swinging on the old tree swing I'd gone to extreme lengths to install so it'd be perfectly safe, and we'd tell each other how our days had gone.

I said, "I didn't reject you! You rejected me, if anything. You got all mad about me not being some kind of lip reader, but I thought you would still come to bed. I didn't know you'd lose all interest in me when I couldn't cheat."

"Well, I didn't just walk off to bed without saying anything," Jane said.

Some other things were said, but I forget what now. The next thing I knew I had my legs wrapped around Jane's hips, from behind her, my mouth up to her left ear, giving directions on how to change the gears of my motorcycle as she steered us down Highway 501 towards Garden City.

FRIEDRICH NIETZSCHE ONCE said, "In revenge and in love, woman is more barbarous than man." He also said that during times of peace, a warrior will end up turning on himself. Suddenly I believed more in Nietzsche than I had in college, as I tried to imagine when I'd felt more at ease with a woman—even though she took the curves at ninety miles an hour on a road she didn't know, on a vehicle she'd never before maneuvered.

We rode the bike into Garden City and parked it in front of where a pier had stood before the storm. I said, "There used to be a pier at this very spot, Jane. People fished off of it. One time I saw a school of jellyfish mating here. Unless they were playing some kind of aquatic tag."

Jane struggled to get off the motorcycle while I kept it from tipping. She said, "Pilings are important during times of stress, Bose. I hope you realize that before we go any further."

I said, "I realize that. I get your symbolism. I'm normal."

"Right," she said. "And so am I."

"It's you and me against the world, as I see it."

My wife-to-be and I didn't speak again until the sun broke out of the Atlantic. We drank bourbon from a flask I'd brought along, then evidently fell asleep, sitting at the base of the invisible pier. We were in the same position as we had been on my Triumph, and that probably accounts for the dream I had of Jane steering it straight into the ocean.

I woke her up by saying, "Hey!"

She jumped, turned to me, and said, "Are you okay?"

I didn't say anything, for I knew that if I told her again that I was normal she'd start doubting me. Nietzsche once said,

"When we have to change our mind about a person, we hold the inconvenience he causes us very much against him."

I certainly didn't want my wife-to-be to be against me. I said, "The house I'm painting now is owned by a probate judge. A woman probate judge. Her husband's a doctor. In the state of South Carolina there's no blood-test law, so a person can get a marriage license from a probate judge with only a twenty-four-hour waiting period. But this judge woman likes me enough to where I bet she'll bend the one-day waiting rule."

Jane said, "So why did you tell me that her husband's a doctor?"

"In case you wanted him to check me our for the clap or anything," I said.

This time I drove the bike. It was around eight o'clock in the morning, and they usually expected me at that time anyway. When the judge opened the door, I unfurled my arms, palms up, towards Jane. I said, "We're not drunk, I promise."

The judge said, "Hey, Bose. I thought you were taking the holiday off."

Jane said, "He's not drunk, ma'am."

And the judge, who'd obviously been in the situation before, saw right through everything and said, "Oh. Oh. Come on in while I find my book."

JACK AND PENNY LEFT a year ago Monday. They left my house with an empty back seat, a lighter trunk, and puzzled faces. They keep in touch but remain skeptical. Jack's last words to me before leaving two days after my wedding were, "Even concubinage has been corrupted—by marriage." Nietzsche, again.

Tomorrow Jane and I are going to the doctor—the judge's husband, oddly—for her final checkup before the delivery date.

We did the ultrasound but asked not to know the sex of our child. The doctor has hinted, though, that we will be proud parents. He said that perhaps he'd not gotten enough sleep the night before, but he would almost swear that our child looked straight back at him, smiled, and winked.

To Jane and me, that seems about right.

# Dialectic, Abrasions,
# the Backs of Heads Again

RITA HID HER LATEST BINGE, and I didn't. There's something
to that obsessive-compulsive argument. I walked out to the
garage to find another pint of bourbon I'd stowed from myself,
and found my wife trying to shove sandpaper into a drawer. The
car was parked in the drive, like I did it when I felt like making
wobbly bookcases out of old barn lumber. Rita just stood there
empty-handed.

I said, "What're you up to?" I did not say it accusingly, I
know. It's an honest question. I think I saw on one of the talk
shows one time that after you get married, it's okay to ask what
your spouse is doing.

Rita picked up a piece of wood she'd scavenged off a fireplace mantle from an abandoned house out in the country
somewhere. She had this idea that she wanted to nail it above
the door to the kitchen. Rita had this idea that most people
would want to nail something as serpentine and lifeless above
their kitchen portals. My wife looked at a lot of magazines. She
said, "If you're looking for your bottle, you hid it in that box of
nails," and pointed.

I said, "Thanks." I even said, "I forgot," and hit my own forehead like a dunce, then meandered towards the box slowly, giving my wife time. Sure enough, when I turned back around that

piece of wood was back in the drawer with the sandpaper. "What happened to that piece of fireplace you just had?"

"You're just going to make fun of me," my wife said. She seemed glued to the drawer suddenly. She said, "Go back on in the house and make yourself a quadruple or something."

The month before, Rita'd spent every waking hour cutting gourds in half, drilling small holes in the lips, and twining raffia through them so they looked like bowls used primarily on the Serengeti. The binge before gourds centered around buying thrift-store china, then painting them completely black with a special enamel. One time Rita thought she found an arrowhead in the back yard—I'm sure it got flinted by the lawnmower's blade—and she dug up all our grass looking for others.

Hell, I went to one of those places up in the mountains and bought a couple dozen real ones to throw around randomly just because I felt so sad for her. I even got some Apache tears.

I twisted the plastic off my pint. I said, "When have I ever made fun of you?" She started listing, and I said, "It was more sarcasm, dear. I know I've done what you're saying."

Rita opened the drawer and pulled out the piece of mantel. She said, "I painted over the old wood, and now I'm sanding over it to make it look old. Like old paint. The thing was stripped bare and looked old already, I know. But I don't want it to look like old wood. I want it to look like old wood with old paint on it. There's a big difference, Glen."

I swear to God I bit my tongue hard, just like in an old slapstick movie. Rita didn't say my name unless she meant something. I said, "There's a fascinating program about Easter Island on one of the cable channels coming on. Right afterwards there's going to be something on the Lost Colony outside of North Carolina. I'm going back inside." I said, "Please don't take the car down to Earl Scheib's and get it repainted so you can drive it home and scratch it up to look old."

"I read somewhere that the natives who lived on Easter Island ate each other," Rita said. She sanded gently on the edges of her wood.

I said, "Sometimes I like to go buy a brand new bottle of Coke, and take the top off so it goes flat, then pour half of it out and pour club soda in it so it gets all fizzy, then let it go flat again before I drink it." It just came out, like that. I wasn't even trying to think up smart-ass things to say.

I'd not noticed that my wife also used an awl—so her new, old piece of mantel wood looked like it got riddled by termites and woodpeckers—until she threw it in one motion and it stuck right underneath my collarbone. When I got back inside, though, I thought about how I could go get some plastic surgery over the hole, then stab myself again.

A DECADE EARLIER my wife believed we were stable enough financially to quit everything sensible and make a living off the flea market, and to a point she seemed right. She believed that we could buy things from flea markets and sell them for higher prices to rich people, and that we could find certain objects at Goodwill, Salvation Army, or Miracle Hill and sell them at flea markets to poor people who thought they got a deal. There was some odd dialectic going on I couldn't explain to anyone, really. I'm sure some of the poor people we sold—say, gourds—to, thought that they could sell the same gourds to rich people, et cetera. In twenty years Rita's gourds would show back up in thrift stores, and she'd buy them back up and probably repaint them, and sell them at flea markets, and so on.

Rita and I taught college English. We taught composition

and rhetoric classes basically, and they were basic composition and rhetoric classes. We scraped by, shook our heads, and laughed out loud in the middle of the night about how kids we taught would end up owning us somehow, some day. We taught English in the low country of South Carolina, and thought of ourselves as Peace Corps volunteers without the farming know-how.

When Rita decided to scrap it all, my theory was that we really couldn't make a living this way, but I didn't say it more than once. I had a collection of good baseball cards so I didn't have to really go to but one show a month in order to cover my health insurance, car insurance, life insurance, house insurance, mortgage, and food on the table. We didn't have children for one reason or another. My old college roommate Clyde worked for Allstate, so I had free coverage on insurance.

I'm talking rookie cards for Mickey and Nolan, Hank and Willie.

I also had a room of Esso, Butter-Krust Bread, Camel, and Yoo-Hoo metal signs waiting for restaurant managers who wanted to decorate their places of business so they looked authentically old. Ten-year-old kids showed up to buy the signs at the flea market. It's as if they went to Restaurant Manager summer camp, and learned. One thing my father knew instinctively when we traveled around the country every summer for no apparent reason, and that was to carry around a crescent wrench and cat's paw in order to steal unusual signs. He'd been a scallion growing up in west Texas and stolen all the Burma Shave signs across the desert. He left them to me in his will. He also left me his tow truck, which ended up being a good idea.

My father took me places in his tow truck when I grew up, places way out on dirt roads to meet old men who carved, and spelled, and built things—that shouldn't've held together—out of car parts, condiment packs, found rusted screws, weathered fruticose pine branches, and weak pensile cones. He'd introduce me and make me shake hands with men whose hands hurt mine, like caked salt, like dry alluvial granite, like the first roots of newly pulled wisteria. My father bought or traded for what they made, and told me to remember.

Right before my father died of cancer he said to me, "If you teach school/You better be brave/Straddle dead armadillos/Burma Shave." It didn't make any sense at the time. It seemed to be one of those morphine statements he'd announce after a one-minute sleep, something like, "When'd we get to Blanco?" or, "The Cadillac's fins look shiny today."

Because of all this, I'm sure, I took an interest only in primitive art works, and bought or made them up whenever possible. At one time, I bet, I owned the largest collection of nativity scenes made purely from grape vines. Even before my daddy died I went back to all the old places and reintroduced myself, and allowed ancient carving men to give me the gifts they possessed. One time I owned two working clocks made from poptops, and four chairs out of thick 6 1/2 ounce returnable short Cokes. I owned gargoyles and mermaids made from knobs, a collection of spoons made from oyster shells and wooden skewers, little log cabins from cigarette butts, lampshades from Popsicle sticks, cut-out silhouettes of rabbits and hawks and barnyard animals out of roof tin, and etched gourds offering no particular story line whatsoever. Lookit, I probably own the largest scary-face-jug collection in America, by Dave the Slave back in the 1860s, on down to Roy the Mute now. I own face jugs what make men shake, is what I'm saying. People in New York try to find me all hidden up here where I live.

At one time my liver wasn't enlarged, and I remembered every significant date pertaining to history.

My father never met Rita, but reminded me to marry a woman willing to change, and only join a worker's union if I was the sole member.

WE KEPT OUR REGULAR table underneath the tin awning at the Pickens County flea market on Wednesday mornings, and an outdoor table at what was billed the Largest Flea Market in the South in Anderson, which is not far from the Georgia line. This cost ten dollars total. Some Thursdays and Fridays and Sundays we set up a booth at antique shows scattered between Virginia and Alabama, Kentucky and Florida. That cost more. Sometimes we didn't. Rita spent money on fancy embossed two-color business cards and made sure that collectors without time to shop had her number. She gave them out at the thrift stores, too, and promised a tip to any man or woman who shuttled a Windsor chair or whatever in the back and hid it until we could come pick it up.

I didn't.

Because I loved my wife more than anything else, I let her do what she needed in order to feel worthwhile. Evidently showing a student how to fix a run-on sentence didn't work for her in the grand scheme of things, I don't know. Or fragments.

I came back outside and found Rita painting over what she sanded already. I walked back into the garage—not looking for another pint of Old Crow or Jim Beam—because I couldn't think of that fruit or vegetable that wasn't an avocado. I said, "Hey."

She said, "Don't start up. Don't even think about giving me shit right now."

"I know most things people eat," I said, "but for some reason I can never think of this one. I want to ask you about something people eat. We've never bought one, I don't think. It's spiky. My mother used to serve it with mayonnaise."

"Artichoke," Rita said. She held a brush the size of a number 2 pencil with the bristle of one donkey's hair sticking out. I remembered her buying it from a guy next to us at the flea market. She said, "A little bit of blue on a good eggshell white will end up a slight gray. A gray sanded comes out what I want. It's what I want."

I said, "I know that's what you want, Honey. I know." I said, "Yeah, artichoke. Listen, I was at the store earlier and this blind woman was there touching one of those things. I'm saying she stood there with her hand on top of an artichoke, patting it like an albino kid's buzz cut. I guess she sensed me there next to her—that's how people missing a sense are, you know—and she said out loud, 'What is this thing?'"

Rita put wood putty in the holes she'd already poked out, then started digging at them again. She said, "This is a joke."

I said, "No it's not. Listen. I didn't even have time to think. First off, I didn't know what it was called. I said, 'Ma'am, you're petting a porcupine.' And then she said, 'What's a porcupine doing in the grocery store?!' all incredulous. And then I said, 'You're at the zoo—run for your life!' like that."

My wife did not look up. She handed me her sandpaper, walked back into the room where I mostly sat, and hid my bottle for me. At the time I could not move. I'd started laughing, and bent over, and put my hand down on the work table there. I'm not sure if my back went out or what, but I do know that I wondered how I ever got involved with the kind of person who'd buy dowels at the hardware store, carve them into intricate totem poles, then buff them back down to plain linear grain.

Rita came back and said, "Don't you have some phone calls to make to Buck Buffington about his whirlybirds?"

I said, "Yes, I do," just like there at the altar. I said, "But first

103

I want to get some good fresh ribeyes, cut them into strips, dehydrate each piece into jerky, and then glue it all together and soak each steak in water so I can put it on the grill." I'd found and held the awl. I said, "I have some ice trays that should be melted enough—I got water, put it in the freezer, let it harden, and then took it out at room temperature so I could drink it liquid, you know."

I heard my wife hitting the buttons on our telephone.

MY SISTER-IN-LAW owns two uteruses, or uteri, and everything for which that stands, if it matters. It does. One time she told me that once a month she could fill any major city's Red Cross quota for type-whatever blood she possesses. I only nodded. I tried not to think about feminine hygiene products that sold by the bolt.

This is not a lie. Get this: Rita's sister's name is Tina, and she got married to a guy named Benny Helpern, so her name came out Mrs. Tina Helpern, but I called her Tuna Helper what with bilateral uteri added. We didn't have the best in-law relationship, obviously. And I have to say that I didn't start calling her Tuna publicly until long after she kept saying I was perfect for dealing in primitives, seeing as how I wasn't but one gene away from being Cro-Magnon at best.

Tina didn't tell just anyone about her internal addition, and she didn't tell me directly at first. My wife did, though, one morning when she complained about PMS or whatever, and then said she couldn't imagine how Tina went through it all. I said, of course, "What?"

My wife explained it this way, "Imagine if you had a blister on top of a blister, or a bunion on top of a bunion. Imagine that, then multiply by about a million."

I didn't get it. When Rita told me about my sister-in-law's

double occupancy down there I said, "Hotdamn! If it's in the genes, you know, and we have a boy, maybe he'll have two peckers. That'd be cool. We'd have a famous son. And popular, too."

Rita said, "It's not like that. That won't happen. Plenty of women have more than one uterus. It doesn't really affect anything, except they bleed a lot when they menstruate."

We drank coffee that morning. This was right about the day we decided to quit teaching English together at a state-supported college, and figure out how to sell used items to people used to needing used items.

Tina'd left her husband, but never changed her name back for some reason. And on that night when I found Rita hiding sandpaper, Tina showed up at our house. I don't think that's who she called when she pushed all the buttons on the phone, seeing as her sister lived a couple hundred miles away in Durham, so she'd be close to science and biology. I'd gone back inside to my room where I sit alone and do what I got to do. What I got to do includes staring at books I've never read, studying up on art, calling people who live next door to primitive artists in order to leave messages—seeing as how a truly honest primitive artist doesn't own a telephone—and rereading Ulysses because I have an Irish background, among other things.

I sat there in a hardback Mission chair no one would buy and Tina walked in to say, "Glen, Glen—estrogen," like that. She said, "Thog want food," and stomped her foot three times. "Thog kill possum and Thog need fire." This was supposed to be funny. She wanted to get me for my love of hand-carved silverware.

Tina wore bell-bottom pants, by the way. Tina's hairdresser insisted on this feathered layered look, with frosted blonde highlights streamed randomly. Although I never told my wife, I always thought Tina should've played a secondary character in a

1970's television program involving cops, wayward teenagers, and a big dog named Bosco. I said, "Hey, Tina. The discotheque's twenty miles down the road," and pointed. I looked at her crotch and said, "If you had two urethras would you have to pee twice, or half as much?"

She said, "Thog does math."

I said, "Your sister's either painting or sanding. She either has a can of Krylon in her hand, or some sandpaper, or both. Rita's ambidextrous, you know."

My wife's sister said, "I bet you're the kind of man who likes to know that men want your wife, but who doesn't understand that your wife might want other men."

I said, "No," knowing that it was just another ploy. I said, "I'm about as worried about my wife having sex with men she doesn't know, as I'm worried about men showing up to repair our roof out of nowhere." I nodded hard once. I didn't say anything about how my sister-in-law looked like an idiot wearing polyester and clogs.

Tina grabbed my crotch, and squeezed twice hard. She told me that she'd always liked me, and if things didn't work out with her sister she'd like a try. That's how she said it, too. She said, "I bet Rita's leaving soon, Monsieur Bubba."

I said, "Why're you here?"

"A week," she said, not understanding, evidently.

I PUT THE LINGUINE in water. There's one thing no one can say about me, and that's that I don't know how to cook noodles or that I'm afraid to be the cook in the family. I can cook noodles. I can cook macaroni and cheese, and I can cook spaghetti and I can cook angel hair. Boy, I can look into a pot of water and figure things out.

Lookit, I didn't have the time or will power to figure out re-constructed ribeyes. Sometimes I talk big, sure.

Rita and Tuna came inside, and my sister-in-law said, "How much garlic are you using? I love garlic, but it's a little strong in here." She held her nose in the air like a mean domesticated hound. With the bell-bottoms she looked like a salt and pepper shaker set I'd found for nothing in Elberton and sold in Atlanta.

I'd sautéed three different colored bell peppers, a couple cloves of garlic, two jalapeños in one frying pan, and two Italian sausages in another. I couldn't remember if Tuna was a vege-tarian. It seemed like she would be, seeing as how a bunch of eating habits changed in the late 1970s. I knew a man who kept trying to sell me a box of granola and a case of Tab he said were the first off the assembly lines.

Rita said, "Garlic's good for your blood."

I said, "I had some whole cloves, but I pressed them up, then pureed them into paste, then molded them back into shape before dicing them up." I said, "I'm not lying," when Rita hit me in the back of the head the way she does.

Tuna took plates down and got silverware out. She said, "I have this funny feeling I'm not visiting at the best time." She said, "I don't claim to have ESP or anything, but sometimes I watch those shows in the middle of the night. Do y'all ever watch those infomercials? Weird. I saw one one time where this girl was a singer with a pretty, high voice. I forget which one that is. I think she was a natural soprano."

I said, "Yeah, that's a soprano. We just use paper towels for napkins."

Tuna said, "Then she got depressed and screamed until she blew out all her vocal cords. She got so depressed and she called one of the psychics, and the psychic told her she would go back to singing. Get this: she ended up having the deepest bass voice ever, and now travels around to churches all over the United States challenging men from the choir to see who can go lowest. She tells her life story, and then they pass the plate for her, I think."

We sat down and I noticed Tuna holding her stomach the entire time she ate. I looked up at my wife, but she seemed enamored with a cube of sausage. I said, "Your sister's mad at me because I made fun of her painting a piece of bare wood, then sanding it down to make it look old. That's it." I said, "I don't think you have ESP, either, Tuna."

"This is a decent meal, Glen," my sister-in-law said. She looked me in the face and said, "I'm not lying," because I knew about her sarcasm, wit, and propensities.

"Just wait," said Rita. "When I start selling scrolled wood for entranceways, you'll see. I want to see you laugh then." I'd laughed before. I'd laughed when I went through the family photo album and noticed how every one of my in-laws turned his or her back to the camera. What I'm saying is, all of my wife's family photos are the backs of heads. Rita said there seemed to be a superstition going on about those creepy red eyes in a picture. I know this—my wife's family can brag about never having their eyes closed in a group shot.

I poured more wine all around. Call me sentimental, but all the talk about scrolled wood, and church-service miracles, and what with the wine right there on the table, I started feeling religious. I said, "I bet you a thousand dollars you could make it on the sideshow circuit, too, Tuna. What we got to do is find us an internist—or gynecologist, or whatever—named Dr. Moses." Then for some reason I thought it necessary to go into all the symbolism with the Red Sea, et cetera.

After my sister-in-law quit crying I went back to my room

and tried to light a cigarette with a spark from two rocks. What I learned there by myself, with an ear to the door, I can't even explain, really. My own wife said too loudly, "It can't be the worst marriage in the history of marriages, Tina," talking about me. I think she cried somewhat, too.

My sister-in-law said, "I'm thinking about converting to Italian," whatever that meant. I stood there next to the door in my room, with fifty face jugs staring down at me. Tuna said, "I don't want to eat pork anymore, and I want my Sundays free."

My wife started to explain how nationalities weren't converted, and how Tuna probably meant Jewish, but stopped when I opened the door laughing out loud.

It didn't matter about the mistake. Those two women looked at me as if I'd been tattooed throughout with the sign of the anti-Christ. My wife took her sister by the arm and led her into what was once my bedroom. The only thing a man can do at this point is wonder if really the sister-in-law lived closer, lying. The only thing I could figure was that Rita called Tuna, and Tuna came to help her take all the clothes out of one closet, and separate into many pieces of attire, then put them into one big suitcase.

I SLEPT IN THE TOW TRUCK. That night I had a dream about a butcher. For some reason I needed to host a barbecue, and Rita let me dig up the backyard for a pit. In the dream my lawn looked immaculate, and there were no arrowheads in the soil. I dug a food sarcophagus and did not need to shade my eyes or wipe my brow or think about anything symbolic-looking, like a tomb. I did not have to think about vegetarians, is what I'm saying. It was that kind of dream.

I grated cabbage and carrots, made my own mayonnaise, baked beans in an iron cauldron, and put out hors d'oeuvres I did not know. I chopped hickory, and pulled up the only mesquite stump outside of Texas—a backyard miracle I'd never noticed. I got jalapeños out of the garden, and my meek habaneros, and mixed those thick-sliced assassins with a hard and unforgiving mustard-based sauce unknown to anyone outside of Eskimos by choice, and Southern tailgaters by lot in life.

When the butcher delivered the pig whole, he asked if I needed help. We only lifted it together, on top of an old judge's desk Rita'd bought at an estate sale. The butcher waved good-bye and shook his head. I knew he knew my trick, and I knew he disapproved.

Understand, people meandered around the yard, and I assume got what they needed. I did not see my wife or her sister. I did not recognize individuals, but knew that they counted, right there among the many people attending that I had never seen.

With a chainsaw I cut that pig up like a jigsaw puzzle, and made intricate and enigmatic angles, ovals, and slight arcs. I nodded in this dream and smiled. Then I got a very long rebar skewer and shoved it all back together.

In this dream, in this tow truck, in this sapper time, I held the pig way above my head and flaunted it above anyone right up until I needed to lay it on the fire. Then the pig fell apart. And then out of nowhere my dead father showed up in his tow truck wanting to teach me how a person needed to love the pig, then detest the pig, before one could eat the pig. He admonished me for not understanding this after my wife and I'd taught at a state-supported school for so long.

My father said, in my dream, that I'd do better selling face jugs and whatnot, if I understood the human dialectic involving thesis, antithesis, synthesis.

I knew at that point my father never used those terms. Then I woke up with my foot attached to the flashing-lights switch.

From the rearview mirror I saw our car there. Tina's car was parked behind Rita's van. I looked down and saw what I'd brought with me the night before—James Joyce, a bottle of booze, an unopened packet of headache powders, a swatch of sandpaper I must've torn off angry.

I thought to myself, I am alive. It wasn't the first time. I thought about how I didn't want to have "Here we go" turn into "Uh-oh, " or "I'm sure about this" become "It might not be the right way" as my last words, later.

When I went back inside at dawn, Tuna stood there wearing the same white lace atropine nightgown my wife wore every night. She held her hands out, and promised she wasn't like her sister. My sister-in-law rubbed her fingers in an odd manner, though, as if she tried to scrape prints off.

# Cleft For Me

HE'D COME BACK. That's how they work. First, they case a place, and then they come back. Other things besides human beings work the same way. I saw a special on foxes one time. I saw a movie about hawks another. Not sleeping seemed the key.

I turned off the lights to my adjacent trailer. I didn't worry about the street lamp outside. First, I sat with my .410 on a three-quarters sized couch with floral designs. After a couple hours I moved over to one of the Chippendale wingback chairs and matching ottomans. Finally, to avoid getting sleepy, I took off my shirt and sat upright in the only Naugahyde chair I have. My theory and plan worked the three or four other times I'd been cased earlier, over in Enterprise and Corinth and Tifton and Waycross. Other times I guess they got spooked, or saw me waiting. That must've been what happened here. Or, I figured, he'd come back on another night, a night when his wife wasn't home off her third-shift job, or a night when his kids were staying with their cousins, or a night when he had just enough to drink to get the dare inside him going.

I'm a patient man.

In a town like Kingdom Come I'm sure there are a bunch of jokes. I'd never been here before, so I don't know for sure. But more than likely people said a lot of things like that "from here to Kingdom Come" thing. I know for a fact that when I realized he'd come back I said to myself, but not loud enough so's anyone would hear me, "I'll blow that guy from here to Kingdom Come." Then I decided that wasn't far enough, seeing as how I lived in Kingdom Come, if only for a couple months. I said, "I'll blow that guy from here to just across the border in Vicksburg."

My job was to say things like, "If you had a channel changer in your hand, you'd look right at home." It's something they told us to say at the pep rally up in North Carolina. Sometimes it worked, I guess. It worked when wives weren't around, or when they inspected something else on the other side of the showroom. What I'm saying is, it worked for men. For women we learned to say, "Hot damn! Queen Elizabeth showed up right here in (whatever town). Then we're supposed to put our hands in that photo-way, pointer fingers touching thumbs in a box like we're some kind of movie camera men, and walk toward the women slowly. I think they called it panning the customer. They said it'd work 'cause it was psychological.

I'd sold office supplies back before carbon paper and slide rules almost became obsolete. I'd sold textile supplies before the imports took over. Before any of that I went to school and got out and sold encyclopedias, and I sold vacuum cleaners, and I sold insurance, and I sold electrical supplies, and I sold appliances. I sold things that were supposed to sell, and I sold them. I didn't have that golden tongue like some guys did, but I kind of made a living. I dated a girl once who sold Avon, but like I said I didn't have a golden tongue and we didn't get too far.

I have a college education, but I don't want to talk about that. Now, it seems like a whole different life.

I started selling and traveling too early. I couldn't meet a woman and marry her. No woman wants to get involved with a man who's already ready to move on to the next town, I doubt.

I sell furniture direct from Thomasville, North Carolina, at 60 percent off the regular price. I set up my shop in a Wilson's Five and Dollar parking lot, a big plastic tent right up next to my trailer. I pull my trailer with a pick-up truck. The trailer's big enough to lug the tent and a generator and my few belongings when I'm driving to the next town, to meet the eighteen-wheeler to stock me up to capacity. It doesn't take a five-star rocket general to call up the warehouse, tell them I've sold blank number of pieces in wherever, and have them load up that many to take on to the next town on their way to deliver sleeper sofas and end tables to somewhere else on the same route.

After I'm all set up I get my generator going so I can work the stove and refrigerator and the outlets so I can watch TV. I arrange my furniture in the same way a funeral director arranges his caskets—I start off with the middle-priced pieces right there at the door, then follow them up with the highest-priced. If anybody has the time to walk full-circle, he or she'd find the cheapest stuff. Usually people buy on a whim, according to the pep rally director up in Thomasville. Usually they're just driving by, see my sign and the tent, drop in and pick something up for the wife or mother on Mother's Day, or for themselves when there's a new rec room involved. When I'm in Georgia I special-order Go Dawgs lamp shades, in Alabama Roll Tide arm covers, in Mississippi rebel-flag seat cushions.

My plastic tent's not fully see-through, understand. It's opaque, more or less. If you've not seen mine, you've seen someone's—the tent looks like an old milk bottle, or a Texas racecar driver's windshield, or the smoke in a fight arena's spotlight.

So this guy shows up earlier in the day and stalks. He goes by the middle-priced chairs, and the expensive love seats and sleeper sofas, and right on back to the eighty-nine-dollar chairs with scuffed legs or small rips in the underside stitching. He doesn't make eye contact with me, even when I come up and say, "These here are the best prices you can find in Kingdom Come, Bubba."

He picks up a price tag and pretends I'm not there.

I say, "Eighty-nine dollars. You can't beat that."

He lets go of the tag. He walks over to the only piece of wicker I got, a funny swirly end table–looking thing that probably couldn't hold a candle on it, and checks the price.

I walk away and stand in front of my cash register, knowing that he'll come back in the night to steal my furniture, or try to break into my trailer so he can get the money I hide every night behind my toilet.

I can go a good week before I need to drive the trailer down to a dumping station and release my toilet, by the way. The smell doesn't even bother me, but that might be 'cause I live alone.

He walks back around the other way and I watch him like a dog. Other people walk in and look at a couple of the matching Strat-o-Loungers but I don't even move to tell them that they would look better with a channel changer or with a crown on their heads. I watch my man. He moseys. He slinks. He wears an old Army jacket and stands five-foot-ten or so, weighs maybe one-seventy with blue eyes and brown hair and three-to-seven days' worth of beard, depending. He's got on high-top tennis shoes, blue jeans sized 33 waist and 32 length, and a T-shirt under the coat that says "a St" because the coat is unzipped but not fully open. I make a note to think North Carolina, Alabama, and Louisiana State. Later I think of Nova Scotia, and much later Montana in case I needed to give a description to the police. I'm no artist. I can't sketch out what someone looks like.

I study geography, though.

That night I didn't sleep when I thought the college boy in

the Army jacket was coming back, but I wasn't exactly sluggish. I stayed alert, thanks to the way the Naugahyde kept my nerve endings sharp. He didn't show, and I concentrated on the lines I learned at the pep rallies plus the few I'd made up myself. One chair a day is good in this business, and I sold a love seat and a sleeper-sofa also, before three o'clock. I remember all this 'cause at three o'clock my caser showed up again, this time wearing a suit and carrying a Bible. And he brought along a woman, younger than me but not much—maybe in her late thirties— who toted a Bible also but wore a green V-neck dress that showed enough cleavage to turn an irrigation farmer green.

He came right up to me, too, and didn't seem to be the suspicious customer he'd been just 24 hours earlier. He came up and said, "I was in here yesterday looking around. I'm Mike," and stuck out his hand to shake. I tried to look at his face but couldn't keep my eyes off the woman he brought. And I remember even thinking to myself, "This is a new ploy. He's still casing the joint and has brought her along as a distraction."

I shook his hand. I said, "Howdy. Doug Grigsby." I tried to make my name sound important. It's not always easy.

"This is Bethany Shipman," Mike said. I quit shaking his hand so as to take hers. She gave me one of those limp handshakes, but I didn't care. I understood. She probably didn't want to jiggle. "We're with the Traveler's Ministry and try to keep up with anyone who might be coming through this area so as to invite them to our services."

I said, "That's nice of you." I didn't tell him I'd not been to a church service since my parents took me to get baptized in the river and the preacher accidentally let go of me just long enough for me to sink and get tangled up in some submerged branches. People in my hometown still sometimes call me the baby Moses, seeing as how when I came out it looked like I

117

brought up an ark of bulrushes between my toes. I said, "I remember you from yesterday. You were kind of quiet."

Mike said, "I didn't want to scare you off. Some people, they get a little jumpy when a man of the cloth's around. And I hate to admit it but a lot of people traveling through Kingdom Come aren't exactly the most desirable types to have in the church — not that the church isn't for everyone. I just mean, we had a couple of drifters one time who put Stick'em on their fingers and pulled quite a bit out of the collection plate."

I think that's what he said. I'd motioned for Bethany to sit down, she sat right across from me, and I could see up her dress. I said, "So y'all are some kind of co-preachers of the church, a husband and wife team?"

Then I gave out a silent prayer.

Bethany said, "My goodness, no. Mike's the preacher. I just do the books. He asked me if I wanted to come out here with him and I said okay 'cause I wanted to look at a little something to get my mother. You don't have any nice mirrors or picture frames or paintings of the sea crashing in on some rocks, do you?"

I said, "I can get some!" I felt my face turn red after blurting it out.

Mike said, "Actually, Doug, our purpose here is twofold. I'd like to know, too, if you'd be interested in loaning our church your generator on Sunday morning." He said, "You wouldn't even miss it if you were at the service."

Bethany said, "I know what it's like to be on the road. Before I decided to settle down in Kingdom Come to write my memoirs, I worked for Mimi Dubose's All-Girl Wrestling Spectacular. It ain't exactly the glamorous life everyone expects it to be, is it? I'll come over and cook you dinner tonight if you let us use the generator on Sundays until you have to move on."

I tried to remember passing a K-mart on the way down here so I could unhitch my truck from the trailer and go find Bethany a mirror or picture frame or a painting of the waves hitting the rocks. Being a man of town-to-town living, I'd seen Mimi Dubose's All-Girl Wrestling Spectacular.

I TOLD THEM THEY could certainly borrow the generator, and that dinner sounded like a great idea, and that I'd be at Sunday's service, but the entire time I couldn't get out of my mind that my trailer was too small to take on company, really. I mean, I couldn't make out whether Bethany'd turned into a good Christian girl overnight or not in our one conversation, so I thought it might be forward asking her to sit across from me at the fold-down table that also served as a mirror when up in the daytime.

I went out to my tent and rearranged the furniture so Bethany and I could eat by candlelight, seated on matching King and Queen wingbacks designed by Simon Dubus. I placed one of the most popular tables I sell, the Nooker, between the chairs and went over to Wilson's Five and Dollar to buy some plastic flowers for a centerpiece.

I had it all ready. I had my generator going so my kitchen would work. I smelled my armpits about every fifteen minutes to make sure. I didn't think about taking off work early and going to a local library to find a book on conversations or party jokes.

Bethany showed up at eight o'clock and said, "I feel bad, Doug. I said I'd cook for you." She held a bunch of sacks in her hand. They looked like groceries to me, for what it's worth. "But what I wanted to make you, the store didn't have. I know what it's like to be on the road. I went by the 7-11 and got us two twelve packs of beer and some two-for-a-dollar hot dogs."

I said, "Hot damn," just like that. I could see already that the floor mirror wouldn't have been such a bad idea.

"I figure we can just sit out in the lot and watch the cars go by, you know. It's more fun with two people," she said. I stood in my trailer. Bethany stood on the asphalt. She wore a different dress than earlier. It was the same style, but black. I could look down it from where I stood.

I stepped out of the trailer and walked by Bethany and went straight to the tent to get the King and Queen wingbacks. I set them on the street corner overlooking the four-way stop. I'd had dreams about nights like this, I hate to admit.

I said, "So, what's with this church you're affiliated with? Is Mike your new husband or something like that? How come you want a person like me in a pew like yours?"

Bethany said, "Do you have any glasses in there? I don't like to drink out of a can." On my way back to the trailer I couldn't tell if she belched or giggled or said something. For some reason I couldn't get it out of my mind the time I sold furniture in Sevierville, Tennessee, between mountains, in a gap.

That night Bethany and I sat and watched people mess up at the four-way stop, and we drank the worst beer ever canned, and we ate a few hot dogs. She let me know that she wasn't the preacher's wife, which mattered at the time. She showed me the tattoos she had on her ankle and the inside of her left breast, far from her nipple. We threw empty cans behind our backs, trying to get them on top of my tent to roll off. She told me she originally came from Oklahoma, but ran away when she graduated from high school—she was supposed to represent her hometown in the Miss Oklahoma pageant—and ran out of money in Baton Rouge on her way to New Orleans. That's when she happened on Mimi Dubose's troupe. It saved her life, she said.

Her talent for the Miss Oklahoma pageant, if it matters, was to twirl a baton while riding a unicycle while the orchestra played "A Bicycle Built for Two." She said she chose that song on purpose.

I said, "And then, somehow, you found religion and came to Kingdom Come, huh?" It seemed like she'd never get to the present.

I tried to keep my eyes on my own beer can. It was generic generic beer. The cans just had a "B" on their sides.

Bethany said, "I was making upwards of a thousand dollars a week, and didn't have to worry about rent or food. Mimi treats her girls good, you know. Our wrestling matches were staged, if you didn't know, and we'd take turns winning from one city to the next. Sometimes I dressed up like an Arab to be the bad girl, and other times I'd dress up like that Gone with the Wind woman. It didn't matter. All of Mimi's girls were friends, and I still try to keep in touch with them, maybe at Christmas when they're always in Bethlehem, Pennsylvania."

I said, "But you're happy to be away from that type of profession, I take it." Two Camaros revved their engines at the four-way.

"I had a vision," Bethany said. "I was slated to be the good girl this one night right over in Monroe, so I got all gussied up in the cheerleader outfit some of us wore when we were good girls. Well, Carthella Mayhew was the bad girl that night, up against me. And she dressed up in the Indian outfit Mimi Du-bose sewed up herself, not counting the rubber tomahawk she bought at a Stuckey's somewhere. That night something got into Carthella and I don't know if she thought what we were doing was real or what. All I know is that she got me in what we called the Boob Buster—actually normally we swung each other around by the armpits but if it was done really fast it looked like we swung each other by the titties—and in all the dizzy

121

commotion for some reason I had this image of the baby Jesus. And in this image—it was more real than a dream or mirage—the baby Jesus told me to get out of this line of work and follow His ways."

I thought to myself that I needed to get out of selling furniture from town to town out of a roadside plastic tent at the time, of course. I said, "Another beer, Bethany?" I said, "Do you want to go ahead and get my generator tonight, or are you coming by in the morning to get it?"

She said, "And the weirdest thing happened. I lost, 'cause I was supposed to lose that night. And when I crawled out of the ring holding my titties like I was supposed to, Mike walked up out of nowhere and said, 'And there shall be no more curse . . .' which is right there toward the end of the New Testament, I found out later. Well, I took it all for prophecy, like it was supposed to be. Then he told me about Kingdom Come and his church, and I guess I just realized that I wasn't supposed to be wrestling with other women any more, you know."

I tried to think of ways for Bethany to leave. I had this feeling that there'd be a prayer session coming up, but no laying on of the hands.

"Mike got me a job in his parents' restaurant working as a hostess. It gives me time to work on my memoirs during the day. I think he has a crush on me, Doug, but that's it. To tell you the truth, I wish I'd have another vision to get me out of Kingdom Come. Mike, he's a nice enough guy and all, but he's always trying to do things to convince me that he's the man I should settle down with. He's always trying to impress me in weird ways. Do you know what I mean?"

She scooted her wingback closer to me and leaned over. I thought we were about to kiss. Just then, someone honked a horn at the four-way and it ended up being Mike. He waved, driving a convertible hearse I learned later he customized himself.

Bethany led me back inside my trailer, crouched low. We didn't really speak to each other. I'm not ashamed to admit that I'd never slept with another woman in my trailer, so I didn't know how tight a fit it is to unfold my home entertainment system down to a bed for two people. I didn't waggle on Bethany that night — she took the bed drunk and I took the hallway. I guess I took the hallway drunk, too, 'cause for some reason I decided that it'd be okay to leave the wingbacks out on the edge of the parking lot.

It wasn't, of course. Those things were nowhere to be found when I crawled to the front of the trailer and looked for Goody's Powders at dawn, then went outside to clean up the beer cans from underneath the edge of the tent's roof. Sometimes Thomasville sends spies down to make sure all of us traveling salesmen are keeping a clean and hospitable showroom, and to match receipts with remaining items.

Like stepfather like son — one time my mother's second husband, the used car salesman, had a one-night-only test-drive party, complete with chip dip and Cokes — and at the end of the night he'd lost two Buicks and an Oldsmobile. He never found the missing cars and he never told the cops 'cause he knew it'd be in the local paper and he'd look like a buffoon for trusting people with the keys to his cars.

I had better luck. I woke up Bethany and said, "It's eight o'clock. Does Mike have a Sunday school class or anything? Do we need to pack up the generator and go?"

Bethany didn't sit up in bed. She had the blanket up to her chin and said, "I had this dream, Doug. I mean, I think I had this vision. You and I were living in Montana, and we had this big ranch house. We were throwing a party for some guy and about a hundred people were in our house. They all sat, too. They all had places to sit."

I said, "That's good. Are you wearing what you're wearing? Do you need a headache powder or anything? I have a suit somewhere around here but I'm not sure it still fits 'cause I haven't had to wear it since I had to show up in court one time a few years back in Atoka, Tennessee, to testify against a guy I saw shoot another man in the foot because they were arguing over bowling shoes." I said, "So."

Bethany got off the bed naked. Sometime in the middle of the night she'd thrown off all her clothes. She still had her Mimi Dubose's All-Girl Wrestling Spectacular physique, too. She said, "It was the same kind of feeling I had when Mike came and got me out of Monroe, this dream I'm talking about. Except in this dream, after everyone left, you and I got on a sleeper sofa and made love. Bizarre."

Bethany bent over and touched her toes. I guess it was some kind of routine with her. I counted every rib on her backside. Then I said, "I have a robe folded up underneath the sink. Put it on and let me show you something inside the tent."

The robe was paisley. It matched the sleeper sofa I pulled out in the tent.

I understand how a man can lose all sense of self-pride or self-esteem or self-control because of a woman he loves, but I only understand him doing stupid things like calling at all hours of the night, or following her around, or sending flowers to her place of work every day. I don't understand talking yourself into believing that a woman will think a convertible hearse looks elegant. Bethany didn't tell me any of this until we'd folded the sleeper sofa back into its original form. She told me about Mike

124

because she wanted to warn me that he might act a little jealous at church. I told her I could handle myself. I told her that I'd sized up Mike before I'd even met him.

She called me by name on that couch.

We took the generator to a church that looked more like a defunct drive-in movie than a church. It was a defunct drive-in movie, for what it's worth—people sat in their cars usually and Mike gave a sermon standing on the top step of an old metal sliding board where kids used to play before the feature began. Instead of amening, Bethany said, they honked their horns at particularly good or inspiring passages. If they felt compelled to speak in tongues, they started their cars and stepped on the gas and flashed their lights in some kind of weird Morse code manner.

We drove up before anyone else besides Mike was there. He said, "Aren't y'all wearing the same thing I saw you wearing last night over at the four-way?"

I said, "No."

Bethany said, "I wish you weren't always so jealous, Mike. I've told you before."

I said, "Where do you want the generator?"

Mike didn't answer. He didn't thank me for bringing it. He smiled but didn't show his teeth. Peripherally I saw my two wingback chairs over in the kids' playground, turned facing the screen. Mike stooped down and took the generator and walked over to where the old concession stand stood. I didn't pay attention to Bethany, who'd walked over to Mike's pick-up truck he used as a collection plate—normally Bethany drove it around and people threw their change in the bed of it. Cars started coming into the lot, taking their favorite places. I noticed how the younger drivers parked in back.

So everyone parked and Mike didn't go to the front. He

plugged in his home movie projector and pulled the cord on my generator and before you knew it we were all watching some kind of staged home movies of Mike visiting a place that was supposed to look like Jerusalem. People on the screen kept opening their mouths and I suppose the film had sound, but no one could hear it above the buzz of the generator. I sat in my own truck with Bethany. We didn't speak. We watched, but we didn't say anything. The film on the old screen showed Mike walking around the Holy Land, and then a guy who looked like Jesus came out of nowhere and put his arm around Mike like they were old buddies.

It wasn't really the Holy Land. In the background you could see a water tower and a radio tower and a billboard that said, "Rent Me." There was the trail of a jet in the sky. The guy playing Jesus wore Converse tennis shoes.

I said to Bethany, "Let's go. Let's leave my generator here, and go back and pack up the furniture and just go."

She tried to stuff my talleywhacker back into my pants and said, "Do you mean it, Doug?"

I said, "Montana. Can you drive this pick-up? Let's go get a U-Haul and get what we need for furniture and convoy ourselves right on up there."

Luckily we sat back together for a moment and thought rationally. Bethany got in Mike's pick-up and started collecting change from the congregation. Then she scooped out the bed of his truck, put the money in her purse, and told me to drive like a pile driver.

So if the law's not after me, I'm sure the Thomasville furniture coalition is. It doesn't matter. God forgives those who admit to their sins—Bethany told me and I figured she knew more about it than I ever would. Here there's no church, whether true or off-beat or sanctified or not. I fish now. I fish and I bring people into our cabin and talk about what it's like living in the South. For some reason they want to know. They bring us food and drinks. They come in and just ask us to talk to them.

Bethany and I make love every night in one way or another. She stays in shape by chopping wood every day. I watch her sometimes from the back window, watch as she lifts her ax above her head and brings in down in a way that can make her breasts look larger than two side-by-side mulch mounds. She brings that ax down on timber, then pulls the log and ax together above her head to wail them both down so the crack's large enough to fit a wedge between them afterwards. Bethany knows what she's doing.

She writes her memoirs, daily. Me, I talk to the locals. I take the good logs that Bethany doesn't split and use them so I can practice making my own furniture, mostly chairs and end tables. I listen to Bethany when she wants to tell me about her old days wrestling, or her old days reading the Bible, or her old days even before that when she ran around with a group of girls named Rhonda and gave the finger to cops driving by.

We make our living. We find ways to find ways. My step-father once told me that the best way to crack open a pecan was to stare at it long enough, say a few threatening words to it, then bite on it right in the middle. He said it'd open right there—in the right spot—so the meat could be dug out easiest. He taught me how to stick a half-scissor in the nut to cleft it evenly.

My biological father taught me how to move when it's time to move, indirectly. He knew his own Bible verses, in his own way, too.

# Caulk

ELAINE INSISTED ON more silicone, and I stood my ground at least twenty-four hours on how she didn't need it. I said there was a reason for honest ventilation, for breathing, and that too much silicone would hamper this process. I mentioned how it would be obvious to her both winter and summer, when everything unnatural in the world either contracted or expanded. This was fall—late October—in South Carolina. At noon the temperature got up to the mid-seventies, but the humidity was a low 60 percent. There existed no other time to paint a house.

"If you don't caulk right then you'll have to do the job again before the year's out," Elaine said. "I know what I'm doing, Louis. Remember—I lived in Mexico City the spring semester of my junior year in college."

I didn't get the connection. We stood outside. I held a caulk gun in my right hand, with about half of the tube gone. It was the first one of the third case. I turned the lever down so no silicone spilled out, so caulk didn't exude out on my beat-up no-name-brand tennis shoes, making me undergo flashbacks of a time at the Auto Drive-In with my first high school girlfriend who almost gave it up. I said, "I've caulked every goddamn seam, Elaine. I've caulked boards that were welded together—

that were petrified, by God—and needed caulk about as much as a goat needs a can opener."

Elaine held nothing. She stood with her hands on her hips and looked at the soffit and fascia. She looked at a point twenty feet off the ground and said, "You didn't smooth that bead down. You missed a spot."

This was near dusk. Elaine had come home from work hoping to find me—I know—not working on the house like I'd promised. Some time earlier in the week I'd been drinking, and as drinkers might be wont to do I'd said the house needed painting unless we wanted someone like Andrew Wyeth hanging out in the front yard thinking we lived in a weather-beaten barn, and that I didn't have much else to do, seeing as I'd gotten mad at my last boss and quit a job driving oxygen canisters around to hackers and wheezers. Elaine said, "It needs to be scraped and caulked hard, Louis. Why don't you let me hire someone to do the job right. There's no need to even talk about it if you don't feel committed to do the job right."

Of course I took all her talk to be a challenge, and didn't understand that she knew how to wind me up like a cheap metal mouse that skitters across linoleum floors. I said, "Why would a complete painting stranger care about how this house turns out?" I felt my one eye starting to travel off. We stood outside, still. I pretended to check the soffit and fascia, too. I said, "Personally I think I'm ready to paint tomorrow. If you want, I'll go over the whole house again with caulk."

And I meant it. In my mind, a person scraped flaked paint and caulked up holes, buckled seams, roof flashings, door casings, and paid special attention to window frames. That's what I did the first day. The goddamn house was airtight, but if she wanted more caulk, then I'd do it.

Elaine said, "You weren't drinking up on that ladder, were

you?" She took my caulk gun, turned the lever 180 degrees, and shot an invisible indention underneath one of the living room windows. Elaine rubbed it four directions, then handed the tube back.

"There's no telling what somebody might charge to paint this place. I don't even know anyone who knows an honest painter. They say to never let a roofer around your wife, and never let a painter near your liquor cabinet." I felt my eye wander back even with the other. I'd drunk about half a good bottle of Old Crow during the day. There are two theories: don't drink and don't fall off the ladder, or go ahead and drink hard so it won't hurt so much in case you do fall.

I've tried both in the past. The second's best. When I worked construction one summer in college sober, I pulled back a shutter where a small but nervous clan of bats nestled daytime. They flew out. I fell off. This is no lie: on the way down the entire history of French literature passed before my eyes. When I hit the ground I got out the "Bo" from "Baudelaire," but nothing else.

MOST TIMES WHEN ELAINE went off on two-day business trip seminars in order for her to push what she pushed, namely new and improved kitchen accessories—there are more conventions held on blenders and whatnot than the average person thinks—I'd either find a way to get time off from my job delivering oxygen, or I'd stay home looking out the venetian blinds to see if Elaine hired a detective to see if I left or invited dancing escort women over. But this last time I didn't get an invitation, even though I'd quit my job and had the time.

"We're doing a fair in Atlanta," Elaine said. "We got I don't know how many rooms downstairs at the Omni to show off the new products. They're saying every new micro-brewery pub is sending someone to check out our line of mid-sized Hemingway sampler stemware.

I said, "Huh. Not to mention the zucchini thing." What else could a caulking boy say? Elaine's company had developed a slicer/dicer/skinner mechanism that worked so clean and easy they thought it might change Americans' attitudes and diets. Me, I couldn't tell the difference between zucchini, cucumbers, or dill pickles. I didn't care to cook or eat any of them, either. As far as the Hemingway line—I'm glad Elaine's company didn't market a set of shot glasses.

I said, "Well, you have a good time, dear. Don't go down to Underground Atlanta all by yourself. Don't show up at the Cheetah 3 with your friends just because women get in a strip joint free."

Elaine rolled her eyes. She said, "I won't have any time off, Louis. And if I did—like maybe if there's a blackout and we can't showcase our wares—I'd find a museum."

"If there's a blackout it might be hard to look at art," I said. It just came to me, fast. Sometimes I thought that maybe those oxygen canisters leaked and gave me extra brain cells or something.

Elaine said, "Caulk. Don't start painting until I get back. I'll call you when I check in at the hotel."

She kissed me on the mouth, but didn't mean it. This happened once a month. I knew she had cutlery on her mind. Me, I could only get out, "If you're going to talk the talk, you better caulk the caulk," like an idiot.

I'D STILL BE MARRIED if it weren't for the weather. In a way, Canada's to blame. If that big Arctic swoop they show during the weather-map section had moved south of Appalachia while Elaine worked in Atlanta, then we'd still be together, I'm sure.

Whereas it got down to the low 20's in places like Johnson City, Tennessee, it stayed in the low 70's in the upstate of South Carolina.

As any reputable caulk tube will point out, caulk cannot be used at temperatures below 5 degrees centigrade, which is 40 degrees Fahrenheit. Hell, the tubes I used even had directions written in French—which I'm sure had something to do with that Canadian Arctic jet stream, seeing as I've never seen actual French people caulking their field stone houses out in the countryside near Dijon or wherever.

Elaine went off, and I got to work. I finished the last eleven tubes of the third case, and then I called a local hardware joint and got them to deliver another dozen cases and put it on Elaine's bill. I brought Jason the delivery boy inside and we feasted on canned smoked oysters and Bloody Marys before I got to work on the house.

I said, "My wife seems to think an entire wooden house needs a layer of caulk before it gets painted," and handed him some ground habanero peppers for his drink. Jason looked like a college kid going to a Baptist school, but this was a Friday morning and he wasn't in class. Later on I thought how he looked a little like someone I saw on television who was a member of a white supremacy militia group.

"A lot of people use primer," he said.

"Exactly! You prime the wood, and then you paint it," I said.

This is no lie: Jason poured a quarter teaspoon of ground habanero on his thumb, then snorted it. Jason said, "Pain. Pain's good so you remember pleasure. That's one of my mottoes."

I poured another drink and put it away. I poured another drink and put it away. I'd made a pitcher, and made a mistake. I didn't want a delivery boy dead on my hands with hot peppers up his nose. I said, "Prime, paint."

"Well, technically, you only prime new wood, man. Or new sheetrock. After your house's been painted, I wouldn't prime it again. Maybe that's just me," Jason said. I looked across the table at him and thought, How can a twelve-year-old get a job as a delivery boy? Jason said, "I only work weekdays, you know. I help out my friends doing jobs they're doing—not as a gofer, either. If you need help caulking and you're willing to pay, I'd be glad to help you out. I can get you references." He nodded up and down ten times.

I poured the last of the pitcher and said, "Am I the only delivery you have today? Here." I handed Jason ten bucks for a tip. I said, "No. This job is something I have to do myself."

Jason sat there with his first drink still full and a red powdery stain on his upper lip. He said, "I understand, dude."

I said, "Say, do you have any other mottoes?"

He didn't blink. He said, "Paining others gives pleasure, too."

That night I slept without my wife. Every light, television, radio, and appliance stayed on. The evening low was fifty-two degrees.


I CUT HALF OF THE nipples down two inches, and the others only a half-centimeter. I needed thick, thick beads and I needed ones so thin I could've worked Hollywood as a make-up artist for villains and swashbucklers. I put the twenty-foot extension ladder up at the far gable and set my stepladder up against the front of the house. There was no need for drop cloths.

When I got four feet down the house in wide rows, I'm sure the bees showed up only because they thought it was the biggest albino hive ever. There are different caulks, I'm sure, but I stuck with siliconized acrylic white. If I'd've used a gray color, then wasps would've shown up, thinking our house was one big paper nest.

My right forearm hurt and pulsed like the furthest moon of Jupiter, and at times I thought the four triggering fingers I used might cramp into a claw so hard no middle-weight boxing champion would have a chance with me. I did not think of Elaine flirting with men from Minnesota who owned slight restaurant chains, with men who didn't come so much for the spectacular as they came for the spectacle — let me say now that I know my wife got hired for her physical attributes more than she did for her culinary or home ec prowess. Elaine majored in anthropology, for Christ's sake, and I know for certain she spent her first year in college as a pom-pom girl.

Our house was thick and white, is what I'm saying, by Sunday night when Elaine came back. She only got a sweeping glimpse of it when she turned her car into the driveway. At the door I said, "Hey! You got back safely. You cheated Death again."

Elaine said, "There must've been too many cars coming my way in the opposite direction. You didn't paint the house all white, did you?"

I grabbed my wife's suitcase. I shuttled her inside as quickly as possible. This was the exact moment when I thought maybe I'd gone too far, out of meanness. I said, "Did people like y'all's products?"

"The house looked really white," Elaine said. She tried to turn around, but I pushed her towards inside. "I could see our house from way far away," she said. "There's a glow."

"Life in the big city," I said. "Boy, that really seems to change your way of looking at things. Of seeing things. Of your outlook on what is real and what isn't."

I held my wife's suitcase. She held a handful of her company's pamphlets. Ten minutes after I closed the door it got steamy in the house, for reasons other than a wife returning from a business trip.

ELAINE SAW NOTHING wrong the next morning. When I awoke due to a cramp in my forearm, Elaine stood above me in her robe at an hour past dawn. She held an eight-inch-wide brush in her hand and said, "You can start now." She had on her robe, and held a blazer outfit she always wore to work, as if she went out to either sell real estate or lead a group of drunks from intervention to committal.

I said, "It's supposed to rain today." It's the first thing that came to me.

"No, it's not. I just watched the local news while I dried my hair. It's supposed to be warm again." Elaine brushed something invisible from her coat.

I said, "How could you hear the weather report with a blow-dryer on? I think you heard wrong. There's no way you could hear anything right with a blow-dryer on."

Elaine smiled, but didn't show her teeth. She grinned. She said, "I went outside to get the paper. I bet it's ninety degrees out now."

Lookit: I swear it doesn't get 90 degrees at dawn in South Carolina during October. There might be 90 percent humidity. It might get to 90 degrees by two o'clock in the afternoon, but not before sunlight. One time my grandmother on my father's side said it reached 110 and rained simultaneously on Christmas day, 1950, but at that point she'd gone through both radiation and chemotherapy—she liked to pull the top of her dress down and show the cavity where one breast existed, then say how smoking was bad for you.

136

I got up and said to my wife, "Did you look at the house?"

"I'm so happy you gave in," she said. "Let me say now that I thought I'd come home and find that you hadn't done anything since I left. I'm sorry. I didn't think you'd caulk the house right." Elaine walked into the laundry room.

I stood in my boxer shorts sober. I said, "It's a joke, you idiot! I caulked every square inch of the house. It looks like a Dairy Queen treat from the road. Yesterday an Eskimo family happened by and asked me the name of our contractor—they said they'd been looking for an igloo like ours ever since they left Lapland, or wherever."

Understand, I caught myself hyperventilating, and my bad eye strayed off even though it was morning and I'd not partaken yet. Elaine came back in the room wearing a pair of bicycle shorts so tight she showed camel-lips. I didn't realize that everything was out of sync. Why did she take a shower and wash her hair before exercising? Elaine held 5-pound weights in her hand and said, "What? One-two, one-two, one-two," et cetera.

I CAME INSIDE from almost painting to find Elaine on the telephone with her college roommate Amy. They planned their tenth reunion. Elaine laughed too much, I thought, as I came up from behind her. Elaine said, "Well, I wouldn't know how to react to an uncircumcised man, either. I've only seen one once."

I tried to step back out of the room, but made a noise. The floor creaked, is what I'm saying, and you'd think somebody who lived there—namely my wife Elaine—would've thought to have caulked the area.

Elaine hung up without saying goodbye or anything. She just put down the phone. To me, my wife said, "Hey," and smiled. She could've done a commercial for toothpaste or dental floss.

I said, "Is there a problem with the phone lines? If you want me to do it, I'll call the telephone company and say our phone's gone out."

Elaine stood up erect. She'd put on the business suit. "That's okay," she said.

"I couldn't call the telephone company if our line was out, stupid!" I said.

Elaine said, "Louis, there're men who don't play this game always. I thought you were outside painting the house."

What could I say? I knew there were other men out there—younger, better-looking men—who didn't have the advantage of taking a logic course on the college level. I don't want to come off as superior or anything, but I've noticed how people without four-year college educations tend to buy more mobile homes percentage-wise, and how people like me have noticed that acts of nature, viz. tornadoes, knock over trailers.

Of course they didn't scrape, caulk, and paint wood, granted.

I said, "So you're looking for a man who ain't circumcised, is that what you want? I guess that's what you want." I'd put mini-bottles in the gutter the night before. I said, "Four fat men stopped by thinking our house was a pilgrimage to the Michelin man. Did you, by any chance, know that the word caulk comes from the word caucus, which means just a faction of a political party? It's Greek. It means the whole goddamn house doesn't need doing."

This wasn't exactly true, but it sounded right. I was pretty sure the word caucus came from some Greek word.

Elaine said, "You're full of crap. Caulk comes from a 304 milliliter tube, which is approximately ten-point-three fluid ounces."

I said, "Does Amy have a ten-point-three-fluid-ounce uncircumcised caulk tube she's worried about? Is that what y'all were talking about, Elaine?"

My wife actually giggled. She turned her back towards me. She said, "Uh-huh." Then she went to work, finally, running late.

IT'S IMPOSSIBLE TO roll paint right, across concentric horizontal loops of siliconized acrylic caulk. After Elaine left I put the brush aside and rummaged around in the garage until I found an old roller with a nap used for rough surfaces. My wife wanted the house a hue the paint company paint-namers tabbed Saharan Winter Sand, which most sane individuals outside of the house-painting business would call "tan." I took my roller and pan outside, my aluminum extension handle, and the long ladder. The beads of caulk were stuck so thick it felt like driving over a Wal-Mart parking lot of speed bumps paved one after another. It didn't take me one hard roll up and down to have a flashback of little league baseball, and that feeling of bees in the hands when you swing and hit a pitch in on the handle. The sound that emanated was not unlike a stick drug across an expensive, tightly cropped picket fence.

"That's a nice mural of the Riverside dirt track stands after a muddy Saturday night," some guy in a Camaro yelled out at me as I stood in the middle of the front yard not admiring my work. I turned around and waved. I laughed, and even thought deep down how this guy probably knew exactly what I did to get back at a wife. I watched him ease by slowly, and paid attention to his gravity-prone mouth sag, and thought to myself, now there's a man who's had destiny knock on his forehead more than once before he thought about answering the door.

I thought how maybe the same could be said about me, too, for about three seconds. Then I looked up at the sky for rain clouds, and wondered if rain might wash down Saharan Winter Sand over caulk lips over and over until one smooth facade showed that might satisfy wife, real estate agent, and prospective buyer alike.

A thunderstorm wasn't in the forecast, just as Elaine told me.

I yelled back, "Come here and tell me that," like fighting words.

I knew this guy—I'd seen him over at Compton's store—and he always meant business one way or the other. He was one of the Shirley boys who ran an auto body shop nearby, pushing and pulling dents out of car panels and hoods. Ray Shirley also ran dirt track at Riverside, of course, in the modified division. One time I took Elaine over there and everyone jumped out of the stands holding their faces. I said, "Someone farted." What happened in fact was that there was a drunk guy raising hell below us, and there was this old woman who had a canister of mace, she blew the thing in the drunk man's direction, and then all hell broke loose. Much like that Canadian Arctic wind not showing up on the weather screen, this woman didn't understand how the wind blowing towards her might send spray backwards.

That's what happened. Elaine and I stood there while everyone ran from the bleachers. Elaine said, "What the hell?" like that.

We smoked cigarettes, too, and didn't smell or feel a thing. This old guy in a wheelchair up top with us shook his head and said, "Again. It's happened again. When will people understand stock car racing?"

I thought about the double-amputee when I returned to the ladder, after the Shirley boy drove off. I thought to myself, there's a way caulk might make his life bearable, if one of those companies came up with a more pliable prosthetic limb.

I got up on the ladder and got my face close, is what I'm saying. This is no lie: I caught myself wondering why a Supreme Being didn't invent regeneration for human beings. And at that moment something picked me off the ladder and threw me to the ground.

I almost broke my first hip at age thirty-three.

"YOU DID IT ALL on purpose, Louis. Don't lie to me," Elaine said when she got home. "What'd you do, jump off the ladder? I bet you had to go up that thing ten times and dive off to get a swelling that bad."

I was in a tub of Epsom salts with an ice pack on the side of my ass. It had been years since I'd bruised myself, and I couldn't remember if heat or ice came first. One time ten months before, I crashed the oxygen delivery van into the front of some old guy's house and tore up my knees. This was winter and I'd lost control going down his driveway. He came outside with his walker and handed me two Darvons. I sang in the ambulance, later.

"Is it raining outside yet?" I asked Elaine.

"What did you do to paint the house? Did you get out a little watercolor brush and draw lines?" she asked.

My ice melted. For a second I wondered if I could create a thunderstorm in the bathroom with enough ice and hot water. I said, "I used a roller instead. Then on top of the ladder I looked up and saw these buzzards circling. They thought they'd found a dead polar bear rolled over, I bet. I leaned back, and then fell off, I swear. Help me out of here."

Elaine walked away. I struggled around, then finally slid out over the edge. When my wife returned she said, "Good. I found six Fine Red Sable brushes from when I took that painting class in college. Fill in the gaps, Louis."

I think she might've meant that in a double-entendre kind of way, now.

SHE DID. ELAINE DIDN'T come back that night, or even the next morning to pick up clothes for work. I waited until noon the next day to call her at work, and then only got an answering machine message about what number to call to order the new chinois with beechwood dowel and stand. Of course I went outside with my tiny brushes and started filling the white indentions by hand. I knew later that the job wouldn't be so difficult if I'd've only used the eight-inch brush and painted from horizon to horizon.

Ray Shirley came by and said, "I seen you fall off the ladder. I seen you in the rearview mirror and felt it was part my fault for breaking your concentration."

I said, "My foot slipped." I felt like an idiot holding the artist brush.

Ray Shirley said, "You aim to fill in every spot you missed with that little thing? Goddamn, boy, I didn't think you'd be good on detail work, what with the way you caulked the whole place."

My hip hurt. I'd put Icy-Hot on it earlier, which burned my fingertips, which made it hard to hold the brush, which felt like a thin branding iron in my hand. I said, "Originally I only planned on teaching my wife a lesson. I think she left me, though."

Ray Shirley stood on the ground, looking across the street. His Camaro idled chugging in my driveway. He said, "I'm on my third. The first two didn't understand racing. Third one's half blind. She don't get scared watching me, ever."

I started to say how I could've used a blind wife—and even got my mouth open to say so—when some hand reached down again and pushed me. I almost broke my second hip, then. Ray Shirley stepped out of the way without looking up. He got me to my feet and held my arms over my head so I'd get my breath back. "You seem to be the kind of fellow what needs a job on the ground, son. Hell, you need a job below the ground, like a miner, or a grave digger."

I tried to say, "Or a cave guide," but couldn't get it out.

OUT OF MEANNESS I finished painting the fouled front of the house, then the rest of it with the regular paint brush sideways. The place looked pretty good when I finished. From afar the ripples weren't even noticeable—like maybe two miles away—and up close it only looked like I'd bought wood from a lumberyard with dull and wiggly band saws.

This process took me less than a week; I forget meteorological lingo, but it may have been Indian summer. What I'm saying is, it was the end of October and early November, and still warm enough to paint at night. There was no need for spotlights. I'm no geologist or chemist, but I bet siliconized acrylic caulk has some kind of phosphorescent properties that make it glow in the dark. I almost needed a welder's mask to see what I did and where I'd been.

In my mind I saw Elaine driving by the house at dawn, checking to see if I covered the caulk adequately. When cars passed by I never turned around for two reasons—I didn't want to make eye contact with my wife, and both my hips seemed fused to the point of petrification. I think there's some kind of toy where this guy goes up and down a ladder, stiff, and I could've modeled for it.

I didn't turn around, but I did yell out, "Dead man caulking," more than once, I swear.

Understand, I didn't call Elaine up at work, and made a point not to look in her closet to see if somehow she'd returned while I went out for booze or cigarettes so she could scavenge up all of her low-cut blouses and slit skirts. I didn't pace back and forth, seeing as how I couldn't. Not once did I get on the telephone and call Elaine's parents, her boss at home, various clients I knew she kept an ongoing customer relationship with, the police, or that guy who has a show on TV about missing persons. Somehow I knew maybe Elaine underwent a seven-year itch thing known usually to people like me, and that she'd return in time all apologetic, spiritual, calm, and ready to patch up anything wrong in our relationship. I felt certain she'd saved vacation and sick days up in order to meditate in New Mexico, or Nag's Head, or some real ashram over in real India.

She didn't.

I never called Elaine's old roommate Amy, on purpose. Already I knew my wife had given up and left her job—that she'd learned from me. I thought about that poor kid Jason with his mottoes, and wondered if he knew Elaine.

My wife called once and I said, "Hello," and she hung up, not knowing we'd gotten that Star 69 device. Elaine had left everything we'd accumulated in order to live with Amy, the woman worried about what uncircumcised people might mean to her future. My wife had moved to Delaware, of all places.

I sat in the living room alone like a man alone in his living room. I thought about how this house now stood caulked beyond what full-time caulkers might agree upon.

Ray Shirley finally showed up again and I waddled to the

front door and let him inside. He said, "I got people working the pits who don't care as much about life as you do."

I sat inside my house steamed for two reasons. I said, "What?"

"I want to ask you if you're working any more in a real job," Ray said. "I know you're not working a real job getting paid and all."

I'd been thinking about oxygen. I'd been thinking about how someone out there needs to start up a business as an oxygen-tent caulker, just in case. I said, "I'm working. I don't get paid, but I'm working. It's hard to explain, man."

Ray Shirley looked out the front window where my eight-foot stepladder still stood. He said, "I have one word for you."

I said, "Uh-huh."

"Pitman," he said.

My whole life flashed before my eyes, with the exception of the time Baudelaire came to me in college. I said, "Right, pal."

Ray Shirley said, "My boy I had working for me down at the garage just quit. He worked Saturday nights when I raced, too. I think you're the man I need for the spot he left."

I nodded. There was no way I could afford my tan igloo another year without a job. I'd called my oxygen boss, drunk and begging, but he'd found someone stupid and reliable to fill my place. I said, "I don't know anything about cars."

Ray Shirley shook his head sideways. He mentioned how I needed to get over Elaine, and nothing could do it better than learning the intricacies of carburetors, pistons, valves, and timing chains. He said there weren't enough people out there who could fill holes left wide and inviting by people who ran four-way stop signs, or followed too closely. I limped each step outside towards his car, on my way to find my new job, the one he said God called upon me to do.

These days I sit on an upside down dry-wall bucket, waiting for customers to offer their dinged and dented vehicles. Let me say that I'm not the first person to notice how modern science should've invented a Bondo of sorts by now, to smooth over damage we've done to what still flutters on beneath the rib cage.

# Rentals

As much as blind Chuck wants to live, I think he wants to die. And as much as I think blind Chuck wants to shock people, I think he'd just as soon live like a hermit, wear sunglasses more often than not, have the local grocery store delivery boy bring canned goods and fresh fish on Thursdays, occasionally drink over at Scatterbrain Johnson's tavern with people like me, and pump his leg to music when it's live and regular. Here's what I know: the day after I moved in next to blind Chuck, he came over and said, "Someone told me there's already a world record for a blind man playing tetherball. Will you come over one night with an ax and cut off my left arm—not my right arm—so I can become the best one-armed blind tetherball champion of the world?"

I said, "I just moved in here. My name's Kilo," because it was, because my parents were way before their time, because my parents smuggled dope even before the 60's revolution and all that stuff that happened with the Flower Children. I was in my mid-thirties when Chuck knocked on my front door with his cane.

Chuck was in his sixties, I could tell—I swear I could work for the county fair and guess people's ages. Weights, I don't know—I couldn't even hold a watermelon and a peach and tell which was heavier, something with the nerves—but I can tell ages right off.

Chuck said, "Chuck. I'm hoping to shake your hand for the last time." Chuck said, "I know you just moved in, I'm not stupid, I heard the truck yesterday and I heard the truck today. I heard Ronnie move out, and I heard you move in. Don't look down on my intelligence, or whatever they call it. Don't disparage me. Don't insult me. Don't discredit or affront me." Chuck snaked his cane between my ankles.

I said, "Come on in. There are boxes, man. Don't trip or anything." At the time I didn't know Chuck. It's not that I thought he might bring a lawsuit on me as much as I thought he might just trip, fall down, and either be embarrassed or not like it.

Chuck said, "I take mine black. I used to put sugar and cream in my coffee, but when my sight went all out, it became too hard judging teaspoons and dollops. Is your kitchen table where Ronnie's used to be?"

I led Chuck by the bicep over to the table and pulled out a chair. I said, "I was never in Ronnie's apartment when it was Ronnie's, so I don't know. Here's mine," and then went over to the counter, pulled my coffee maker from a box, found the filters in another, and made ten cups.

"Booze I can handle in coffee," Chuck said. "As a matter of fact I sort of like to misjudge pouring amaretto in a cup of coffee. Or Irish whisky. Kahlua."

"I hear you, Chuck," I said, and opened another box.

I poured plain bourbon in his coffee, and I swear when he heard the bloop noise he said, "Double that." And I'm not ashamed to say that I did one of those hand waves in front of Chuck's face to see if he was faking his blindness, and that he said right away, "I'm truly blind. What did you say your name was again, son?"

I told him and said, "I can't do the arm thing, Chuck. I can't

148

come into your apartment in the middle of the night and chop off one of your arms."

He laughed and nodded and pointed right at me. He drank from his cup and made a grimace, rubbed his palms on the tops of his jeans, and said, "Whoo. Ronnie drank wine coolers. You're all right." He said, "Well, do me this, then: it takes me forever to look in those record books in Braille to see what's there. If you'll just look through some things and see what it is I can do for a record, and I'll set out to do it."

I said, of course, "What's the fascination with setting records, Chuck?" and poured bourbon in a glass straight. Then I poured another when I saw his nostrils flap.

"I just want to be remembered," he said. "Hell, it's hard enough being remembered when you ain't got a handicap. Try it blind, Kilo. What do you do for a living, anyway, and why ain't you married?"

I stepped over to Chuck and handed him a glass, touched his hand with it so he'd know where it was. I'd been brought up seeing a blind great uncle twice a year and knew some of the required unspoken procedures. Still, I looked into Chuck's eyes— he wore those dark glasses but they weren't so black I couldn't see that his eyelids were up—and did an abracadabra finger roll like I threw salt on a fire to see if he'd react. Chuck didn't. He said, "Well?"

I told him the truth. I told my new neighbor blind Chuck that I sold textile supplies, and that my ex-wife got bored and left.

BEING IN THE textile supply business doesn't offer so much money, seeing as Reagan went nuts with allowing imports to kill cotton mills, but it does offer a lot of free time. It's the perfect job for an artist who needs to supplement his or her income, or for someone involved in a religious cult who needs to pray for a half-hour every forty-five minutes during daylight hours. It'd be the ideal occupation for a person who'd rather daydream, or watch a 24-hour news channel, or a gambler who needs to check with his bookie frequently. Or a heavy drinker. And it fits hand-in-hand, really. If you sell textile supplies, there's no need to care about art, and there's no way possible to believe in a Higher Being worth worshiping. There's no need to daydream about better times because you've been pommeled beyond hope, and no need to care what country outside of the United States undergoes an uprising, and there's no money to bet.

I moved into the new apartment next to blind Chuck and arranged my bleak furniture around the room so as to make it look like I cared, stocked my cupboards with what booze I needed for me and anyone who ever visited, and got the telephone installed so I could call customers when I needed to do so. I called the last few cotton mills in the Southeast and said things like, "How're you looking for replacement belts, or check-straps? How're you looking for bobbins?" If they needed something, I put in the order. If I needed to show my face to a purchasing agent or supervisor I did so, and found a way to find a bar with a happy hour that lasted all day.

And I got out that Guinness book to see what blind Chuck could do so his life would be worth living. I didn't see him for a week after the first time we met, but when he did come over rattling his cane against my door the first thing he said was, "I can't play baseball, obviously. I can't shoot baskets. I know about sports like that—I listen to baseball and basketball all the time on the radio or TV but I have no idea what's going on. I was born blind, Kilo. My mother had some kind of bad gene going on in her body, but I don't blame her."

Chuck walked right in and didn't even use his cane to feel

himself around. He said, "Everyone who's moved in here has put furniture in the same spots. I've lived here going on thirty years, you know."

I said, "Can you jump rope? Can you eat goldfish or jalapeño peppers? Can you grow a mustache? Can you do a standing broad jump?" I said, "How much money do you have, Chuck? Can you buy enough seeds to grow the largest sunflower crop? Can you start a coin, seashell, baseball card, beer can, bottle top, screwdriver, record album, designer plate, shot glass, thimble, model car, comic book, carnival or milk glass, mini-bottle, Barbie doll, gun, lunchbox, hotel ashtray, autograph, or wedding-cake figurine collection?"

Chuck said, "What're you talking, man? That's boring. I need physical prowess."

I didn't say, "Eat me, Chuck." I didn't say, "Fuck you, old blind man, I'll kill you, why am I even trying to help?" I said, "There's stuff for blind people in golf and tennis and squash and racquetball and distance running. Blind people have done it all in large amounts in fishing, hunting—this blind guy killed a hundred-ninety-pound buck in North Carolina one time—water skiing, dog sledding, snake-catching, snow skiing, and dirt-track racing. There was even a fifty-dollar-bill forger who was blind."

Chuck walked over to my cupboard, opened it, and started feeling the bottles. He said, "You don't drink Scotch, do you?"

I said, "Un-uh."

He said, "You want some of this vodka? I'm in a vodka mood."

I said, "Okay." I said, "I can only have one, though. I'm supposed to meet this buddy of mine tonight to play some pool."

And then I thought about how I'd never seen anything in the record books about a blind man playing pool, about him

151

running a table, or running consecutive balls down in nine-ball. I said, "Did I say 'pool'? I mean, I'm supposed to meet this friend of mine to play darts," but it didn't matter. Pool or darts, it didn't matter. Chuck could've done either, in his way. Chuck knew either sport involved physical prowess. And I knew that I'd not seen anything in the books about a blind man playing either pool or darts.

Chuck said, "Pour me some bourbon. Here we go. I'm so glad you didn't move in and try to push me towards shuffleboard, Kilo. I'm so glad you didn't try to make me the blind king of croquet."

I BROKE THAT NIGHT. I broke for a week, but when I started losing I made Chuck break, even though he asked me to do so. There's a pool table over at Scatterbrain Johnson's joint up in the mountains, and I took Chuck there for the first time on the day he came over to complain that I didn't find enough events. I broke and I said things like, "Well, I didn't make anything in. Your shot," and took him behind where he needed to shoot.

We started at eight-ball just so Chuck could get a feel for hitting cue to ball. When he got good—which was exactly seven days later—we started playing nine ball and I'd tell him about cue and ball position. I said to Chuck, "Did you go to school as a kid?"

He said, "Of course. Blind kids can't just sit at home and watch television, Kilo."

I said, "What was your best subject?"

I knew the answer already, but just wanted to make sure. He said, "I'd have to say geometry."

It was the truth. He seemed to picture angles so well and be sure of them that when he missed a shot he'd say to me, "That ball was closer to seventy-five degrees off the cue than eighty,

Kilo. It hit the left bank, didn't it? That's seventy-five degrees, not eighty." And he understood English, too—and not the kind taught in school. Chuck quickly figured out that he needed to place his cue from shot to shot, and after I'd say something like "Six ball in the side pocket, straight-on shot," he'd say, "Where's the seven?" and adjust his stick to one of the four corners of the cue, hit the shot, make it, and say "I should be right at about sixty degrees from the seven," or whatever.

It got to the point where I didn't really like Chuck. I wished that we'd taken up darts, 'cause then in a game of cricket or 301 I could lie and say he missed the triple twenty. The dart board sounds the same all over, but there wasn't a way I could tell Chuck he missed a shot when he heard his ball rolling down the innards of the table.

And Chuck may have just been one of those people who say things jokingly, but the humor got old quickly. Every night when I took him up to Scatterbrain's place he'd say, "Did you sell anything today?"

I'd say, "No."

"Well, did you get any leads, Kilo? Did you make a phone call, and have someone tell you about someone who'd be interested in one of your products?"

I'd say, "No." It's not like I didn't know how to lie. I should've. You'd think that night after night when he asked the same questions I'd come up with something on the lines of, "Uh-huh, I just sold ten thousand 192-by-35-millimeter replacement belts to a mill in Caracas, Venezuela," which I'd done, really, once, my first year selling, before the trade problems.

Chuck would say, "If I don't make it in playing pool maybe I can take your job. Hell, son, a blind man could do better than you're doing. No wonder your wife got bored."

I tended to enter Scatterbrain Johnson's gravel parking lot up on the curve at about fifty miles an hour and hit the brakes hard to see how far I could skid and fishtail. I tended to secretly estimate how many degrees Chuck's forehead came from the inside windshield before his seat belt caught.

But I couldn't hurt him. He was old and crotchety, and every time I did my little trick in the parking lot he'd say, "I might need an agent if this works out, Kilo. You're the man, what with your selling capabilities."

And indeed there seemed to be some truth in that. People started coming from miles around to watch Chuck play pool, and after he'd beat me, someone would have quarters up to play next. I'd stand behind him and direct his shots, and he got to forgetting my real name, seeing as how he called me "Eyes," as in, "I need my Eyes to tell me where to shoot this one," or "Where'd my Eyes go off to?" if I stepped out back to take a leak.

More than once I saw some guy wave his cue stick in Chuck's face, checking to see if his blindness was a hoax. More than once I heard Chuck say to someone, "This is pool, not fencing."

More than once I went up to Romaine, Scatterbrain Johnson's widow, and asked for a six-pack to go. More than once I went up to Romaine and asked her if she had any nieces I could call up some time, and told her I wasn't all that bad a guy when I was outside of a bar, and sober.

SO THE NIGHT CAME a few months later when Chuck was going for a big record of consecutive balls made by a blind man. Like I said, there was nothing in the record books about it anyway, but Chuck wanted to go right up there with the record for a sighted pool shark. I'd gotten in touch with two people: one from the International Billiards Association, and the other from

Guinness. They both said I only needed some trustworthy eye-witnesses willing to sign affidavits or whatever, saying they were present and paying attention to Chuck, that he didn't make any shots he didn't call ahead of time, and so on.

I was in a particularly good mood because my ex-wife had called that week saying she'd had time to sit down and think about what went on in our marriage, and how she may have made a bad move. She'd gone through rehab and counseling, and promised me that she was on the mend. I said to her over the telephone, "Caroline, I've changed, too. I've befriended a blind man!"

She said, "A blind man?! Goddamn you, Kilo, you haven't changed. Are you giving him all your money like you did that Salvation Army woman right before we had no Christmas to-gether?"

The one thing about Caroline I didn't like was that she came from a Republican background. I said, "I'm not giving this guy any money. As a matter of fact, he's about to make me a bunch."

She said, "How can a blind man make you a bunch of money? I don't understand you, Kilo. Have you joined the church or something?"

I said, because I always did—Caroline always asked me if I joined the church and secretly she wanted me to do so—I said, "The Church of Love and Forgiveness."

She said, "You haven't changed."

I said, "Come on up to Scatterbrain's on Saturday and watch blind Chuck shoot pool."

I'd gone to Scatterbrain's before Caroline and I wed, and during our marriage. It wasn't her favorite place. First off, she didn't understand all the mountain people who grew pot, and she didn't understand moonshine, and she didn't like the jars of

155

pickled eggs, sausages, and corn cobs on the counter. She didn't like the fact that the little shotgun building had an out-house.

She said, "Well. Okay. I'm a changed woman, now, Kilo. I want you to understand that."

I said, of course, "Uh-huh. I just made a sale to this big mill in Caracas, Venezuela."

Chuck was ready when I walked over to his apartment. He'd put on a suit, for he'd heard that the best pool players did. He asked me if any photographers would be there, if he should put on his special sunglasses, if this might be reported on the local news. I told him everything had been taken care of. I told him that there was a full moon that night, and that more than likely the boys would come down from the mountain to see what he had to do. I told him that if things didn't work out, I'd still be his neighbor and friend, for some reason.

Chuck said, "Are you sure I look okay?"

His suit was nowhere close. Chuck had someone come pick up his clothes and take them to a laundry, and I guess they knew he was blind. Sometimes someone mixes things up, probably thinking that he'd never know. Chuck wore green pants and a purplish sport coat. I guess people messed with him when he was in stores, too. I said, "You look great. Come on, let's go."

"The reason I'm so good at pool, Eyes, is because I've been practicing for years with my cane," Chuck said. "I never told you that, did I?"

I said, "You didn't tell me that."

He said, "Do you have any bourbon left? I feel as though my nerves need calming, a lot of calming."

I said, "Whatever," and took him one door over.

Inside, at my kitchen table, Chuck said, "You seem a little giddier than I've ever seen you. Did you make a sale today?"

I said, "Caroline called. She's coming to watch you play pool tonight." And then I thought about it. With Chuck, it was best to think ahead what he might ask, and what you might answer.

"Caroline!" he said. "Your ex-wife, right!"

I said, "Uh-huh. Yeah, that's right."

"Are you sure I look okay? I mean, I wouldn't want first impressions to be bad," said Chuck, but he laughed and didn't mean it. He rubbed his palms again and I gave him a motel-sized glass full of bourbon, no ice.

I'd forgotten about my ex-wife Caroline, evidently. I'd forgotten about how she didn't like my friends, how she didn't want me to have friends, how she didn't have any friends of her own, how she didn't like both men and women, how she wanted to be an artist but couldn't do better than being a cosmetologist and had to settle on it. Chuck didn't forget, and he didn't even know her. While I sat there, right before Chuck's big night, I thought about how I'd read something one time about a blind guy who could see better than anyone else, and how he was a fortune-teller, and about how some other guy got so upset that he had to stab out his own eyes.

CHUCK PULLED HAIRS out of his nostrils. Chuck felt around his ears for stray hairs, found none, twisted his cue stick in circles, and looked straight forward. He slicked down his short hair. Chuck took the toe of his right shoe and scratched his left ankle, and did the same with his left toe to his right. Caroline showed up. I didn't say anything. Everyone at Scatterbrain Johnson's clapped in unison, waiting. Two men stood with banjos around their necks, and another five or six stood with guitars. Old J. D. sat down with a lap-top steel guitar and muttered about how he'd had two strokes already. J. D. held a pick in his mouth.

157

I'd picked me and a boy named Bad-Check Johnson—not that he had money problems, he claimed to be an ex-hockey player from up North who ran into too many offensive players on the opposing team—to witness Chuck's record. Romaine went to a Mr. Microphone and said, "Tonight we're to witness histry," like that. She said, "Let the game begin."

Everyone quit playing his banjo, right on cue. Everyone hushed and placed their beers down on a table or floor. People came from inside, leaving their Mason jars.

I said, "Tight rack, Chuck."

He said, "Good. Thanks. Take me to the end of the table," like he didn't know where it was.

He broke, as I remember, and the six ball went in. I took him over to the cue ball and showed him the one, and then the two, and then the three. And then Caroline said, "Get your claws off of me!" like that, which I had to pay attention to. I had to pay attention to my ex-wife yelling, no matter what. There were a bunch of people there at Scatterbrain's, all of whom had the potential of pinching a butt, and I reacted. I took the pool cue that I always held and went for the scream. Chuck was on his second or third shot, but I reacted to where I heard my ex-wife yell out, "Get your hands off of me!"

It took about the time for me to take two steps for everyone in the bar to pick up a cuestick and start swinging. It took about the time Chuck said, "Eyes, where's the three ball, now?" for me to get to my ex-wife, dressed in a nice pants suit, to look at who pinched her rear end, and take a swing at him.

Chuck said, "I can do it myself."

I took a swing at this boy like I knew what I was doing. Let me say that he wasn't a regular, for I wouldn't hit anyone who came in all the time. I hit him in the stomach, he doubled over, I grabbed the back of his head and pulled it down to my up-pulling hard knee, and after his nose blew up I took two or three swings to the sides of his face, fast. Around me everyone started swinging, too. What I'm saying is, a free-for-all started, and there wasn't much anyone could do about it.

Chuck said, "Hey! Hey! This is a special night, ain't it?!" I turned around to make sure he was okay, and just saw him standing there with his cue stick over his head. He held it with both hands and looked like he wanted to do some pull-ups.

The guy who molested Caroline was big—bigger than me—about six-two and 220 pounds, and he caught his breath a little faster than what I'd seen on late-night TV when they showed karate movies. He said, "I'll kill you," like that, and tried to pull his arms down on the top of my head like he shoved an ax, but I moved. I didn't know what to do. Whatever that little Chinese guy taught on the TV didn't seem to work. I didn't know any of those other moves, to tell the truth. I didn't know leg-kicks, or any judo flips.

I kicked him in the nuts as hard as I could.

Around us all, chairs flew and Romaine yelled. I got hit in the head with the pickled corn cob jar, and a man named Dink got caught with the Penrose sausages. Through it all I heard Chuck yelling, "Stop, stop, stop!" like that. He never said anything about him being blind, though. He never said, "Stop, I'm a blind man and I can't defend myself." Two or three times I looked up, though, and he was picking up balls from the table and winging them anywhere.

Caroline crawled under the pool table, safely. I got one tooth juggled, but must've knocked out three, I figured, from the marks on my fist. Later Caroline told me that she'd never felt safer, that she wanted a pool table in our house, should we ever have a house.

———

CHUCK DROPPED THE three ball in on the break. He missed at the one ball right away. It didn't matter for him. He could've easily started over, but he didn't. Chuck said, "Drinks are on me," like that, and held up his cue stick. He said, "Who's got the table next?"

I said, "Come on."

Caroline said, "Chuck."

We were in the Rack Room, down the mountain in town, amongst a bunch of lawyers playing pool. It was a regulation table just like at Scatterbrain's place, and there was no reason to pull back. There were people to witness—me and a boy named Little Jackie—and we were ready. My ex-wife wife Caroline was there. Everyone was standing around to watch Chuck hit his balls. But Chuck said, "Next!" right away. He said, "I don't want to play anymore." He said, "Sorry, Eyes. Sorry, Kilo."

I walked up to Chuck and said, "What're you doing, man?" I almost said, "Say it ain't so!" but didn't.

Chuck said, "I'm an angel." He said, "I don't need anything, now that you and Caroline are back together. I don't need anything now that things are straight."

For the first time I remember, he didn't look at me. Chuck just kind of spoke out to the ceiling, holding his cue stick in his right hand. He looked more like he stared at smoke than a person. He said, "Tetherball. There're no fights on the playground in tetherball. I should've stuck to tetherball, Kilo."

Caroline didn't speak, for the first time. She stood there. Caroline stood and looked down at the carpet. These two guys took over the table, and one of them broke balls. One dropped. One boy said, "I'm low," like that.

Chuck said, "I'd like a bourbon the way you fix them, Kilo," in a low voice, and walked past me using his stick for a white cane. Chuck said, "Bowling," like that.

160

Caroline said, "He said, 'Bowling,' Kilo. Chuck wants to take up bowling." I pretended not to hear. I went to the bar and got two bourbons straight up, and a spritzer for Caroline. I honestly believe deep down that what split us up the first time was that she drank spritzers. Call me queasy and sheepish, but there's something about carrying seltzer water around in a grocery store I don't like. Up at the bar I even tried to muffle my voice when I made the order.

I'd never played bowling, and had no interest in playing. I'd seen it on television before, and knew what a pain in the butt a seven-ten split was, but didn't really care that much after that. The barmaid gave me my drinks and I tipped her and thought, "Chuck bowling." That's all I could think. That's all I could see, too—Chuck bowling, a blind man strolling down the lane not knowing where the stripe was so he could quit walking and start rolling.

I came back with two bourbons and that thing I can't understand how my wife drinks and I said, "You can't start playing bowling, Chuck. I don't know anything about bowling—I don't know how to keep score and I don't know the nuances. There's no English in bowling. There's no geometry as far as I can tell."

Chuck still held his cue stick. I had hopes that he'd not given up. Caroline stood there and said, "You didn't bring me a straw, but that's okay."

"Bowling," said Chuck. "Bowling, or Frisbee golf. You never brought up either sport, Eyes. Frisbee golf sounds fun. I've felt one before."

Caroline pulled from her drink and said, "It's not all that hard teaching Frisbee."

I said, "Chuck."

"Or you could come in and chop my arm off like I asked you to do way back when—like I asked Ronnie to do, too—and

161

we could go back to tetherball," Chuck said. He stood there grinning. He held his bourbon and his cuestick and he smiled. He had on his best glasses.

I said, "Come on, man." Some guy broke behind us. Some guy laughed hard.

Caroline said, "I don't see what's so important about a world record, anyway. Do you see what's so important about a world record, Kilo? I don't. They get broken. They're like rental property. They aren't forever."

Caroline wasn't the woman for me. I decided right there that Caroline wasn't a person I could spend my life with. I said, "What you're wearing wasn't made in the United States, probably, Caroline. You're hurting me." I said, "Hey, I don't know what you think is important any more."

Chuck said, "Stop."

I said, "If Chuck wants to set a world's record that's his business. That's Chuck's business. That's what Chuck wants to do, Caroline." I tried not to act like the bourbon affected me. I said, "Leave Chuck alone about all of this."

Chuck said, "Stop."

Caroline said, "See," and looked elsewhere. She looked over at the bar, like someone watched.

I grabbed her above the elbow and yanked a little too hard again and again. Chuck said, "Stop," over and over, a thousand times over, until we left. We said nothing on the way home, me driving, Caroline in the passenger seat, blind Chuck in back.

# Sanyayana Speaks Through Me

IF YOU HAVE attention deficit disorder then stop reading right now, as if it'd matter. I mean, if you have A.D.D. then by now you've forgotten what I first said—la, la, la, la, la—I might as well start singing for all it matters. I might as well go off into a slew of Esperanto. Since this new syndrome seems something no one suffered from when I grew up—we had class clowns, sure, but they owned dogs that ate homework, or rode open-windowed school buses that vacuumed out their homework papers and books—I can only conclude that something's going on differently between the beginning of organized education and about the mid-1980s when parents, students, talk show psychologists, high school counselors, and various other whiners started all this crap up. I won't go into the theories I have concerning the Reagan-Bush years. I won't even mention MTV, the disappearing fear of nuclear holocaust, environmental concerns involving the ozone layer, or video games.

I will mention school lunches.

I'll spend some time on the Sloppy Joe sandwich.

Lookit: the school lunch menu pre-1980—the beginning of Reagan—offered two, maybe three alternatives. It'll be difficult for future generations to understand this, but as you know— since you don't have attention deficit disorder and have made it these 200-plus words or so with me—we ate a bunch of Sloppy

Joes, lima beans, mashed potatoes with no gravy, either kerneled corn or cornbread, dark pudding, canned peaches, and whole-fat white milk one day from expiring; fish sticks, lima beans, mashed potatoes with no gravy, either kerneled corn or cornbread, dark pudding, no tartar sauce, canned peaches, whole-fat white milk one day from expiring; meat loaf, et cetera.

Sloppy Joe day was a treat, really.

All of this came to me in a deluge one day 'cause I ran out of gas in front of a junior high school and went in to use the phone. I mistook the cafeteria for the office and walked on in. It was eleven in the morning. Inside, it looked like one of those "A Taste of Our Town" carnivals or festivals — Del Taco, Taco Bell, Pizza Hut, Burger King, and Long John Silver's all had booths set up.

I walked right in. No one stopped me, like would have happened when we went to school and had a hundred assistant principals walking around all over carrying large paddles with holes drilled into them. For a second I thought I stood in a mall's Food Court, until I saw a student order two cheeseburgers, forget he'd done so, and walk over for a personal-sized pizza, order, forget, and so on.

I remembered the way it was, because I could. Right off I thought about how that dopey JUST SAY NO campaign might have been behind it all, seeing as how some people seem to forget that pickling is a preservative.

At least that's my theory.

Well, let me tell you I got out of there right away, when I completely understood how the ex-president's wife willed herself into thinking if everyone got brainwashed enough, things wouldn't seem so bad. Understand, somehow she'd been told by some advisors that clear heads meant exactly that — really, really clear heads, like those of cave salamanders, or albino tadpoles —

and that we could stay under the power of people like her husband for ever and ever. Luckily we had enough citizens left over from thinking times, like 1949 or 1963. Maybe I exaggerate. Maybe I've gone a little too reductio ad absurdum and veni, vidi, vici, I don't know. Maybe I'm hoping for a little deus ex machina coming down to save us all, like it did me at least two dozen times during my childhood, right after possible electrocution and brain death due to short-lasting household fuses and sideboards on cars.

I walked back to my empty car and thought about the times my mother sent me under the house. We had this frigid water heater, evidently, and about every month Mom sent me down to stick in a new fuse. I don't understand electricity. I don't understand how something can be completely out and put you to the unfinished clay floor. But I know after the first time I always asked my mother to cut all the breakers just in case. And I know that on more than one occasion I came out from under the house cussing. My mother'd be on the phone, or fixing a Saturday lunch of Sloppy Joes, lima beans, mashed potatoes with no gravy, kerneled corn or cornbread, dark pudding, canned peaches, and say, "Oh! I forgot!"

I don't think she had attention deficit disorder, though. I think she only had other things on her mind, like how to tell my father the Volkswagen bug might be a collector's item in six thousand years but it wasn't worth killing me over.

I don't want to call child abuse on my dad, but it's true he liked to pull that VW far into the carport, get me clung to the running board and open window, and have him zip in reverse thirty yards out the driveway only to stop hard to see if I could hold on. I did, a few times. Mostly though I followed one of those laws of physics and kept on going, then hit my head on the cement. Sometimes even now I wake up hard from a regular sleep yelling out, "What day is it? What day is it?" like I did when I came to on our driveway.

What the kids need today is a little more electricity and a little more coma, I'm convinced. I don't condone spanking. I don't condone a nose in the corner, for that matter. I'll say this: sometimes our cement half-basement flooded when I grew up. One time my mother handed me this mop and bucket and told me to get up the six inches of water. I started to, then noticed this metal industrial vacuum cleaner there, already plugged in. At the time I just thought, I can lay out the hose and suck this water right up. I remember noticing the standing water ripple, but that's it.

Summary: New and better technology, namely long-life fuses and aerodynamic cars without running boards, cause our children to forget, or not even know anything in the first place, from the get-go. Everyone should eat Sloppy Joes regularly.


I WENT INTO THIS PLACE for lunch and ordered what I wanted. Two minutes later this three-hundred-pound guy comes and sits down a door next to me on the stool and says, "Corndogs. Give me four corndogs. I eat corndogs Thursdays and Saturdays."

I looked straight ahead. I looked at what was behind the counter, which was a few small boxes of Special-K cereal, some Ohio Blue-tip matches, a bottle of Tabasco, and one of those glamour shots of the owner's high-school-age daughter, with the blue fake puffy clouded background. I'd just been caught without gasoline and found out some things I'd never thought. To say the least I wanted to jot on a napkin more than talk to a man about his eating habits, whether he had a reason or not. I'd known fish-on-Friday Catholics. I once met a Jew who explained all that kosher belief concerning hot dogs, pickles, and why he had to hate pig.

I'd ordered what I had to order, of course, so's not to get that Attention disease. I came in worried, and the waitress even asked if I wanted a little something she kept behind the counter to put people at ease, or if I wanted a Goody's powder. I just said, "Sloppy Joe and a milk," before I even looked at the menu. Afterwards I added the lima beans and so on. It's not like I don't know all about cholesterol levels, heart attack chances, and so on. It's just that after weighing out the options, I'd rather remember having the heart attack, whatever.

The corndog man turned my way and said, "Race tonight."

I said, "What?"

"It's Thursday. My boy's racing tonight. Thursday's Riverside and Saturday's Copperhead Bend. You want to come on out? I got an extra ticket or two." He held his mouth in a tiny O the way people do when they think they've come across a secret, or said something awe-inspiring.

I said, "Drag or dirt-track oval?"

"Hell," he said, and his corndogs were ready. "Look at my shoes. I practice with the boy." He turned and held both his feet my way. The right shoe had an inch less tread, as if he'd stuck his foot out of the door on curves. He said, "I'm Gene," and stuck out the hand.

I said, "Lee Toomey," and shook. When we got through, he wiped his palm on his pants like I'd contaminated him or something. I said, "The oval track. Like most NASCAR. Like down in Darlington."

He bit his first corndog in half and slid it off the stick. Gene turned away as if we'd finished our conversation. The waitress brought my Sloppy Joe and asked if I wanted hot sauce or mayonnaise. I said I didn't, and then Gene turned to say, "Howdy, I'm Gene," and stuck out his hand again.

Right away I felt like I had to reconsider my new notions

about the downfall of America's youth. I said, "Lee." Gene sucked some batter and mustard off the side of his face and nodded. I looked at the waitress for one of those international signs letting me know Gene was nuts. She poured sugar in a pourer like the world depended on it. Gene said, "This is good."

I said, "Alright."

"You need to come up here on Friday and Monday nights. They got amateur nights where you sing songs to one of those screens that gives you the words," Gene said.

Still staring at the sugar canister my waitress said, "Anybody sings. We're getting a beer license soon, too."

"I sing and play harmonica at the same time," Gene said. "Right through the little reeds. I'm that way. I can do things."

"He can," said the waitress. "He can do things."

I had out my napkin and pen. I wrote down so many ideas it wasn't funny.

"Been married thirty-three years to the same woman. Still know my times table through twelveses. Can take an engine apart and put it back together fast and tight. Can name every heavyweight champion up till they gave it away to just about anyone."

I finished eating as he went on and on about everything he'd done before and could still do again if asked. At the end of it all, Gene said, "I'm Gene," again, and I realized that earlier he hadn't just forgotten introducing himself to me, as much as he wanted me to know that he knew who he was and what he was about, unlike the kids standing around a Taco Bell booth aimlessly, when they'd be better off reciting state capitals like we did back in junior high school before they'd even let us go to lunch—say, if somebody said the capital of somewhere far away like Washington was Seattle. As a matter of fact Gene probably thought I was nuts for saying, "I'm Lee Toomey" again to him.

The waitress said, "That's ol' Gene. There's only one Gene. Gene-Gene-the-corndog-machine," and looked up at me. She poured ketchup into containers. I felt good and safe and hopeful there, in the Berea Family Diner, Home of Fresh Grits Hourly.

Right as Gene got up to pay his tab I said, "Are you from around here?"

He said, "All my life."

I said, "You went to public schools here?"

"My daddy whipped me when I didn't," he said.

I didn't go into any details about my theories, unfortunately. I just kind of blurted out—and this question could be taken the wrong way, I understand now—"Were you shocked, or knocked out a bunch as a child, Gene?"

Summary: Corndogs on Thursdays and Saturdays might take the place of Sloppy Joes, lima beans, white milk, et cetera, but the end result's a short temper and causes you to punch out people sitting on stools at diner counters. It's good to know how to tune up an engine and multiply 12 X 12 off the top of your head, sing and play harmonica at the same time. Carson City's the capital of Nevada. Columbia, South Carolina. Boise. Bismarck.

IT'S LIKE THAT DUMB No Pain No Gain chant, only nowadays it should be something like No Fear No Hear, seeing as how all these students evidently can't concentrate long enough to listen to instruction, and that's why they never have their homework, and the teachers have to set aside an hour out of the day to write notes home, and the parents call up at all hours angry saying, "But my child has A.D.D.!" like that, and the teacher hears the roar of three television sets in the background and understands the problem immediately. Without fear, the brain can shift to

neutral and stay there forever. The longer it's in neutral, the easier it is for first through fourth gears — plus reverse — to collect
excess grease, clog up, and become virtually useless without a
major jolt of fear to unkink everything.

Electricity, or a high hard fall, cures this problem, of course,
as I've established. Any of those fight or flight scenarios aids in
Attention Surplus.

Example: Years ago, when we grew up on two-lane roads
mostly and might have to drive two hundred miles to find an interstate, there wasn't a McDonald's, Burger King, Taco Bell,
Del Taco, Hardee's, or Waffle House on every street corner in
America. Even after you got on the four-lane, there wasn't an
exit every quarter-mile or so down the road with eighteen different fast-food joints and self-serve gas stations with shiny rest-
rooms mopped at twenty-after and ten-till the hour by some
poor kid with attention deficit disorder, who had a manager who
only had to point in one direction or the other to get the kid to
do his job. What I'm saying is, students nowadays get a full blad-
der and just pull off to Shangri-la, complete with automatic
warm air blowers. They don't have to plan, which involves
thinking, logic, and back-up get-away excuses.

On more than one occasion when I was in high school and
college I'd take these long road trips to Myrtle Beach or Savannah or Atlanta or Washington, D.C., or wherever and end up
having to pull off at the only possible place to use the bathroom,
and that place was always called a Rest Area, either in the middle of the median or off to the right, either cement block or pale
brick. Sometimes now when I drive I guess I pass the old rest
areas but I don't notice them so much, seeing how I'm keeping
mind of traffic going on and off exits, probably high school students needing to pee, play some video games, and watch some
television.

I try to forget rest areas but I can't, seeing as I got brought up before short-term memory problems right up there with Korsakoff's Syndrome. I can still see the phone numbers etched into small partitions, and feel the threat of presupposing perverts.

Listen: maybe it was one of those theories of synchronicity, but as I recall, every time I went into a rest area toilet I'd read the limericks, racial slurs, look at the pictures of body parts, and then see some kind of meeting proposal that went something like, "If you want a good time with a studly buck, please meet me here at four o'clock on Friday," and I'd look at my watch to see it was 3:59 or thereabouts. I'm not lying. Every time I went anywhere to pee growing up, there'd be this threat-like invitation on the wall, and I'd be there. It's a wonder my pee-hole isn't as big around as a bowling ball's thumb space, seeing how hard I always pushed wanting to escape embarrassing and indubitable consequences.

Now, how I'd fix the situation is twofold: either I'd knock out all the exits, or I'd know about all the places with clean toilets, or I'd try to convince perverts to spend less time haunting the rest areas and more time with Magic Markers inside Ronald McDonald's stall. Then kids could get scared of using the bathroom there. Then they'd stop eating cheeseburgers and French fries and happy meals. Then they'd realize that the Sloppy Joe — served mainly at all-American diners where MEAT ME graffiti doesn't exist — is better for their gastrointestinal systems and psyches in the long run. Then their attention deficit disorder might quell and relapse and disappear.

And then they could start concentrating on fearful things like driving around on two or three beers, instead of forgetting altogether and blankly tooting their horns like messiahs, or forgetting altogether and getting drunker than minnows in Japanese sake gardens. What this country needs for her kids isn't a prohibition-style mind-set. What this country needs is a mandatory driver's education school, followed by a mandatory drunk-driver's education school. There need to be different lanes, too, for the beer drinkers and the liquor drinkers, subdivided into amounts, ages, tolerances, and so on. Some kind of mathematician needs to incorporate pot smokers and other drug users, so we could get this thing under control. It's an equation beyond my capabilities, but it's an idea.

I'm only trying to think up new techniques, seeing as the old ones don't work whatsoever. Anyone who messes up should be shocked, hit in the head hard, or forced to eat Sloppy Joes, lima beans, mashed potatoes with no gravy, and kerneled corn, and drink whole-fat white milk one day from expiration, for at least a month. The dark pudding and canned peaches need to be omitted as a punishment of sorts.

Summary: No Fear No Hear—if you can't learn to drive drunk then you can't learn to drive sober, either. Driving sober's as exciting as a fast-food bathroom. God doesn't like people who don't take chances. Popping an electric hand dryer with your elbow doesn't take the brains or coordination of pulling down a cloth spool foot-by-foot. Even if there are more perverts per capita, they can't keep up with the extraordinary increase in take-out restaurants springing up on our nation's highways' exit ramps, plus their clean bathrooms, and this is a direct cause-and-effect situation vis-à-vis A.D.D.

THE TROUBLE STARTED when this seventeen-year-old boy in the class said, "Huh?" after everything I said. What I'm saying is, I could look him right in the face and say something like "What do you think about how it happens that people plan to go to some Point A, haphazardly end up on their way to Point B, and end up in trouble?" I said, "Or, how do you think it happens that they plan on Point A—let's say a day at the lake—take a wrong turn, end up at Point B—let's say a diner that serves good Sloppy Joe sandwiches—meet the woman of their dreams, get married, et cetera?" That's what I said.

We weren't even reading that famous poem by Frost about the fork in the road. We weren't reading about that Misfit guy story by that good dead Catholic woman writer from down in Georgia, either. It was the beginning of the day and I just wanted to throw out something existential.

He said, "Huh?" I went through it all again. I gave concrete examples. He said, "Huh?" I didn't pay attention to his shirt, which had a bunch of demons prancing around a tombstone. They held skulls with bleeding eyeballs, of course.

I couldn't take it. This wasn't the first time, and he wasn't the only student. I said, "Hotdamn, boy, has your hearing gone overnight?" I said, "We've just gone through a dozen stories that have to do with the notion of Chance. Can you get it?"

His name was Ronnie, and I knew I held it against him, what with the president. Ronnie said, "I'd kill them. Every story we've read could get fixed if they'd just kill someone when things got bad."

No one said, "Huh?" They laughed, though.

I said, "That doesn't happen in literature. The conflict gets resolved." This Ronnie kid must've thought a four-minute story took too long. He must've thought that the first conflict that came along—my boss told me to float down the river and look for some out-of-control guy named Kurtz, I didn't want to, so I killed him, The End—needed resolution right away so he could goddamn keep his attention up. "It doesn't work that way in a good story," I said.

He said, "What?" Ronnie said, "Not in what I read. and it's

been published." I knew right away I was looking at one of those fantasy readers, a guy mesmerized with unicorns and the wizards that rode them.

I said, "Hey. Menus get published. Some menus are better than others, though. If you pull out a Waffle House menu it'll list eggs, bacon, sausage, hash browns, and waffles." I swear this came to me right then and there. I said, "And you can take a menu from some high-class expensive joint that might have vindaloo, cordon bleu, lobster thermidor, and whatever. An egg means an egg. Vindaloo means either chicken or shrimp or pork, and curry, and vegetables. One's dopey and blunt. The other's intriguing and exotic and imaginative. See?"

My boy Ronnie in the front row did that "Huh?" thing again, and then he got up and punched me right in the face. He started screaming, "You're making fun of me! You're making fun of me!" et cetera, and went storming out to tell the principal.

I said to the class, "George Santayana once said something about history being cyclical, and that we needed to know history so we wouldn't make the same mistakes over and over. Get out your journals and write about what just happened so it won't occur again." I was smart, and figured that thirty witnesses could back me up when it came time for my reprimands.

Let me jump ahead to say that Ronnie's parents were rich, held pull in our little town, and wanted action. Furthermore, the attention deficit disorder syndrome came to my, well, attention, when I brought in my thirty journals as back-up evidence, just to turn to pages that read things like, "Mr. Toomey talked. Ronnie left."

That was all! It was like a bad music video with the sound turned down—Mr. Toomey talked and Ronnie left.

In a way it's my fault. I didn't pay attention myself, oddly.

Every day I worked teaching high school English I brought my own lunch in and sat in the teachers' lounge. I didn't wander over to watch my students eating the same food I assume they still served. Get it: I didn't even know until I ran out of gas and walked into the junior high cafeteria.

I had no theories until that point, basically. I went from being simply forlorn into being scorned and forgotten, up until now when I've figured out the problems and solutions.

I took courses in how to sell real estate, of course, like every other disgruntled human being. I sold things over the telephone, and heard televisions in the background, if they weren't drowned out by students chomping on Cap'n Crunch and popcorn.

I realized there was no hope whatsoever, and gave up. Driving became less a pastime and more an obsession.

Summary: A boy named Ronnie said, "Huh" one too many times. I couldn't take it. A fracas may or may not have occurred. I got let go from my responsibilities even though I cared about educating the masses more than anything else—a lofty, naive goal. Some people don't even notice there's a path to be not taken, except for Santayana, who started showing up more and more in my life. Don't trust journals.

SNORTING GOODY's headache powders on a dare, ordering anchovy-jalapeño-onion pizzas, and clapping when it seems the logical time to applaud some string quartet, are the simple things I can no longer tell young people not to do, seeing as how attention deficit disorder ruined my life. No judge pelted sentences down on me, but I've given myself restrictions, such as walking one hundred yards from any school, driving my car through school crossing zones at eight or three o'clock, or buying long chocolate bars that might remind me of the candy drives we held to help send our glee club to New York City every spring break.

I taught high school for sixteen years. I sent kids out of the state and kept up with how and what they did. My voice started out calmly, but rose with each subsequent Reagan year. I'll be the first to admit that I didn't keep up with what went on—the exact blindness for which I chastised my growing number of disordered students—by eating my lunches outside of the regular cafeteria, opting for the faculty dining area along with my chalkboard-banging colleagues who couldn't handle attention deficits, either.

I didn't even know about Burger King moving in. I must've called in sick the day Taco Bell held its grand opening at our school, complete with piñata. As a matter of fact, I remember waking to no hot water that same day, and crawling under the house to change a fuse.

I assume I got shocked.

I assume this was a day when my wife lived with me, and went off to her own job—get this—as a marriage counselor. (Talk about obvious attention deficit disorder.) I assume the afternoon my students quit eating Sloppy Joes, lima beans, mashed potatoes with no gravy, and whole-fat white milk was the same day my ex-wife sat around on a couch with some guy who couldn't get it up with his own wife but could with his marriage counselor, who couldn't remember the vows she'd taken so many years before.

Sometimes at night I think about some things.

I think about voter turnout, and people who give up everything to make their own house and furniture out in the woods by themselves away from the rest of humanity. I think about dogs left dead in the road. I think about sober people I read about, lost in the mountains on church outings, and bagboys who complain when people either don't tip or say they have the biceps for their own groceries. I think about people who say things like "Snatch-o/Grab-o" when they play rummy, or pinochle, or go out to find hubcaps randomly.

Sometimes at night I wonder how a kid named Ronnie with attention deficit disorder remembered enough to call his parents on vacation in France and tell them about me shaking him hard and harder, how through his disease he could recall me almost snapping his neck against the blackboard right there in front of a group of kids who said they cared about getting into college.

I try to figure out how all these disordered students can actually drive to school, and imagine their excuses when they undergo the road test portion of the driver's exam—"Red means stop?! Well, I have a learning disability called A.D.D. and you can't hold it against me 'cause it's been diagnosed and documented," et cetera.

And sometimes I sit alone and almost wish I, too, hadn't eaten Sloppy Joes, mashed potatoes without gravy, fish sticks without tartar sauce, lima beans, either kerneled corn or cornbread, dark pudding, canned peaches, and whole-fat white milk one day from expiring. I wish I'd've contracted attention deficit disorder. Then I could forget getting let go. Then maybe I wouldn't always remember that poor kid Ronnie saying "Huh?" until I lost my temper and snapped him in half like the undercooked string beans they used to serve us when anything else seemed out of season.

Summary: Red means stop.

# I Could've Told You
# If You Hadn't Asked

DESMOND WANTED to make a movie called Chickens. He wasn't sure if he had the imagination to pull it off, and he had no hope of grants or investors. The one thing he did possess was a beautiful but crazy wife, though I didn't know about her right off.

I had no money either, of course, but was getting some notoriety as a visionary what with the patch of gray hair on the back of my head that looked just like an eyeball, added to the fact that I'd predicted three Kentucky Derby winners in a row, the date of Black Monday, and Hurricane Hugo's strength, time, and place of landing.

I could see, understand.

Desmond said, "Weldon, I know what I want to do will be a big seller. I just want you to give me the green light, guy. I call it Chickens for two reasons. First off there will be chickens in every scene—somewhere strutting in the background, maybe. Second, I want to train the camera on people and ask them about what they fear more than anything else. I want a man to look into the camera and say, 'The gang violence around here is scaring me more than cornered rats.' Meanwhile he'll be eating a piece of fried chicken. That's subtext, man. I want to see a kid riding a homemade go-cart in circles around his parents' shack, going through a herd of chickens."

I said, "I don't think it's a herd. I think it's a clutch, or a brood. You might want to get that down before trying to approach investors. It's a bed of clams, and a cloud of gnats, and a sounder of boars. It's a troop of monkeys and a knot of toads — that's my favorite, a knot of toads." I'd memorized the World Almanac, 'cause it had this kind of information.

Desmond stood there in the small kitchen of my small cabin. I drank Old Crow mixed with ginger ale and milk thistle to help replenish my liver. I'd been sitting there almost nonstop — not always drinking, of course — since getting fired from my job a year earlier at Coca-Cola in Atlanta. I had worked in an advisory and public relations capacity, but I'd been on a downward run with the higher-ups ever since I said publicly that the new Coke they wanted to market wouldn't work whatsoever.

Desmond said, "You know I'm not as smart as some people think I am. I'll admit that. You know my wife wants to leave me because she has fulfillment issues. She says I'm not performing to what she saw as my capacity when we married."

I said, "You're going to have to give me a minute to think this one out. It might take me some time to puzzle out what Hollywood wants, and what the people want."

Desmond said, "I need some time to write out the script anyway."

He wore a pair of khakis that didn't quite fit any more. They hung down low, and his stomach stuck out like a silhouette of Stone Mountain down in Georgia. Desmond and his nutty wife moved from New York down to Christ Almighty, North Carolina, about the same time I made enough money to move up and buy a summer cabin, long before I understood that I might have to move there for good. Desmond thought he'd absorb some of the South for the best-selling novel he planned to write, but the South absorbed him.

Desmond pulled out the chair across from me and sat down. I said, "There's a job down in Tryon with First Realty. They're looking for someone to put up For Sale signs. I think they pay ten bucks to put up a sign, and five for pulling it down once the house is sold. Here's what you do: Get the job. Put up the signs. At night drive around and knock the signs down. They'll ask you to put the signs back up and you'll get paid twice. Let's say you only have ten signs a week. That's only $100 a week. But if you keep knocking them down, you could make fifty bucks more. Plus you get the five dollars for what sells." I mention this conversation to show that, contrary to his subsequent claims, I told him all these scams before I ever laid eyes on his wife.

Desmond said, "I want to make movies. Films, dude. I've given up writing novels about upper-middle-class people trying to find out about themselves in new and exciting ways."

I got up and made another drink without as much milk thistle because I felt dangerous. I said, "After you make the money by peckering around with real estate agents, go put down money on a lush apartment. You put down one month's rent and the security deposit. Pay in cash. Lie about your name. Then place a want ad in the papers for the apartment for about half what you pay."

Desmond said, "Weldon. I don't want to go to jail."

"You ain't going to jail, man," I said. "You're a film maker. How many film makers are in jail, outside of that guy who can't come back to America for what he did with an underage female?"

Desmond held his head funny. I told him to get some nice furniture, tell prospective renters that he'd gotten a one-year job somewhere and wanted to keep the apartment. I told him to get a post office box and a telephone his wife wouldn't know about.

Desmond said, "Five people a day come in for one month. I show them the apartment, say it's furnished, and take their money?"

I said, "Ask for cash. Say you don't believe in checks. Give them receipts. In no time you got enough money to make your movie." Before Desmond could think about it I said, "Three hundred dollars for the first month, three hundred for the security—that's six hundred. Six hundred times a hundred and fifty people. That's ninety thousand dollars. Hell, rent out three or four apartments and you can go beyond documentary-style black-and-whites. Goddamn, boy, I see a major motion picture in your future."

Desmond said, "My wife's not a patient woman, Weldon. This has to happen fast."

I said, "Go rob a bank. Rob a bank, then make your movie. I wouldn't, but you might."

Desmond shook his head. He pulled his khakis up, then combed his hand through where he wanted more hair. Outside, a hawk circled above Lake Christ Almighty. I tried to think about people in a theater, watching a movie with chickens in every frame, but couldn't.

I FOUND DESMOND'S wife dumping ice deliberately, a ritual I'd heard about but taken for myth. Desmond's wife went in the back door to their added-on house and brought back one of those styrofoam chests for transporting good meats or vital organs. She stepped softly. She was wearing padded bedroom slippers. I didn't speak, because what she was doing looked a lot like what I imagined ancient Asian religious folks did during their somber ceremonies, or how a talented seer might act outside in times of rare planetary alignments. Desmond's wife sprayed Numz-it first-aid medicine between her ice mounds.

"Are your soles soft rubber?" she asked with her back turned. I swear to God this is true. What I'm saying is, this woman was both cosmological and ontological somehow. She may have been teleological, too, but I don't remember all my metaphysics from college.

I said, "I just wanted to come and see if Desmond was doing OK. I just wanted to see what he's working on these days." I wasn't sure if he'd told his wife about Chickens. I didn't want to give any secrets away in case he kept plans to himself. It's a male code.

Desmond's wife stood there holding the styrofoam. She wore a thin cotton print skirt that let light flow through—her upper thighs could've been used as sturdy, solid thin masts, is what I'm saying—and a T-shirt that read Vote Your Uterus. It kind of gave me the creeps, but I swear I couldn't keep my eyes off it. She had big knockers. Desmond's wife said, "The earth is our mother. Walk softly. I'm about to plant a garden, and I don't want my mother to hurt whatsoever. I'm numbing her skin before I dig. I'm numbing the dirt before I dig or hoe or scrape."

I couldn't say anything except, "Shew—I don't want to hurt the earth none. I wouldn't also want to disturb a grist of bees or a down of hares." What the hell.

Desmond's wife said, "You didn't major in geology, did you? I hope you didn't major in geology."

I about told her I never went to college. I said, "No. I majored in philosophy in undergraduate school. Then I went on to law school and quit before the year was over. I never was good at the sciences, really."

"Geologists become miners. Miners end up drilling holes in the earth. You wouldn't go to a dentist and have him drill into your teeth without any kind of pain killer, would you?"

I said, "Tell Desmond I came by and I'll try to get in touch with him later." I started to walk away, back around the cold shallow lake to my little cabin. I kept thinking how men down here pride themselves on not coon-dogging what's already been treed. We don't actively pursue a married man's wife, is what I'm saying. We kill the husband more often than not, or at least get him in a situation that involves a long prison sentence. Thinking about it almost made me have a Pentecostal fit, all thick-tongued and spastic.

"You ever been to a proctologist?" Desmond's wife asked me. She didn't seem to squint as much as she seemed to want to cry, or pass two stones the size of a bad carpenter's thumbs.

I said, "I just sit in my room and think, ma'am. I work as a freelance consultant these days, when admen can't come up with ideas and don't want to lose their jobs. Please don't judge me or anything, please."

Desmond's wife said, "My husband went down the mountain to do some work. He won't be back until way past ten or eleven tonight." This was a Sunday. Realty offices were closed. I knew what Desmond was doing. I laughed and said, "Hey, do you cover your land in sheets of plastic when it hails?"

Desmond's wife took out a little memo pad notebook from the elastic band in her skirt, and wrote down something. She smiled, and raised her eyebrows. She looked like God let her down on a handmade sunbeam.

I didn't understand until later that maybe women from up North kept track of when their husbands returned. Maybe I'd gotten too caught up in my own ways to realize Desmond's wife was sending me a signal.

I LEFT DESMOND'S wife and went home until the sun went down. Then I made my way backwards towards every sign I'd seen lately from First Realty, knowing he'd be nearby in stocking cap and black gloves, sweating from the humidity. I found him hidden halfway down in a carport adjacent to the sort of solid cedar-shake shingle house admired and purchased by people who have a thing for armadillos and alluvial outcroppings.

I said, "Desmond! Get out of there, man, it's me!"

Desmond shimmied goofily, holding his hand up against my pick-up's beam. He said, "Weldon, you scared the shit out of me."

I said, "I meant to. Your wife said you wouldn't be back until late, so I surmised that you got a job doing what I said."

"Well," Desmond said. "I got to do what I got to do in order to do what I want to do, you know."

I said, "Uh-huh."

We shook hands. He'd already thrown down the For Sale sign a good twenty feet from where he had planted it earlier.

Desmond said, "You didn't tell me to wear different-sized shoes when I did this. But I'm wearing different-sized shoes. I went down to a Salvation Army place in Spartanburg and bought three pairs of boots ranging two to four sizes too big than what I wear. I wear a normal ten. I figure no one would be able to trace it back to me—unless they open the woodbin where I keep them during the day."

I said, "There are no cops in Christ Almighty, Desmond. I think you're pretty safe."

He said, "You didn't tell Fiona where you thought I might be, did you?"

I thought, Fiona. I had never met a woman named Fiona, but it seemed like a Fiona would be either the kind of woman who'd numb the earth before digging into it or the kind who welcomed strays. I said, "When she told me you wouldn't be

185

back until ten or eleven tonight, I told her you probably drove all the way to Charlotte looking for a strip joint. Now don't go committing suicide with that post-hole digger."

He said, "OK."

"It's a joke," I said. "I didn't tell her anything, you idiot."

"You don't know my wife, Weldon," he said. "I'm not real proud of it, but I have a girlfriend back in New York. I tell my wife I'm going back to deal with an agent or editor. Actually I lost both my agent and my editor. It's a long story that involves a favorite uncle and his cousin's wife's daughter."

Desmond laughed. I tried not to make eye contact and found myself staring at his chin more than anything else. I said, "That's OK," though I didn't think it was. Listen, I took those marriage vows seriously—even my ex-wife would have to back me up on that one.

We stood while two jets flew overhead, almost side by side. In the brush beside this house a doe rambled, bedding down. I thought about my ex-wife in my ex-city, living not so far from my ex-job. I handed Desmond a beer out of the bed of my truck and said, "There are no chickens living nearby. What're you going to do about that?"

"When I wrote novels I didn't care about truth," he said. "I published a novel about Vietnam and the women's lingerie industry. To be honest, I didn't know squat about either. I'm from Brooklyn. All you need to know applies to both subjects—camouflage only works for so long."

I did not say how it was the same thing in advertising. I didn't say anything because it looked like we were bonding in the dark, and that scared me. I said, "Chickens."

He said, "I put ads in some magazines up North for the apartment. People come down here in the winter, you know. I even said it was a condo."

It would've been a good time to tell Desmond that I was only joking, that I made everything up about how he could make money. But his wife worried that the earth hurt, and I worried that she hurt, too. That's all I could think about there in the dark, with one For Sale sign down and another fifty or so scattered around the mountain. No comet, or shooting star, or UFO showed itself. No Dodge Dart skidded around the curve carrying a trunkload of moonshine. I did not smell marijuana burning anywhere, though I felt hungry and responsible, as always.

"Desmond," I said. "Desmond, Desmond, Desmond. I may have made a mistake by telling you how to make money to support a movie. Don't you have any family that believes in you?"

I turned the lights off in my truck and left the engine running. I barely saw him, is what I'm saying. Desmond said, "My dad's dead and my mother thinks I'm still going to write the great fucking American novel. I can't let her down." He shuffled a foot in sparse gravel and said, "I don't have any brothers or sisters, and I wasn't that popular growing up."

I didn't ask if Fiona had anyone. I kind of knew. I said, "Fiona numbed the earth so she wouldn't hurt it any when she planted a garden, or something. Have you thought about keeping the camera turned on her? I don't want to make any judgment about you and yours, but I bet a documentary about your wife would be interesting. Hell, all you'd have to do is buy some security cameras and set them up."

Desmond took a draw from his beer and threw it back into the bed of my truck. He said, "That might be an idea, paisan."

I said, "When's the last time you saw a movie about a person who did things a whole lot differently than anyone else?"

"I don't remember offhand," Desmond said. "I could've told you if you hadn't asked."

With that response I knew Desmond needed to go back up

North. No one in his or her right mind below the Mason-Dixon line answered questions with "I could've told you if you hadn't asked." It didn't even make sense. If it did, people would just walk around aimlessly spouting out answers like, "Carson City is the capital, not Las Vegas or Reno!" or "Robert Duvall played Boo Radley!" or "Jupiter's equatorial diameter is 88,000 miles," or "Tonga's chief crops are coconut products, bananas, and vanilla."

I said, "Goddamn, if you got such a hard-on for chickens, maybe you can buy a couple roosters and keep them on your property so they'll show up in some scenes with Fiona."

I did not, of course, mean this in an odd, poker-night, jokey way. Desmond took off his watch cap, wiped his forehead, and laughed without thinking about how it might be heard all up and down the mountain, through two valleys, past his job at the real estate agent's office, and into whatever apartment he rented there at the foot of Mount Christ Almighty on the Pacolet River, "Where Retirees Can Enjoy the Splendor of Country Mountain Living."

I DO NOT KNOW the cost of spy gadgetry, and didn't ask Desmond how many signs he set up, knocked down, and reset over a two month period. He bought his chickens first, over the complaints of the home association, and later set up cameras one at a time when Fiona drove down the mountain for ice, Bactine, gauze, Neosporin, and whatever else she used to help heal the mother on which we live.

I know I found myself looking across a quadrant of lake water too often. I used binoculars, hoping to see Fiona bent over in a less-than-modest dress. I thought about how my wife was long gone.

The first time I met Fiona she knew I was watching her

188

numb the soil, so I should have known she could feel me watching her two hundred yards away. One morning she knocked on my door and I answered. When she said, "You want a telescope?" I could only hope that I heard wrong.

"Hey, Fiona. Come on in for some coffee," I said.

She said, "Is it one of those flavored coffees? You know those flavored coffees have chemicals in them that they don't advertise on the box."

I said, "It's regular coffee. I have some bread, too. I was just about to have breakfast. Come on in."

She stood there wearing the only skirt I'd ever seen her wear, the one that sunlight ravished without much effort. Fiona said, "Weldon, right?"

I said, "Uh-huh."

She said, "I know when you're watching me, Weldon. You aren't doing anything weird up here, are you?"

I said, "I'll confess that I watch you. I've never seen anyone care about blemishes so much. I apologize, and I'll quit, but I promise I'm not doing anything perverted. I've had a wife and I've had girlfriends. Not at the same time, either—I took a course in ethics one time in college."

That wasn't true. I mean, I had not taken a course in ethics, which I figured gave me the right to tell a lie. Fiona said, "Did you use any preservatives in your bread?"

I told her I washed my hands between each knead.

WHEN WE FUCKED daily for the next six weeks we did so slowly. Fiona wasn't sure about my cabin's pilings—whether or not they were planted loosely—or whether our rhythm might tamp down into her mother like the misstroke of a blunt-ended toothbrush that jabs your gums. I did not her tell her about her husband's uncle's cousin's daughter. I did not break male code in that way.

And there was no love between Fiona and me, at least that first week: We only whispered about the earth moving, often.

But I said more than once in her ear, "Where were you when I thought I should get married?"

"Probably getting married. Or in Santa Fe learning massage therapy," Fiona said to me more often than not.

DESMOND CAME OVER finally in midsummer. I felt uncomfortable, of course. We hadn't spoken since I told him to scrap Chickens. Desmond said, "Weldon, I've been thinking. I don't want to be nosy, but how do you live? You don't work in advertising any more, do you, Weld-on? You don't have a home office upstairs so you can just fax what you're thinking, do you, Weldon?"

Desmond seemed to have something to say.

I said, "I saved money well and invested OK. I work as a consultant sometimes but don't seek it. I don't like to brag or anything, but people in the industry know me, and when they're out of ideas they get in touch and offer me money. An adman without an idea is an ex-adman in about a thirty-second spot."

Desmond said, "Huh."

I said, "I thought you'd be wearing a beret by now. How's it going?"

"Oh, I'm set, amigo," he said. I poured bourbon. "I ain't got a story line or anything but figure I can do it through editing. Are you sure this'll work out?" Desmond didn't sit down when I shoved the chair out for him.

I couldn't lie. I said, "Well. Maybe your wife's not as quirky as I thought."

"So you're saying Fiona's not odd enough to star in my film, is that what you're saying? You saying my wife's too average to care about? I don't think you know what you mean, Weldon."

Desmond had a different edge to him. He bowed up on me good. People in the South sometimes think Northerners display a certain curtness, a certain broad and blatant cruelty towards other human beings. It's a misconception that thrives with others—such as how dead blacksnakes on fence posts end droughts, or crossing a downhill stream will stop a specter. People from the Northeast are kind, really. Unlike me—and the people I know—they don't constantly scheme at ways to kill friends, acquaintances, and relatives.

I said, "I'm saying I don't know what I'm saying."

Desmond held his fists at his sides. In this short time I'd already considered throwing him off my porch headfirst, taking the fire poker to his temple, even rigging a clipped and frayed electrical wire from an outlet into my toilet so when he peed out his bourbon it'd shock him hard. When I stuck up one index finger and shook it like a scolding mother from a fifties movie, Desmond evidently thought I foreplayed a shot to his nose. He decked me quick, then. He said, "I know about you fucking Fiona, Weld-on. I got movies and I got a lawyer."

I'VE REALIZED THAT the more isolated a person attempts to be, the more people know about him. I'm sure everyone on Mount Christ Almighty, and the valley towns of Tryon and Columbus, even smaller Lynn and Green Creek, knew that I had a scalp condition that required dandruff shampoo. Or that I had the occasional bout with athlete's foot when I worked in scawmy conditions, or that I had hemorrhoids from worrying too much about my goddamn feet. People knew these things because I could do my grocery shopping at one place only—a family-owned store down the mountain called Powell's.

When this buzz-cut kid handed me a subpoena to show up

at Fiona and Desmond's divorce proceeding, he held a hand-kerchief to his mouth. I said, "Have you got a bad cold or some-thing? I took a bath this morning."

"I don't want to get the tuberculosis," he said.

"I ain't got TB."

"Well, you had to go down to the doctor last week, and you haven't bought any cigarettes since, and you had a coughing fit down at the Waffle House," the kid said.

"Oh. Oh, yeah. It's not tuberculosis, man," I said. "It's ra-bies." I took two quick steps his way so he jumped clean off the porch, eight feet off the ground.

I'd gone to the doctor to get some shots because I'd been hired to check out the chances of a Disney project in Kuwait. I told them to save their money, but they didn't. That Gulf War thing took place soon thereafter. There you go.

I lied in front of the judge and jury, in front of the packed house at the Polk County courthouse, in front of Fiona, Desmond, and their respective lawyers. I said, "No sir, I never had sex with her in my house. It's true she came over as the films indicate." Then I said, "On more than one occasion Fiona came over looking for Bactine, Neosporin, and gauze." I made it sound like Desmond beat her or something, but I didn't care.

Desmond had the brains to point one of his little cameras towards my front porch. The jury saw something like forty-two clips of Fiona walking in my front door, all but one of me hug-ging her there. When Desmond took the stand he swore I'd told him about my scams just so I could lure his wife over my way. He'd put his hand on the Bible and everything, and looked the jury straight. Obviously they believed him. Luckily, no chicken followed Fiona over or we might have been sentenced to the electric chair. This was the South.

Of course she lost everything. Juries from the mountains of

western North Carolina don't care about mental cruelty or impotence or abuse. It's as if "Stand By Your Man" is piped into the chambers.

The prosecutor asked me, "Do you know what kind of person you are, breaking up a marriage?" I sat silent. "You're nothing but a coward, lying like this. Do you know the meaning of coward?"

I tried not to shake. I didn't look up or down, or sideways back and forth haphazardly, like an animal confused by rain.

I didn't mention to Desmond's lawyer how the mountains of North Carolina are filled with garnets and rubies and emeralds and mica. I didn't say how one day when Fiona came over she made me lie naked in the sun, and placed semi-precious gems on what she understood to be pressure points on my body.

I understood, too. I'm talking sundial—she put a rock right on the end of my pecker. Fiona said, "I'm trying to learn the proper and beneficial uses of magnets, but I don't feel sure about myself yet."

In the distance we heard Desmond's roosters crow. Fiona put rocks on herself, and we both fell asleep. I got a sunburn, and when I woke up it looked like someone had written tiny Os on my body. I'd never felt better in my life—when Fiona rolled over on me our white marks fit like pistons, I swear. Let me say right now that it was at this point that I knew I loved Fiona, and could work as the conductor on her trainload of neuroses. Call it luck or predilection on her part, but those stones made me feel different about myself and the rest of the world, and the way things would end up in the future.

The prosecutor said, "Boy, I believe you got some Sherman in you, what with the way you burned a marriage with a perfect foundation." He pointed over at Desmond and said, "What else could you have done to this poor man?"

YEARS LATER ON, reading about how Chickens won those independent film competitions, I had all kinds of reactions, most of which involved duct tape, a hard-backed simple chair, a pistol butt, and a smile. I read that in France the movie was called Les Poulets, of course, and audiences considered it some kind of classic. In Holland or Denmark the film went by plain Peeppeep. Because Desmond won the divorce, he also got the house and half of Fiona's worth, enabling him to back himself on his own project. Fiona came from a wealthy family, too. What I'm saying is, I damn near forgot that women named Fiona either numbed the ground when they walked, or took in strays, or had a trust fund the size of influenza.

We live quietly these days and we compromise. Sometimes Fiona circles that gray patch on the back of my head as if she were mixing a drink with her finger. She says I'll come up with a vision for us both. I don't make fun of her when she goes outside at night and cries with the stars and moon. And unlike most people, I'm now allowed to stomp on this earth.

# The Ruptures and Limits of Absence

IF I WERE TO SEE THINGS in a fateful manner, more than likely I would have gotten a job with the telephone company straight out of high school. I'd've been one of those pole guys wearing a silver hard hat. If I'd not gotten a job with the telephone company, maybe I'd've become one of those daredevils who circled a stadium until getting enough motorcycle speed, then jumped fifty parked junkers. I could've gotten a job selling new cars, probably, or ended up asking students if they wanted pizza or a cheeseburger in the high school cafeteria. It seems like I would've turned out to be one of those lawyers fighting against the tobacco industry. If I believed that everything happens for a reason, then these were my only choices.

I always thought my story began when, at the age of fourteen, the woman who served mashed potatoes daily in my junior high school cafeteria serving line hit me from behind at sixty miles an hour. I was on a Schwinn ten-speed going up Powerhouse Road in first gear. She drove a big light blue Ford Galaxy, and later on told the police that she'd looked down for a second in order to push in her cigarette lighter. I don't remember any of this, of course. Someone estimated that I flew something like thirty feet before a telephone pole stopped my flight ten feet up, that I hit the thing upside-down and backwards, and slid down the pole slowly and landed on my neck and shoulders, feet in the air, knocked out.

Twenty-five years later I'm able to understand that this was my re-birth—that sliding down that telephone pole head first was similar to sliding down the birth canal, et cetera. Whenever any of those goddamn stupid Pentecostals and Baptists ask me if I've been borned again, I can say Uh-huh and not think anything about it. I can take a lie detector test and pass that question.

If I were to believe in fate and whatnot, maybe I should've started training immediately for the Tour de France or something, but that would've been nearly impossible. First off, I hurt my hip and limped for the rest of my stay in Gig, South Carolina. Secondly, the concussion was lasting, and for a few years I kind of forgot where I was, or why I went, or where I meant to go. If I'd've begun a training regimen, more likely than not my father would've had to come pick me up a hundred miles from home, once I realized I'd forgotten to drop bread crumbs along the way.

The bottom line is this: instead of understanding that nearly dying at the age of fourteen should've given me some direction in life, it only pissed me off. It kind of got me frost-hardened, like a good pepper plant in late March when freak weather tests it. As soon as I woke up three days later in the hospital where my father visited almost hourly, I crawled over the hospital bed guardrails and thought only one thing: I have to get the fuck out of Gig.

Now I don't think of myself as more pessimistic than the next boy brought up in a town where the high school drivers ed teacher works as the coroner also, but the entire getting-hit-by-the-mashed-potato-lady episode only made me think that—if the telephone pole wasn't there—perhaps I'd've been knocked clean out of the county, that I could've landed in a town with a local newspaper that came out twice a week, or sold square pieces of cheese in the grocery store. I took the accident as an omen, sure, but not the kind of sign my old childhood neighbors took twenty-five years later, that caused fake tornadoes to scatter their trailers, so their entire lives could be unwrapped on national television.

"You have to go help your father out," my wife said to me. "The least thing you could do is pull mobile-home axles out of the way so the search goes better."

I said, "Everyone could go to jail for this, Davida. Understand, it's against the law."

Here's the story: I crawled out of my hospital bed and tried to hitchhike away. My father caught me on Highway 25 and said that if I promised to stay in Gig until the age of eighteen, then he'd make sure to have enough money to let me go off to college twice and never come back. And that's what happened. Let me make it clear that I got along with my father well, and we saw each other often. He took road trips at least once a week, whether I lived one hundred or three hundred miles away.

Now. Basically, the town of Gig hadn't kept up with the nation's economic recovery, no new business had opened up in two decades, and the closest towns with factories—Columbia, Augusta, Charleston, and Greenwood—stood between 70 and 120 miles away, which was too far a commute for anyone with a car that still had fins. My father called me up just as I started a new semester teaching pop-culture courses at a college in the mountains of North Carolina, a place where rich parents sent children who didn't have the grades or standardized test scores to get in one of the state schools. Each term I helped team-teach two humanities courses that incorporated literature, philosophy, and art, plus I got to design a new course a year involving my area of interest. This particular semester I taught something called Movie Set Backgrounds—the Signifier and Signified.

Anyway, my father called, asking my help in pretending to look for victims in this fake-tornado scheme. I put him on speaker-phone because my wife never wanted to miss a word my father thought up. "We need you here, son. We need someone here who can speak right and convince the media that what happened actually happened. We're down to a population of less than three hundred." Then he hung up and called back presently.

I knew he was up to another scam. Whenever my father thought up things that he shouldn't have thought up, he called and talked in one- minute intervals, seeing as he thought the government tapped all phone lines. I probably should mention here that my father is the drivers ed teacher and coroner. In Gig—as in most small towns—the coroner didn't have to possess any kind of medical background. The coroner needed to know that a person burned like barbecue probably died from a fire, and that someone with a bullet hole in his or her head probably died from a gunshot wound. The coroner needed to understand rope burns and elementary mathematics. There was no test: just a vote and a slight post-
election ceremony.

Of course, my father got voted in as coroner back when people only died of old age and car wrecks. I guess the towns-people figured he should be coroner, seeing as it was his fault for not teaching kids how to drive well, and that he only needed to know basic mathematics for people who died of natural causes. My father named me Park, because of his job. It could've been worse. He could've named me Brake, or Signal. My father and I got along, even though I told him he had no right to let people call him Dr. Bardin just because he was coroner.

When he called, I said, "This is going to be like your pet-ting-zoo trick, isn't it?"

My father said, "Bigger." He'd once helped Big Jim Shorts fit deflated footballs on plain opossums. Big Jim told people they were special armadillos. He didn't bother to paint them or any-thing, so the animals were known as Spalding and Wilson. My father got the idea from an old man up in the mountains. It got Big Jim a letter from the SPCA.

I said, "I had another dream that I should never come back home. I had a dream that I'd get hit by another car." For some reason I'd made a yearly point to tell my father how I considered myself born again when I slid down that telephone pole, that my rebirth involved a Ford Galaxy, et cetera. My father made a point to tell me that my birth involved a brand-new 1957 Oldsmobile, a trip to Myrtle Beach, and a supper involving fried oysters and calabash shrimp.

My father didn't hear me then, either. He said, "The whole town got together. We polled everybody old enough to pee standing, and it came out unanimous. We've got a guy with a wrecking ball he ain't used since the last silo, and two tow-truck drivers who promise to donate their time and money knocking over trailers and jerking entire roofs from their rafters. We got enough bulldozers. I know you're not one to ever get your hands dirty. I know you people living in your ivory towers fear blisters and calluses more than anything else. But I bet your dean would be proud of you on the TV when they ask where you're from and you say you teach at that college, and so on. It'll make you look like a humanitarian and everything."

I stood in my kitchen and stared at the clock hard, trying to make the hour hand spin backwards. I said, "Y'all don't even have insurance. Most people down there don't believe in insur-ance. I don't get the scam."

My father hung up and called back. He said, "We just want some attention. Federal funds will take care of what the insurance don't. Listen, every other American gets prayers sent their way when there's a flood, earthquake, hurricane, tornado, or killing spree. Gig deserves it. Hell, influenza don't even visit us any more every winter, Park."

I thought this: my people want pity. It's the first time, ever, I'd thought about the citizens of Gig as "my people" since leaving for college. I didn't break down crying or anything. I said, "You know I'm not worried about blisters and calluses, Dad," and he hung up. I nodded when Davida came out of the bedroom with a packed suitcase and our tent. At that point I realized that my story would begin elsewhere.

I PICKED THE TIME I got hit by a Galaxy at random, really, because I spent more than a few months out of my childhood wearing white gauze wrapped around my head, slightly bewildered. It's not like I was uncoordinated. To be honest, most of my dozen concussions occurred right after my father said, "Hey, Park, see if you can . . . " either jump off the roof, or slide down a steep hill on a snow disk without going in the creek, et cetera. One time he put my bare shoulder against the back of the house and let me shoot his thirty-ought-six. It backfired, my head hit the bricks hard, and I was out. I think I was seven years old that time.

My mother—who left us when I was only four years old— was a deep-socketed woman, and my father said that's the only feature of hers that I owned. I'm no psychologist, but I'd bet that somewhere in his subconscious he wanted me to hit my head until my eyeballs properly popped forward and filled their surrounding and protective bones so he wouldn't have to think of her every time I walked into a room. Throughout my childhood my father offered only non sequiturs about my mother, things like, "Your mother went off to work at the eraser factory."

I never knew what he meant, and didn't ask. Usually I sat somewhere off in a corner, my head lolling back and forth uncontrollably. I know this: my mother called herself a professor, though she only taught typing and shorthand at a technical college in south Georgia. Somewhere along the line I got it in my head that she was a true feminist, and that she taught future secretaries little tricks so that they could fuck up their bosses and whatnot, and later take over entire corporations. To be honest, I think she taught regular old shorthand and typing, though, out of those odd-shaped Gregg hardback books.

Davida and I drove back roads south to Gig, as if there was a choice. The interstate systems that criss-crossed South Carolina—namely I's 95, 26, and 20—didn't come within a hundred miles of my hometown. There was a giddiness about my wife I'd not noticed in a while. Our trunk and back seat were packed, and she carried two books: one on first aid, and the other Thucydides's History of the Peloponnesian War. I said, "I don't know if I need to tell you that this is all a secret, honey. You understand how this is the dumbest scheme my father's ever told me about."

My wife pulled her left leg sideways on the front seat and turned halfway. She looked like the number 4. She said, "It's another adventure with Dr. Bardin. I think it's a cool idea." Among other things that I'll get to later, Davida worked at the local School for the Deaf. She was the librarian. She spent most of her time in total silence, outside of someone dropping a book on the carpet. "You're going to inherit your daddy's land some day. There's no reason why it shouldn't get a boost no matter how."

Davida signed while she talked. It was a habit. It's the major reason why she never drove when we went somewhere. I never picked up the language, for I knew enough of French and bread-making. I figured my brain was filled up enough. Sometimes when I kneaded dough, Davida would say something to me like, "You just signed out 'Hot dog OK, Coffee, Land of Fuck-Whip,'" or whatever. Sometimes I couldn't even eat what I'd baked, after she told me what I signed making the stuff.

I said, "All these television stations now have Doppler radar, and Super Doppler. I don't know how the people of Gig are going to be able to convince anyone that a tornado hit when the weather map showed no storm activity in a two-state area."

Davida said, "That's what makes this so exciting. That's what makes it a challenge, Park. How're you going to explain it, seeing as you've been voted spokesperson?"

I said, "Deus ex machina. That's the only solution." I felt confident that I could pull it off. I'd once taught a course called What the Hell Was That?—a Look at Greek Tragedy Through Textual Hermeneutics.

I dodged dead animals. Davida repositioned herself and said, "Hey, I hope that old clothing store's still open in Gig. I bet I can get some good old mannequins out of that place, seeing as they'd have to be scattered by a fake tornado."

This is Davida's other job, her real job, the job she does before and after work signing Dr. Seuss and Uncle Remus stories: my wife makes chip-dip holders and hors d'oeuvres trays out of mannequins. She cuts through their bellies with a jigsaw, sands down the rough edge, repaints the torsos, and sticks a Tupperware container in the cavity. What started off as a minor escapade at flea markets has turned into a legitimate money-making business. Her pieces sell between one and two hundred dollars at boutiques and art galleries, mostly in New Mexico and New York City. When she's not making dip holders out of the torsos, she's making smoking stands from the legs.

202

"You've never been to Gig," I said. "How do you know about a clothing store? There's nothing in Gig. People who want to wear clothes need to drive far away, or make them out of feed sacks. A lot of people in my hometown go naked, honey. I didn't want to tell you that."

We'd only been married two years. We drove up to Gatlinburg to one of those wedding chapels, and honeymooned in Dayton, Tennessee, where the Scopes Monkey trial took place back in 1925. Davida and I met at the School for the Deaf when I got hired out through some grant money to come over and teach a week-long seminar on the History of Silent Movies and Their Impact on Existentialism.

Davida said, "Your daddy brought me pictures. Your daddy thinks that even if you're not happy about your growing-up years, I need to know about it. He's right, if you ask me. I don't want you to think I'm loose or anything, but I've met a lot of men before who felt it necessary to send me pictures of their sons. Or of their boys' homeland. You aren't special in that way, Park. There's a whole brotherhood of solipsists out there, both daddy and son. And personally, I bet I've met a dozen men in the Southeast who were exactly like you."

The town council voted to use some tax money to buy my father a camera so he could take pictures of dead people. My father rode around in the passenger seat of the drivers ed car more often than not, slamming down the instructor's brake in order to take snapshots of things he thought interesting. Mostly he took photographs of birds and farm animals. I suppose it's possible that somebody's cow got loose in front of Fashions by Lemuel, next to Gig's Froggy Diner.

I didn't hear what Davida said. I drove south, trying to think of how to describe a tornado without saying it sounded like a freight train.

HERE'S THE LAYOUT: to the south, north, and west of Gig stands the Savannah River Nuclear Plant, a place where bombs were supposedly made back when I grew up falling down, where now only forty-nine other states—and no telling how many foreign countries armed with merchant ships—sent their toxic waste to be buried. The governor of South Carolina says that the money received from this storage rental will go to the education system, so that glowing students can sit in front of computers or something. The legislature votes yearly that gambling and the lottery's a sin, and that even though every other state amasses enough money to put their students in state colleges for free, South Carolina's children are better off in the long run drinking tainted water, et cetera.

I don't get it, but don't need to, seeing as I left Gig for good a few years after I thought my story began.

Davida and I drove down Highway 25 until we reached the 125 obtain-pass-at-gate road that no one used any more, then five miles south took an illegal dirt road to the left that I remembered. I knew that either no one would be monitoring the little hidden cameras nailed to various withered trees, or that they wouldn't be in working order anyway. We crossed over steamy creeks with wretched half-trunks poking out, past clumps of moss that weighed down their shriveled hosts. Davida quit signing after about the third creek.

"Welcome to my old stomping grounds," I said. "Gosh, I remember playing hide and seek out here at night with my friends when we were kids. It didn't take much to find anyone."

Davida clucked her tongue. She said, "Every sci-fi movie about the apocalypse should be filmed down here. This is creepy."

I drove right at ninety miles an hour. It's not like any cops, pedestrians, or oncoming traffic would be around, outside of bad drunks lost between Florida and New York. I said, "We're about twenty minutes away. We'll be coming up on the west side of town."

I knew that if what Dad told me was true, then he'd have people up and down Old Spook Pond Road watching for strangers. He'd have some kind of walkie-talkie system going on in case someone drove up confused. The people of Gig wouldn't want anyone seeing them knocking down their own trailers, of course.

Davida and I entered the area from a road that no one used, and that probably half the people of Gig were scared to traverse, seeing as talk always abounded of lizard monsters and other assorted nuclear swamp beings. We crested the only hill in the area and I stopped. Below us, in a beautiful panoramic way, the townspeople of Gig worked hard together: a wrecking ball swung purposefully and knocked down a little single-wide with one stroke. Both tow-truck drivers hooked their lines to cars and stood them on end. People crouched atop their own houses and ripped off shingles, whole sheets at a time. Big Jim Shorts practiced with his fainting goats and his small herd of cows he taught to play dead. Right in the middle of things I saw my own father, standing atop his drivers ed car, bullhorn in hand, giving either directions or a pep talk, nodding up and down like a preacher on a trampoline.

My wife and I watched my people pushing mopeds and bicycles into ditches, and some woman on a bulldozer driving around aimlessly, pushing over pine trees. Behind her, two boys with rakes tried to hide the tracks. I said, "Those Irish Travelers don't live that far away, really. Sometimes I wonder if I come from a sect of people who broke away from the Travelers, like maybe everyone around here didn't like picayune scams."

Davida nodded. She said, "It's not unlike watching an ant

205

farm, Park. I'll admit that this is a little weirder than I imagined."
In town—which basically consisted of Lemuel's clothing store,
the diner, a barber, and ten vacant storefronts—people broke
plate-glass windows and scattered the glass out on the sidewalk,
as if they got sucked out completely by a tornado. It might be
easier to see my hometown by what it doesn't own: there were
no 7-11-type stores, no grocery store, no laudromat. There was-
n't an old-fashioned feed and seed, no dry cleaner, furniture
store, pharmacy, Army-Navy surplus, ice cream parlor, no H&R
Block. People had to lose a quarter tank of gas to go fill up at a
station forty miles away. There used to be all of these things, but
they no longer existed. Hell, there was once a drive-in movie not
far from the outskirts of Gig, but the last movie shown was De-
liverance and I think everybody around quit going, once they
thought Hollywood only made realistic movies that offered no
means of escape for the citizens of Gig.

I watched the town idiot—who used to be my English
teacher in high school—throw his unicycle up into an over-
grown wisteria.

Both churches, long vacant and out of use, were leveled. I
wasn't sure if anyone held faith in Gig anymore, but I knew that
believers must've driven to Augusta or some place on Sundays.
The two ministers who used to tend First Baptist and First Pentecostal left right around the same time as Nixon got im-
peached. I remember one old preacher telling my dad that he
couldn't live off of IOUs in the collection plate.

I said, "It's not unlike one of those Broadway musicals." I
reached under my seat and pulled out a Thermos of martinis I'd
brought along. Davida opened the glove compartment and
pulled out two plastic fold-up travel cups. When we clicked our
glasses together there was no appropriate toast to make. Davida
signed something that I didn't quite catch, outside of the mo-

tion for insane. I said nothing when I decided it was time to go on down and help my father.

Get this: I put the car in Drive and drove slowly about fifty yards before someone noticed that a stranger approached. I'm not sure who gave the signal, but the people of Gig—even the fainting goats—all fell down in place at once, as if something from the heavens picked them up earlier and dropped them down scattered simultaneously.

ONE SUMMER WHEN I was twelve—only halfway through my series of concussions—I somehow got a job helping Daney Mitchell clean up his barn and out-buildings, load up what he could sell on the back of his pick-up truck, drive to Columbia, and sell off his things at a flea market. Daney Mitchell needed to move out of the state. He said he couldn't take the pressure of being a celebrity where the last famous person happened to be a member of the Confederate army.

Daney Mitchell gained fame, according to everyone in Gig, because he'd gone on a killing spree down in Charleston. Evidently he poisoned some rich people, and stabbed some other rich people, and shot a lawyer or two, and maybe even burned down a jewelry store. His actions kind of multiplied each year. Whatever he did, according to everyone, got him a death sentence. On the morning of his execution the guards came in and asked what he wanted for his last supper. Daney Mitchell supposedly sat there staring off.

One guard said, "You can have anything you want. Steak. Shrimp. Macaroni and cheese."

Daney Mitchell said, "I want a tire. I want a big raw rubber tire."

At six o'clock that night—of course he was to be electrocuted at midnight, just like in the movies I showed my students when

I taught a seminar course called Gangsters, Molls, and Hegelian Dialectic—the guards brought him a Goodyear, but no knife. Daney Mitchell said thanks, et cetera.

According to everyone in Gig, he only got about halfway through eating that tire bite by bite, holding it on his lap in the little cell like a giant doughnut. At midnight they led him into the execution chamber, strapped him up, and pulled down the lever.

He just sat there with a hood on his head. He didn't exactly shake, throb or have his eyeballs pop out. According to my people, Daney Mitchell had so much rubber inside his body—and he rubbed trace amounts of the tire all over his skin, too, an invisible sheen—that he'd become non-conductive. Somewhere in his death sentence there was a loophole, too, that stated if he survived the shock, then he'd be let free, et cetera, which is just what happened.

Every one of those Believe It or Not–types of magazines and books had big write-ups on Daney Mitchell, though I never saw one. As a matter of fact I never looked, seeing as I didn't want to know the truth. For me, Daney Mitchell was one of those guys who found out a way to beat the odds, and I'm sure that the time when I tried to hitchhike out of Gig, somewhere down in my unconscious, Daney Mitchell's story is what made me stick out a thumb.

I didn't ask Daney anything, either. We loaded up his pickup with old single- and double-trees, yokes, plow stocks, barrels, barn spikes, and whatnot, and drove to the capital to sell them off at a place that became the state fair once a year. One Saturday morning Daney drove and said, "I got this story to tell you, Park. I want you to listen closely, okay?"

I said, "I promise." I thought he might let me in on how to chew a tire correctly, should I ever practice heinous and horrific actions in such a way that would earn me a death sentence.

Daney rolled his window back up so I could hear better. He said, "One time the ears died, and the rest of the body tried to figure out who needed to bury them. All of the organs voted on the eyes, seeing as the eyes could go out, bury the ears, and find their way back to the body. But the eyes didn't want to go outside the body, and said they might just bury the ears and never return, what do y'all think about that? The lungs said they couldn't go, because they were like fish out of water when they left the body. The spleen and liver chimed up saying they were needed to stay inside the body to clean up what the blood brought to them, and mentioned how the rest of the body would wither off by the time they got back from burying the ears."

This is no lie: about this point I thought about jumping right out of the truck. I'd already had a couple concussions at thirty miles an hour, and figured fifty wouldn't be that much different. I said, "I've never heard this one," hoping it was only a joke, and not something with inner meaning.

Daney Mitchell said, "You won't hear this one around Gig. You won't hear this one in all of South Carolina, boy." He said, "Okay. The heart went the same route as the liver and spleen, and the intestines said they might get mistaken for a snake outside the body and some woman with a hoe would chop them in pieces. So. The body just lay there with dead ears for a while until the organs all said, 'I think the larynx should go. The body can live without a larynx for a good few days, in case burying the ears takes time.' The larynx said, 'I don't want to go out there,' and so on, but he got outvoted and had to go. The other organs shoved him right outside of the body.

"Well, I'm not quite sure what a larynx looks like, but the larynx never came back. I don't know if it got chopped up like the intestines thought they would, or if it just dried up and died outside the body, on its way to bury the ears. But I know this: once the larynx was gone, the rest of the body died soon thereafter. When the lungs started to hurt, and then the heart, the larynx wasn't there to mention it to the brain. When the kidneys failed and the intestines formed tiny holes in themselves, the larynx wasn't there to explain some things, to yell out a warning, if you know what I mean."

This was summer. Men on tractors worked their fields. I couldn't get out of my mind a pair of ears in a little box underneath the soil. I said, "They should've picked the appendix. It's not much use any more, from what my daddy told me."

Daney Mitchell, the man who beat the electric chair by eating a tire, nodded. He said, "That's not bad thinking. But you know what? Even the appendix still had hope of doing something. You just can't vote for something to go out and risk death just because it seems to have no potential. The body needs to understand that, Park. The body needs to understand that it needs a larynx maybe more than it needs anything else."

Daney Mitchell honked his horn and laughed out loud. When I was a first-year college student I realized that he probably didn't eat a tire and miss the electric chair. I realized that Daney Mitchell, more likely than not, only left his parents' farm and went to further his education, that his parents were embarrassed about a kid from Gig wanting to do something outside of farming, that more than likely it was Mr. and Mrs. Mitchell who made up the story of Daney going to jail.

I realized that Daney Mitchell was a communist.

DAVIDA SAID, "I SEE a couple of them trying to crawl under debris. Man, they got this thing down to a science," when we continued down the western dirt road into Gig.

The first person I made out besides my father was Daney

Mitchell. Daney never fell; he walked around in circles with his hand to his forehead and didn't make eye contact with the car that penetrated the ruptures and limits of my hometown which, of course, happened to be my car. Daney patterned the berm a hundred yards from the first church demolished, and I pulled up next to him and said, "I knew you'd be back."

Daney said, "It was terrible. It was something no one expected. It sounded like a train, man," which reminded me to think up similes for the television crews my father told me to expect.

I leaned over my wife and said through her open window, "Mr. Mitchell, it's Park Bardin. I know all about the tornadoes." I wore my seat belt, and remembered how there wasn't a real cop within a hundred miles.

Daney Mitchell, who wasn't but fifty years old—I'd thought of him being fifty when we didn't sell any single- or double-trees, any yokes, harnesses, or farm implements at the Columbia flea market some two-and-a-half decades earlier—put his hand in his pocket and said, "Hey, Park. Your daddy told me you'd be showing up to help us out." He bent down and stuck his hand out past Davida. "Hotdamn, that was a close one," he said, then turned around and yelled to everyone acting knocked out, "It's okay; it's only Dr. Bardin's boy."

My people got up as if they'd practiced doing handsprings. I blew the horn a couple times, just like Daney did driving to the flea market two generations ago. I said, "You're back, again," to Daney. I put the car in Park and got out my side. It wasn't like I had to pull over on the berm or anything. Davida opened her door but just sat there.

Daney said, "I come back and forth, you know. I go away, and then I come back, and then I go away. And then I come back. I go away. It's not all that much different than being a

211

human tide, Park. Sometimes I think I can get out of here, go to Detroit or some place that needs some common worker's sense put in, and then the next thing you know I need to come back here where people still know me for who I am. For people who still respect me for beating the odds and all. Your daddy tells me you're teaching college. I guess you understand what I mean."

I didn't say anything about the tire. I said, "I know what you mean. This is my wife Davida. She's got her own communist tendencies," even though she didn't.

My father came running up and said, "Park, Park, Park," like that. I'd not seen my father in a few months, and he'd grown a look about him not unlike a man standing beneath the shadow of a sudden dark and fishy wave.

I said, "Hey, Dad." I said, "I still think this is a dumb idea even if y'all have gotten it down to a regular ballet. I thought you needed us here to get our hands dirty and whatnot."

Davida got out, kissed my father on the cheek, and grinned. Daney Mitchell put both his hands in back pockets. My father said, "Ah, hell, I just said that to get you pissed off and down here. We've been turning the town over for a week now. We're just about ready." Then he looked at the sky and said, "How's the world of meteorology? Today's a good day for meteorology, ain't it?"

I looked at my wife. I said, "I don't know."

My father said, "You teach meteorology. Give us the go-ahead, boy. There are some cloudy conditions in Alabama. How long you think it'll take for the storm front to hit us?"

I said, "I teach a ton of things, Dad, but I don't teach meteorology. They teach that at state colleges. They teach meteorology at schools with real science departments."

Everyone from my hometown started back working at what

they needed to tear down. I knew the faces, but not many of the names. There seemed to be an inordinate number of dogs roaming around. My father said, "Oh."

I said, "You're thinking of anthropology. I teach a course sometimes about how human beings are different because they have opposable thumbs. I don't know about the weather."

My father said, "Well, a tornado just passed through here, as far as I'm concerned. I'm the coroner, so I guess I know tornadoes as well as you do. Goddamn, it's been bad." He waved his arm behind him. He did one of those sweeping game-show things for me to look at all the destruction. He said, "I think we're about ready. We're going to crawl under some things, and then we need to get you to call up all the television stations or something."

Daney Mitchell said to me, "This might be the best idea I've come across. Understand this wasn't my idea, but it's a good one."

Davida said, "Where should we pitch this tent?" and pointed in the back seat. She hitched her pants by the naked buckles, as if she grew up in Gig.

My father, Daney Mitchell, and I said, "Not yet," at the same time, which kind of scared me.

I said, "You got the Doppler radar thing and the Super Doppler radar you got to worry about. How's everyone going to explain a series of tornadoes when the radar showed nothing?"

Davida closed the passenger-side door. She walked down an embankment to help people scatter picnic tables and whatnot. My father said, "We thought you'd be able to explain that."

Daney Mitchell bowed up. He said, "Doppler don't mean shit. Super Doppler don't mean jack shit. Let me tell you this, and I'm a man who knows: they keep telling you and telling you about their radar, but in reality it's just a few guys they hired to stand in fields twenty, fifty, and a hundred miles away. They got cellular phones. When things look bad they call up the TV station and say things look bad. That's it. Think about it. There've been enough tornadoes and hurricanes no one expected, not to mention plain old thunderstorms. Fuck America. Fuck everyone."

I looked at my father and said, "See."

My father said, "Your head's been hit hard too many times, remember." He said to me, "You're still the man who's going to talk to everyone. We voted."

Daney Mitchell looked at me and nodded. He motioned for Big Jim Shorts to go ahead and knock down the power lines, seeing as no one needed to use their tools anymore. Daney handed me a telephone from his pocket. Daney closed his eyes and made a noise not unlike the air escaping a body's lungs when something of consequence was about to take leave.

THE FIRST WOMAN to talk to me wasn't from one of the big networks, technically. She wasn't a woman who'd worked her way up from college, from a local station last in the television ratings market or whatever. She was from Augusta, Georgia, where everyone waited and waited for a golf tournament once a year. The first reporter on the scene was a woman named Jill Shore, and she bobbed her head at the end of every sentence.

I'd been the one to call her, of course. Daney handed me a few telephone numbers, I called people in Charleston, Augusta, and Greenville, and I suppose regular idiot weathermen interrupted regular programming to say there was a tornado warning for central western South Carolina, that they had reporters going to the scene, et cetera.

Jill Shore's cameraman's name was Clint Winchester—and with a name like that I knew he wanted to somehow work his way up from cameraman to anchor, from anchor to daytime soap operas. Clint wore blue jeans one size too tight and put mousse in his hair. When he shook my hand he went past my palm and grabbed my wrist. It was like some kind of hipster handshake, or some kind of Star Trek cult handshake. I didn't get it. It kind of gave me the creeps.

Or maybe it was Gladys Phillips moaning from beneath her house trailer, pretending to be trapped.

Jill Shore said to me off camera, "I need to get some facts before we go live. Are you from here?"

Davida sat on a nearby stump with her head in her hands, faking sobs. I said, "I'm from here originally. I just happened to be visiting my father. I come to visit my father, you know, maybe once a month." I gave her my name, and so on. I could feel my face turning red from the lie. At that moment I realized that I wasn't a good son, that I wasn't a good Gigian, or Gigite, or whatever people from Gig called themselves.

Jill Shore bobbed her head. She said, "Was it like a freight train?"

Two EMS ambulances screamed in from Barnwell, the nearest town. I pointed to where Gladys Phillips screamed, where ten or twelve men—including my English teacher, Daney Mitchell, and my father—
pretended to move awnings, statuaries, pink flamingoes, whirligigs, garbage cans, and a lawn mower from the front door facing skyward. I said, "Yes, it sounded like a freight train. And it was very windy."

Jill Shore said, "Okay." She turned to Clint Winchester and said, "Are we ready?" Clint nodded, and a red light came on his little mini-cam.

Someone behind us yelled out, "My baby, my baby," like that, realistic.

Jill Shore said into the camera, "We're on the scene in the small town of Gig, South Carolina, where a number of tornadoes have set down. All around us are death and destruction. I'm here with Park Bardin, and Park, you were just visiting here, right?"

She turned her body ninety degrees and pushed the microphone my way. I froze. It wasn't so much that behind me a bunch of people I barely remembered screamed out, knowing their lines and places. It wasn't so much that I felt some kind of moral obligation to report the truth, or that I felt deep down that my wife would judge me for playing along with my people's scam. I didn't think about any of those sell-my-soul-to-the-devil scenarios I liked to teach to rich kids without proper college-board credentials. I said, "It sounded like a hundred crazed women screaming all at once. It sounded like a hundred crazed women, all angry at their husbands, on their way to one of those conferences where people chant out things non-stop. It sounded like all of this."

"I've heard that it sounded like a freight train," Jill Shore said to me.

I thought, Do not say that it was windy; do not say that it was windy, like every other trailer park tornado victim says. I said, "It came out of nowhere. It sounded like a hundred crazed screaming women aboard a freight train. It's all melted now, but that tornado brought along with it hail the size of hermit crabs, or gallstones, or Amish dumplings, or shrunken heads."

Jill Shore turned around to face the cameraman. She said, "Our meteorologist Gene Frank is back at the studio to tell us what we can do to escape catastrophe during tornado season."

Evidently the people in Augusta, Georgia, saw something we didn't see in Gig. Of course my father and his comrades had knocked down the power lines. Jill Shore turned to me when we were off camera and said, "Amish dumplings? What are you, some kind of weirdo?"

Davida quit crying immediately and got up from her stump. I said, "Well, at least I can pronounce words. I've seen you on TV before. At least I know the state capitals, and how to say them, pinhead."

Some real reporters showed up soon thereafter, including stringers for CNN. I stood on my spot with the town of Gig behind me and waited to give answers better than the first. In my mind I developed images of funnel clouds descending. I thought about a course I could teach in the coming year called Theatre of the Absurd and the Aerobics of Country Music Lyrics. The people of Gig feigned sighs, moans, applause, and cheers. Stray dogs roamed freely. Clint Winchester tried to turn his camera in the direction of what happened. Someone got out some generators, and got some spotlights going so we could work all night long picking up debris and investigating the damage. The EMS men and women got Gladys Phillips out of her fake flipped trailer.

Lookit: Gladys was the woman responsible for Gig children's growth. She used to teach Sunday school before the preachers left. She cut hair all day Saturdays, and most weekday afternoons. Gladys sewed the cheerleaders' uniforms and spent her own money taking kids to the Governor's School for the Arts auditions, though none of them ever got accepted.

Gladys shoveled mashed potatoes on Gig children's plates at the junior high school, and made me the human being I turned out to be.

THE NEXT MORNING I stood on a makeshift sound stage made out of pallets recovered from the old Devore lumberyard, a place that hadn't been in business since someone around Gig either discovered bricks or mobile homes. I tried to look in the cameras and appear both concerned and honest, and even conjured up a tear when we got word that one of those Saturday morning fishermen with his own show set up a fund for the people of Gig because he'd had help with a flat tire on his boat trailer one time nearby. Davida stood behind me, signing like crazy for deaf people watching television.

My father said that someone from one of the stations said that the governor said that Gig had been declared a disaster area and that federal funds would be showing up soon after the Red Cross volunteers got working on what needed to be done. I could only think to myself: my wife's dead mannequins with guacamole bellies make more money than what's coming here. There's something wrong with the way things work.

When the cameras weren't rolling, both Davida and I pretended to clear away paths, comfort men whose dreams appeared shattered, et cetera.

"Now we're getting the attention we deserve," my father said to me between reporters. He didn't move his lips or anything. "Look at all the women." He pointed at reporters, camera crews, and volunteers.

It was at this point that I realized that there were no women left in Gig to speak of—that they had either died off somehow, or taken the same road out of town that my mother took. There weren't any children, either, under the age of puberty. Maybe I'd thought that the fake tornado was so well rehearsed that all the women and children left for relatives' houses far away, or L-shaped motels up and down the little-used two-lane roads that used to be major New York–to–Florida thoroughfares.

I said, "Is this whole thing going on because y'all couldn't get any women to stay in Gig?"

My father still spoke without moving his lips. He said, "It's almost a shame that a bunch of men are going away in the Red Cross van way over to Columbia. They're keeping up a front, you know. We held a lottery to see who'd go and who'd stay around. I'm thinking that even the ones who have to go are going to meet some people, though. Old man Becker broke his own ankle on purpose just so he'd get to meet a nurse." My father wore this khaki outfit that, I suppose, he was sworn to wear during crises. It had a badge on the left front shirt pocket and everything. My father stood next to me surveying fake damage. He said, "We could go into business doing this, Park. Goddamn, I might send a letter to the president of Bangladesh next time they need to fake monsoon season, so those Hollywood people get everybody to send five bucks a month."

Davida came walking down the street lugging two mannequins. She said, "Look what Lemuel gave me. He said that he'll tell the insurance people they flew away." She walked up and kissed me on the cheek.

I said, "Don't talk to any of the men again, Davida. Promise me this: don't talk to any man from Gig. I'll explain later."

She put the mannequins in the tent we pitched and never crawled into, ten yards from where I'd done all the interviews. The only chance I had to speak with Davida during the entire evening of the catastrophe was in between my interviews and her looking for someone's pet rooster. She said to me, "This is what I imagine football to be like. These are all like plays in a huddle."

I thought about saying, "Let's get in the tent and do an end-around," about ten minutes after she'd vanished, of course.

As the sun hit mid-morning my father said, "Here come the contractors," and pointed at two vans driving slowly into town.

"They'll need a place to stay. We already got Johnny Bishop's Rest-a-Bit cleaned up and ready for strangers out on Old Savannah Road. We didn't tear off its roof."

I said, "Dad. There aren't any kids in Gig any more. Who exactly are you teaching out at the high school?"

This man stuck a microphone in my face and said he was from Channel 9 Live Action News, like there wasn't but one of them. He asked me to give a description of how everyone down here deals with tornado seasons, year after year. I said, "The South blows. It really blows in the South."

My father said, "Can't you see he's been through a devastating experience?" and pushed the reporter away. To me he said, "There ain't no kids at Gig High. We haven't had a child in school since ten years after you left. We make up names and pretend. We send in fake test scores to the Department of Education, fake attendance rolls. All of us go into work everyday, but mostly we play cards. I ain't ever told you this one?"

I said, "You must've had something else on your mind."
My father said, "We're real proud. Last year our kids scored fifty points above the state average on the SAT. It was a regular minor miracle. It's also a miracle that no one's ever shown up from the state and checked on us. We got it figured out if they do, though—field trip, the flu, cut day." My father looked off in the distance and gave a thumbs up. Big Jim Shorts fired up a bulldozer. "Sometimes just for the hell of it I go out for a ride in the driver's ed car and still sit in the passenger seat. I like to think that I'm only teaching a ghost how to drive."

I called out to Davida, "Pack up the tent."

WE GOT HOME in time to turn on the Weather Channel and see both replays of my interviews and more updated segments. Sure enough, each meteorologist got on there and said that Doppler radar just missed it, and sometimes the heavens opened up within a micro-nano-second not yet known to man or machine.

Daney Mitchell took over as spokesman for Gig, evidently. He didn't cry or anything, but he looked right in the camera and said that if anyone out there could find it in themselves to send money, the people of Gig would appreciate it. He said, "We don't really need toys or clothes. This was a freak tornado. Nobody's clothes or toys got injured. Hey, if any of you womens out there got a vacation coming up, we could sure use some help with the cooking," which I'm sure went over well with the feminist set.

Davida said, "I know you're embarrassed, Park, but it's not your fault. Sure, I know that some members of the psychology profession think that environment plays a part on the psyche more than anything else, but don't worry about it. If I were you I wouldn't think twice about maybe later on in life thinking up ways to scam people out of their time and money and emotions."

I pressed the button on the answering machine and got bombarded with every student I'd ever taught, calling to say they saw me on television. Instead of writing down their phone numbers on the pad of paper I kept nearby, I scribbled down an idea for another special course to teach: Friedrich Nietzsche and the History of Counterfeiting God. I said to my wife, "Man, this is trouble. Somehow all of this is going to come back to me. I don't want to spend time in prison for something this stupid."

My wife pulled her two new mannequins inside the front door. She said, "What would you want to spend time in prison for?" She stood up the mannequins and said, "The fingers are cut off these things. I bet Lemuel cut them off on purpose, so people in Gig would feel at home in his store."

I said, "I don't want to go to prison for anything. I don't want to do anything. I don't want to teach, and I don't want to work a regular nine-to-five job. I hate to say it, but if my people pull off this stupid fake tornado, truly I can't see what use there is to live a regular life."

Davida walked into the room she used for her workshop and pulled the jigsaw and extension cord out into the living room. She said, "I'll vacuum up the mess," and excavated the mannequins' bellies within two minutes. Davida said, "I might paint these things with an eye towards what happened in Gig. I'll paint overturned trailers all over the body."

I walked into the kitchen and fixed a bourbon and bourbon. I sat at the kitchen table and thought about what I needed to teach in the morning, or what I'd say. "My father told me he still had all the receipts from everything he ever bought my mother. He said he was going to tell the insurance agents that her jewelry box went missing."

My wife didn't look up. She said, "I'll admit that your daddy might get himself into trouble. I'll admit that the guy who never really ate a tire and everybody else might get in trouble. You don't have to worry, though. Believe me, Park, you have an alibi for all this."

I didn't want to hear it. I said, "I'm right on camera telling the world about a phantom tornado, you idiot."

My wife laughed. She said, "There's that old cliché. Behind every successful man, you know."

I didn't get it. I understood Kant better than I understood my wife's non sequiturs sometimes. "I'm not exactly successful," I said. I drank from my bourbon. I strummed my fingers on the table. I looked over at Davida setting a Tupperware bowl in a new old mannequin. I thought about a woman from CNN wearing a dress and rubber galoshes. "What did you sign behind me when I gave those interviews?"

Davida looked up. She said, "Let's just say that you won't be getting in any trouble should word leak out. Let's just say that I may have mentioned how it was a terrible scene — just like you said verbally — but that it wasn't your fault. That you didn't have anything to do with it. That you didn't even know these people any more."

I did not answer my wife. I didn't look up, or thank her immediately. I thought forward, and could only wonder how my father and his friends would defend themselves later on, and speculated that their only argument might be similar to temporary insanity, except they might need to persuade a jury that living in such close proximity to a nuclear dumping ground caused a certain paranoia and lack of understanding reality. I saw myself on the witness stand, too, explaining how I grew up in a place where the most famous person ate rubber, where the drivers ed teacher felt it necessary to teach specters what they needed to know most, namely how to operate a vehicle on their way to a more conducive place to haunt, a place where their own stories could begin.

# Crawl Space

M Y FIRST HOUSE was built by newlyweds on the verge of divorce. They bought two acres, got married, and went to work doing a couple things they'd never done before, namely dealing with lumber and tape measures. From what I understand from the neighbors, this man and woman tried to dig their own footings, then hired out a backhoe man. They tried to lay brick, then brought in a mason. After the foundation set, the newlyweds—I understand both husband and wife taught junior high, so they had one complete summer, every weekend, twenty days mid-winter, a spring break, and fake sick days—laid out plywood flooring and did their best at walls. They hired an electrician. They got a plumber to do the hard parts.

The neighbors say that this couple separated right when the last shingle got tacked on, but I imagine this to be untruthful. Any one of those how-to-build-your-own-house books has shingles on it before sheetrock's installed properly, before picayune detail work gets started, before anyone even thinks to drive to one of the major hardware chains to buy finishing nails. Plus, the roof's fine. I knew right away that the people who tried to build this house separated directly before completing the master bedroom's adjacent bathroom. At the other end of the house all the molding fit perfectly. There weren't spaces between the baseboard and floor. The walls were painted without drips or roller marks slapped on in Y-patterns. At the other end of the house, though, it looked like a goddamn Funhouse.

The drain-waste-vent system at the good end of the house was attached perfectly, with wood supports between the floor joists. The good end of the house, too, had a crawl space five feet high. At the bad end—the end where my newlywed construction workers gave up—it wasn't two feet. My wife and I only figured this out after an armada of slugs entered our bathroom through the strainer, and then the next morning we found a field rat's nose sticking through.

"I ain't going down there to shove the pipe back up," I said. "Forget about spiders, mice, and snails—I'm not going down to the low end with rats living beneath us." This was out in the country, away from getting invited to dinner parties. Unfortunately, we lived beyond zoning laws, too. There were field rats because the surrounding woods got razed daily for subdivisions and mobile home parks. My wife Ardis and I had been married a while. We rented before. At the time she worked painting murals on small towns' wrecked bricked buildings. I did PR for a number of immoral clients.

"I'm not going down there either," Ardis said. "Don't go under the house, Lure." We'd been married long enough for her to only call me by my last name.

I got out the phone book and looked for a plumber. A receptionist on the other end asked some questions, then said that only Stitt could work on such a project. I assumed that the receptionist knew Stitt long enough to only use his last name, too.

STITT WASN'T FOUR feet tall, and he wasn't allowed to make appraisals, offer suggestions, or linger on the front porch once the job got finished. Stitt scared people. "Normally they send someone out with me and make me sit in the truck and wait," he told me. "We're backed up, though. I guess they thought 'cause you live out here in the country, you've about seen everything." Stitt's head was the size of a continent. He combed his eyebrows up to make his forehead look less the size of a chalkboard.

I said, "We've seen about everything out here. One night I was outside with one of the dogs and an owl swooped down to pick us up. Or at least the dog."

What could I say? Ardis left a minute after Stitt showed up. She said she had to look at the side of a shoe store down in Greenville, which I knew was a lie. I was there, beside the tiny door that led beneath my house, beside the tiny man who could walk halfway underneath my house before having to stoop to re-attach my drain.

"An owl swooped down," Stitt said. "You sure it wasn't a bat?"

I said, "I imagine there's going to be a lot of water down there beneath the shower. You want a towel or anything? I got some old galoshes you can have." I looked down at Stitt's tiny feet. He wore kids' no-name-brand tennis shoes. I thought, I have some condoms you can roll up your legs.

"Any rat traps down here?"

"No."

"Then you'll have rats. You didn't tell me you had rats."

I said, "I don't know if there are rats down there. Hell, there's no telling what's down there. A possum might be living underneath our house, for all I know."

Stitt stared at me as if I'd spoken trigonometry. He re-cinched his toolbelt, which looked more like one of those her-nia protectors than anything else—he only kept a flashlight hanging off of it, plus a tube of joint compound. "The only way people find out if their drain's unattached is if they see slugs or mice coming through the little holes. Tell me you ain't seen one of them things I'm talking about right now."

He uncrossed his arms as if he might punch me in the thigh. I said, "I believe you and me should drink a beer or two before this job gets started."

ACCORDING TO STITT, no one realized he'd grow no further until about the sixth grade. By age fifteen he'd had it with everyone calling him Shit, Little Shit, Spit, or Li'l Bit Stitt the Half-Pint Half-Wit. This was a time before kids shot people over names and rumors. He quit school, ran away from his normal-sized parents—cotton mill employees like my daddy—and made a point not to join any of those traveling county fairs. Stitt made a vow not to join the circus, or attempt to make it in Hollywood as some kind of stunt child. He thought about submarines but never talked to a Navy recruiter.

"I got work—and it's hard to believe I'd even admit it—with a shrimper down on the Georgia coast near Brunswick. I fixed nets. That was my job. Because of my little fingers it came easy. There's a ton of work made for midgets, V. O. It just takes telling people."

We sat in my half-built-right den drinking a pitcher of mimosas. I'd bought a couple bottles of champagne the night before after learning I'd gotten the anti–Strom Thurmond account. From the far side of the house I heard a scratching underneath I hoped Stitt didn't hear.

I need to point out that Stitt used the term "midget." If I'd've said anything at all I would've said "little person," et cetera. I said, "There are jobs out there for everybody, I imagine. The House of Workforce has many windows."

"Attic insulation man. Shetland pony polo player. Tombstone engraver—I got friends in that field down in Elberton, the granite capital of the world. They're vicious."

It was nearing noon. Here's me—I almost asked him if he wanted a little lunch. I said, "I hope you're not charging me by the hour."

Stitt said, "The reason why I like what I'm doing now is because of the ephemera. There's a word I bet you don't know, buddy. Ephemera."

I knew the word, but said, "Ephemera."

"Listen, you go into a crawl space of an old house—I'm talking about an antebellum house, or at least something made before 1920—and you'll find things husbands wouldn't let their wives have. I don't know how many times I've gone down to those spaces reserved for cobwebs and found old compacts, and packs of Chesterfields, and empty half-pints of bad bourbon. I've found love letters written to people who never lived there. Don't think I can't do research, man."

We sat together on my couch. Stitt's legs stuck straight out. He held his mimosa with both hands. Listen, I poured it in a fucking jelly jar, and tried not to think about him looking like one of those blow-up clowns that bounce back once punched. "You should collect everything you find and go on the antiques roadshow circuit. My father does that with fishing lures, seeing as our last name's Lure."

Stitt bobbed his head up and down. "I should stick a bottle-rocket up my ass and fly to Mars. My brother's a midget, too. He works as a barber and stands on a box. He should invent a hydraulic device to get him to scalp level. Should, should, should." When Stitt went to crunch on an ice cube for effect, it only filled up his mouth like a snowball might fill mine.

229

I smelled my armpit, thinking it might be a hint that I hadn't taken a shower and that I wanted to do so. "My wife will be happy when this gets fixed."

Stitt handed me his empty glass. He said, "Memorabilia." He said, "Mem-o-ro-beel-ee-uh."

I WOULD GET DRUNK, too, if I crawled beneath houses like mine for a living. When Stitt finally entered the half-door on the east side I stood there like a cub scout den chief. I wanted to say something like, "Take care," or tie a rope to his torso should things get bad.

"This won't take long, V. O., I swear," Stitt said from about twenty feet in. "You go make us some more drinks and I'll be out by the time you pour them."

Here's what I did instead: I walked to the driveway and looked at his pick-up truck to see if anyone drove him to my house. There was a bench seat with a dozen local phone books on it for him to sit on, plus specialized accelerator and brake pedals fashioned from rebar.

Ardis drove up as I stood there mesmerized by geometry. I looked towards the house as if in excuse and said to my wife, "He's still here."

She didn't have to look at me twice before saying, "You invited a workman in our house and drank with him, didn't you?"

This had happened before when we needed to hire a locksmith, but that's another screwed-up story. "We got a little person under the house," I whispered, even though we stood fifty yards from where he stooped. "How'd the brick look on the shoe store? What're you going to do, paint a mural that's fifty feet?" I said, "Ha-ha," like that. I could. I'd done the anti–Strom Thurmond campaign, and pretty much had the Hemp-As-Viable-Fabric account ready.

Ardis didn't get out of the car, a regular car—a Volvo. Me, I drove a pick-up truck not unlike Stitt's, seeing as we lived out in the country, seeing as I didn't like locals giving me the finger. She said, "You don't invite a workman to drink. He gets paid by the hour."

This is no lie: I said, "This guy gets paid by the half-hour. Come on in and talk to him. You'll like Stitt! He's like you and me, only half-so."

My wife turned off the engine and sat there. I tried to think about what I could ever do so as not to appear the idiot. Two weeks before I'd killed a good copperhead, slit it down the middle, showed Ardis how its heart still beat four hours after death; then I rubbed the skin down with rock salt and mounted it on a piece of scrap cedar the original divorced home builders left off in the back section of the lot. It's something I learned as a kid, something that amazed teachers on show-and-tell day from about third grade until right before I fucked my French teacher senior year. I goddamn counted on snakeskins for extra credit, and pretty much believe I got in college because of what teacher recommendations I received due to those three- to six-foot lengths I showed them off-hand. Maybe they feared me coming back, I don't know.

"It shouldn't take thirty minutes to crawl under the house, shove the pipe back up to the shower stall, and re-attach the thing, V. O."

I said, "I know. I'm aware of that. But Stitt's really interesting. He's giving me ideas. You know how hard a time I've been having coming up with ideas." That hemp-as-fabric had me stymied, outside of something like "You thought you could jump high before . . ."

Ardis said, "I don't want to act like I have a fear of little people, but I do. When I look in their eyes it seems as though they're looking back at me thinking, 'I scare you, don't I?' When this guy showed up I felt that way immediately."

I shook my head and held the top of her car. "You're being a wimp. Come on. I swear to God after you meet Stitt you'll want to take up painting regular paintings again, using him as a model. And it'll only take half the canvas."

From under the crawl space, out of the vents, we heard Stitt yell, "Brown recluse, brown recluse!" like that, all excited. If he would've been of normal height the next thing we would've heard was his head banging on every floor joist on his way out.

When he did appear around the side of the house my wife only got a glimpse of him, before backing out of the driveway and taking off, like a person might do if an owl or specter swooped down.

YOU'D THINK A MAN working in crawl spaces would carry a can of bug spray with him. You'd think he'd carry a pistol. Stitt walked up to the driveway and said, "I saw your problem. Well, I saw the problem you called up about, plus another hundred."

I said, "I hope you didn't get bit by a spider."

At the time I didn't notice how he wore three rings: a man's wedding band on his thumb, a woman's on his index finger, and a diamond engagement ring on his other index finger. "I cheated Death again," he said. "Hotdamn. Let's you and me make another pitcher of those wisterias or whatever you call them."

I said, "Well, okay, then," and walked him back towards the house. This time we sat down on the back porch—a regular stained-wood back porch with nail heads poking out of the two-by-fours. I went inside to make more mimosas, looked out the kitchen window at Stitt sitting there, and walked to the master bedroom bathroom to see what my shower drain looked like back normal.

It looked the same. He'd not used his joint compound whatsoever. Outside I said, "There's still a hole between the stall bottom and the pipe. The drain's not re-affixed."

"I ain't got to that yet. I tell you what, though—rats have torn down your insulation. I'm surprised when you walk across the floor in winter it doesn't feel the same as swimming in a mountain lake fed by springs. You know what I'm talking about, Lure—shafts of cold every so often."

I said, "I know what you're talking about." For the first time I thought about how I shouldn't be drinking—I looked at Stitt and only saw that little feral kid in the Mad Max movies, or this one scary munchkin in The Wizard of Oz.

"Oh, it's bad down there. I bet you you'll have to hire an electrician soon, too. Wires are everywhere, and they've been gnawed upon. Half the wood's eaten up with termites. You better run for your life, man."

He wiped his forehead and I noticed the rings. I said, "Did you find those rings down there?"

Stitt looked at his hands as if he just noticed that he owned appendages. He said, "I wear these for good luck."

"I didn't see you wearing rings when you got here."

"Listen, pissant," he said. This is where I understand Ardis's fear of little people—he kind of looked like a pit bull all of a sudden. "I kept the rings in my pocket until I entered your crawl space. Then I put them on. It's hard enough for me to drive the truck outside without rings to distract me on the steering wheel."

The sun overhead beat down like stolen Buddy Rich drumsticks, like the heads of hogs slurping blood from their sliced-neck brethren, like a chambermaid working dust out of a mattress in a motel open only May through September in the upper peninsula of Michigan.

I can kill an analogy, which makes me one of the best PR and anti-PR men in America. I said, "How long's it going to take you?"

"Ten more minutes and a pint of bourbon," Stitt said. "Feel lucky that I'm not adding in tetanus and rabies shots."

The diamond ring on his other hand still had red clay stuck to its edges.

I TOLD STITT I'd drive to the liquor store and buy bourbon, but wouldn't pour him a drink until the job got finished. I never studied psychology in college, but did enough crossword puzzles to know that _____'s dog came out "Pavlov." I drove to town, some fifteen miles away, thinking this: some fast food restaurant should come up with a hamburger called "The Urge," seeing as "burger" couldn't be spelled without "urge" in the middle.

That's what I thought all the time, by the way. Even each night when Ardis came home saying something like how she had a hard time painting a portrait of Jefferson Davis on a drugstore in Abbeville, South Carolina—because he slept there, surely—I thought of things like how somebody running a Chinese restaurant called China Pearl should take off some letters so it only said "hi earl," to at least get the population of men named Earl inside each day for the buffet. I could've cared less about the deficit, unemployment rate, or unrest in the Middle East. Me, I only cared about what people wanted to pay me for what people probably didn't want to buy in the first place. Fuck me.

"I got bourbon and I got sweet vermouth and bitters. I stopped by the store and bought a jar of bad cherries. We're drinking Manhattans and we're going to pretend there's a skyline outside," I said when I returned.

Stitt sat slumped over on the table beneath our umbrella. He woke up. "Manhattans!" His voice held enough phlegm to oil a steamroller's cogs. "I had to call the shop and see what was next. I haven't had time to get under the house again."

"Well then, I'll fix these up while you fix the drain."

Stitt hopped off his chair and walked towards me. "I'm there," he said. Then he jumped off the porch at its lowest point and chugged his way to the crawl space door. Those rings glinted off his hands like sparks from an old Chevy's bad muffler drug on asphalt, and I knew deep down that whoever built my house—the newlyweds on the verge of divorce—threw their vows down one drain or another in an act of desperation.

I said, "I'll be in the kitchen if you need me. Knock on the floorboards, buddy."

He nodded.

Of course I didn't go directly into the kitchen to make Manhattans. I took my bottle of bourbon and accessories right into the bathroom, tipped the toilet lid down, and sat on it. I opened the shower's sliding glass door and stared down to where Stitt needed to fill in what darkness occurred between floor level and clay. I breathed slowly and heard Stitt walk like a regular fullback to where he could no longer stand upright, then crawl to where my problems started—where the husband and wife who built the house ended their squabble.

Ardis drove up in the driveway again, waited, then got out. When she walked inside through her studio door—what was once a regular garage—she said, "V. O." as if she ordered a drink from Louie the bartender down at Addy's Dutch Bar in Greenville where we went after I came up with ideas that worked. We saw Louie twice a year.

"Is there some kind of problem?" my wife said.

"I'm just sitting here." I spoke low, and held a finger to my lip for her to be quiet. "Stitt's fixing it."

"I saw his truck still here. What're you doing—pouring shooters down the drain for him?"

I held my bottles. "Go outside and wait. I swear. Wait'll you see what I have for you coming. Trust me on this one."

Ardis unbuttoned her blouse, unsnapped her bra, and shook her tits towards the drain like it mattered.

STITT CAME OUT unscathed, and I had our drinks ready. I held a pitcher, and kept three glasses on the back porch table, underneath an unfurled umbrella. "For the champion environmentalist!" I said, holding my glass up. "For the only man able to keep our soapy, dirty water from draining straight out into the ground."

Stitt stood below porch level and looked at me as if I'd peed on his head. He shaded his eyes with one hand, veered towards Ardis, and said, "Ma'am."

She said, "Thanks for coming."

He said, "I was just breathing hard. Don't mind me. It's my job. Where's my drink?"

I stuck my arm down to pull Stitt up so he wouldn't have to walk around the porch. He came up like a scrap piece of dander, no lie. He weighed nothing. Ardis said, "I'm pleased to make your acquaintance," like we were in some kind of 1950s movie. I watched her shake the hand that wore two rings.

Stitt said, "Jeepers." I didn't think he was off base. "You're all fixed up. The Lures can now brag about being plumbing-correct," he said laughing. "You might want to call an exterminator, or the National Guard. I forget my biology, but I think rats reproduce about every six minutes, and they have a hundred fifty babies at a time. Oh, it's a mathematical equation."

Stitt acted differently around my wife. Out of nowhere he thought he could have her. I said, "We'll do that," and handed him a stiff eight ounces. "What do we owe you?"

He looked at his wristwatch. He said, "I've been here five hours. I've worked one hour. I don't know. We'll figure it out later. It's $75 an hour, not counting parts. We'll figure it out later."

"We can't pay you for sitting around drinking with us," my wife said. Listen, in the past I'd told her that the easiest way to deal with workmen was to smile, offer them things they wouldn't take anyway—celery stalks filled with cream cheese—and say they did a perfect job. It kept them from coming back later with guns and crowbars. I read it in one of those magazines.

Stitt handed me his glass. He wanted more. "I'm off the clock, ma'am. I'll tell my boss that I had a hard time finding your place, that I spent an hour working, and that I got lost going home. Nobody's worried anyway. My beeper didn't go off or anything."

My wife reached over with her empty glass. She didn't drink often. Here was our marriage—I drank, and she fell down. It was like some kind of symbiotic relationship that no one outside of Darwin would understand. Ardis said, "They want a picture of fish beneath water on a building in Barnwell. The nuclear plant's right there. No fish have survived in twenty years. I feel like painting two-headed fish, out of meanness."

There was no way that Stitt knew what my wife did for a living. I'd not mentioned it. He said, "You could do what you did down in Greenwood, with that old mill owner they wanted painted on the side of the Coca-Cola plant."

My wife had made the mill owner look like a snake, pretty much. Ardis said, "You saw that?"

"I see everything," he said. "The lower the crawl spaces, the more I see. They got me traveling between here and Charleston. I pay attention to buildings. I guess I've probably seen all your murals."

If there's one thing that will turn an artist around, it's people talking about the artist's work right there in front of her. Goddamn Hitler could go up to any artist in America, say, "I like your negative spaces," and get handmade Christmas cards for life.

My wife poured Stitt another drink. She said, "Those are interesting rings."

I said, "He got them under our house. He'll tell you that he came with the things in his pocket, but I know for a fact that they were under our house. The people who built this place threw them down the drain. Somehow when the pipe unhinged itself the rings fell out of the pee trap. I took physics, Stitt. I know."

Stitt sat there with his legs stuck out. I took geometry, too: he was a perfect right angle on our back porch, beneath the umbrella, drinking Manhattans. He took the rings off and set them lightly between us. "Well, you ain't got no ephemera down there. I couldn't find anything else worth keeping unless I wanted rat fur for trim on my parka." He poured his drink into the monkey grass. "I hope you people know what you have."

And with that he got up and left. He floated right off the porch, got in his weird pick-up, and drove off. Ardis said, "I told you he'd get scary. I told you."

That night we didn't make love. We didn't sleep. Ardis made two pots of coffee and rechecked the flood lights a dozen times. I left Stitt's three found rings on the table outside—not so much as bait, but for not wanting to test what vows my wife and I took years earlier. Would we end up like our predecessors, tired and miserable with each other? Would we forget what brought us together, and how human beings cannot possibly live without certain dependencies?

At dawn I went outside with a whisk broom, swept the rings into a dustpan, and buried them beneath the crawl space door. Two days later we got the plumber's bill, with No Charge scrawled across it.